RECOLLECTIONS OF A SOUTHERN BELLE

DONNA DERDEN

Recollections of a Southern Belle

To learn more about Donna Derden visit the author's official website at www.donnaderden.com.

ISBN: 13-978-0-9801177-1-4

Printed in the United States of America

THANK Y'ALL!

The stories in this book are loosely based on my real life family, whose names were changed to protect the innocent. But, y'all know who you are…thanks a lot for sharing your memories with me!

Also, thank you: Kimberly Bates, Sandra Lewis, Angela Parker, Alyson Messenger, Jaumonta Roberts, Pamela Chalmers and Pastor Joseph Robinson. Your support is much appreciated!!!

DEDICATION

To those Belles who've gone to glory
Emma Jean Finch (Jean)
M. Sue Frazier
Kelly Hill-Greenwade
Michelle Finch Morton
Robin Bates Renberg

Your lives have inspired me!

BABY GIRL'S GUIDE TO DETERMINING IF YOU ARE A TRUE SOUTHERN BELLE...by my own self

I'm a Southern Belle.

Y'all the first people I've told because, to tell the truth, I just found out my own self. I was sitting here, minding my business, pondering stuff, when it sort of came to me... This business about being a Southern Belle.

At first, I rejected the thought of my being a Southern Belle because, well, I'm African American. I don't think I have ever heard hide, nor hair of a black Southern Belle. The thought of that gave me pause. But, do you know what? That's the old way of thinking. This is a new day! I have overcome! If it came to me while I was busy pondering stuff that I'm a Southern Belle...then that settles it in my mind. I'm a Southern Belle.

And you can't tell me no different.

Now, it's not like I sit around all day pondering on being a Southern Belle. I have other things to ponder on.

Big things!

Important things!!

Things like, if it's safe to leave work early when the boss calls in sick. Or, when the boss calls in sick, is it really considered a free day? Or, should a person feel guilty about taking a three hour lunch when the boss calls in sick? Or, if a vendor sends the boss a huge box of cookies on the very same day the boss calls in sick, and those cookies are just sitting there going stale, is it a bad thing to open the box, pass the cookies out to your coworkers and eat three peanut butter cookies your own self because they are your very favorite?

I had time to ponder all these things because my boss called in sick today.

In fact, that's what us Belles do, we're intellectuals…we ponder on things. Pondering takes way more time than thinking. Let me explain; you think a thought and it's gone. You move on to the next thought. That's it. But pondering…that's taking it to the next level. Pondering takes time. When a person ponders, its best to close the door, kick off your shoes, put your feet up on the big desk in the corner office, lean back in that big comfortable leather chair, and let your mind just ponder away.

So, I'm at my boss's desk pondering on stuff like that when I get a text saying that a friend of mine's mother, M. Sue, in Columbia, South Carolina died. The news really hurt my heart because she was a lovely old soul. Dainty and ladylike. Just remembering her made me smile. That set me to pondering, *She was such a Southern Belle.*

And that's when it hit me.

I'm just like her.

Well, not the dainty part. I'm not old either, not much. I'm plenty ladylike though. Ladylikeness practically oozes from me. And, I'm from the south too. So there you have it. I'm a Southern Belle!

Belles are brilliant due to all that pondering. That's how I knew it was true about me.

Now, I know what you're thinking. You're thinking you might be a Southern Belle too. Well, I don't know about that. There's more to it than pondering. There's a whole list of stuff you have to go through before you can say you're a true Belle. But, don't worry yourself 'cause I'm gonna help you out. That's how I am.

Okay, if you're thinking you might be a Belle but you want to know for sure, I'm gonna define it and then you can decide for yourself. I believe I'm qualified to list the qualities of a true Southern Belle, being as I'm a Belle my own self.

First off, here's what being a Belle is not. You aren't born into it. You aren't promoted to it. You don't have to be pretty or skinny either. It don't have a thing to do with the color of your skin, hair or eyes. You don't have to be beautiful, either. In fact, you can be a bit homely, but you can't be butt ugly.

'Cause that's just wrong.

And it's definitely not *just* because you're from the South-- but you do have to be from the South to qualify. Sorry, but I'm pretty sure that why it's called "Southern Belle"...'cause you're from the South!

Now, if you northerners or any other direction wants to start your own group of Belles, have at it. That's your own kettle of fish. But you're coming to the dinner table pretty late. Please recognize...Southern Belles are the real deal. Everyone knows that.

So, what is it? What are the characteristics of a true Southern Belle? Well, I'm fixin' to tell you if you can hold your horses for a cotton pickin' minute. Dang!

A Southern Belle is patient.

A Southern Belle carries herself well. She's a lady. Like my friends mom, M. Sue, she's stylish and dainty.

She walks with her head held up and there's a bit of a bounce in her step. She's dignified but approachable.

Southern Belles walk to the beat of a different and much slower drummer. She's comfortable taking her time and living life at a leisurely pace, taking in the sights and sounds of everything around her. But it's also knowing how to pick 'em up and put 'em down when need be.

She's down to earth and honest. She has a love for family, even that crazy cousin that nobody likes to talk about. Y'all know the one.

There's something about her that's just different. If she has moved and lives outside of the South, people are always asking her, "You aren't from around here, are you?" There is a genuineness and openness about her that is an automatic people magnet. They want to be around her.

She helps people. In the South, we call it being neighbourly. When there is a problem, people know they can come to her and she would give them the shirt off her back if she thought it would help.

She acts like she has right good sense.

Her words are seasoned with wisdom.

She minds her manners. When walking down the street, she purposefully looks strangers dead in the eyes and says, "Good Morning." She knows to speak when she enters a room, regardless of who's there.

It's having a love of all things Southern. Even though she lives in other parts of the country, or even the world, she still carries the values, the warmth, and the beauty of her Southern heritage in her heart. It's a state of mind.

Now, that list is from my own self. And it's just off the top of my head. But, are you still tying to determine your Belle-ness? Now, if you're a sister (as in African American) and don't fit into any of the categories listed above but you still want to be a Southern Belle, there's still hope. I have just created the following quiz to see if I can get you into the club through the back door. Extra credit, so to speak. So, ask yourself:

Do you know someone named "Peaches" and that's her legal name?

Do you refer to your family as "Momma 'nem?"

Do you call the hair at the nape of your neck "the kitchen?"

Do you only eat bologna, spam or hot dogs burnt?

Do you rarely put g's on the end of words?

Have you ever been told to go somewhere and sit down?

Has your mother ever threatened to slap the taste out of your mouth?

Did she? (Extra points if you answered yes to this question.)

If someone were passing around a petition to make fried chicken its own food group, would you sign it?

Did you start that petition in the first place?

If you answered yes to at least five of these questions…well, I don't know if it makes you an honest to goodness Belle like my own self, but you are certainly down to earth enough to gain an honorable mention.

And that's good enough for me!

* * * * *

So, after I finished pondering stuff, I progressed to the third and final stage of mental awareness…recollecting. Now, recollecting is what you do after you've finished pondering and you need to call stuff back to your memory. That's what I'm fixin' to do right now. I'm gonna recollect a bunch of different stuff. I hope y'all can keep up, 'cause I got a smorgasbord of recollecting to do.

If y'all thought I could ponder, I will dazzle you with my recollecting abilities.

My favorite thing to recollect on is my crazy family, which takes a lot of my time because my family is huge, especially on my momma's side. My momma, Beulah Mae, was the tenth child out of sixteen, but a pair of twins died at birth and another child died after less than a year. But still, that's thirteen siblings who survived.

And then, when you move on to my immediate family, there are eight of us. Five girls and three boys born over a twenty-three year period. So you see, I've gathered a lot of ammunition…uh, I mean warm fuzzy recollections to tell y'all about.

I could sit here recollecting and pondering on the stories that have been passed down from generation to generation. It could take days to tell them all, but I flatter myself if I think I could hold your attention that long. I will just start recollecting back as far as I can and try to bring this story to an end before y'all get tired of me.

But, I better make it quick…I just heard my boss is feeling much better and will be coming to work tomorrow.

PART ONE

HOW WE GOT OVAH

CHAPTER 1

THE USUAL ROUTE

Anderson knew to run like his life depended on it...because most assuredly, it did.

Working in his favor was the fact that he was experienced in this sort of thing. Running, that is. Running away, to be precise. Because that's what he was doing at the moment. Running away and taking the usual route.

If the phrase, "feet don't fail me now" had been around while he was taking his dangerous journey in the summer of 1875, it would have been appropriate for the situation at hand. But, that was another saying for another day.

The slap of the branches against his chest felt like he was getting a whippin' and the sting of thorns and thistles pricking the medium brown skin on his face was most unpleasant, but he'd felt worse. He knew he'd look a bloody mess by the time he made it to his destination. *If* he made it to his destination.

Don't matter, he thought. *If I git caught, dat whip gone feel a whole lot worser dan dis.*

He ran like nobody's business.

At the age of twenty, speed and agility were on his side. Also working in his favor was that the fact that he'd come this way several times before. Like I said, it was the usual route. His feet neither stumbled nor fell over the fallen trees and branches that littered his path. His pace was slowed as his feet sank in the nasty, mirky, muddy waters of the swamp, thick with brush and vegetation. But his steps were strong and sure. It wasn't like the swamp was about to swallow him whole.

The dense brush was so thick you could only see a few yards ahead of you. It provided just enough cover for him to make his escape. The only problem was snakes. The swamp was their natural habitat…they were everywhere. Anderson knew the possibility of him running across one on his swift journey was a very likely one.

He shivered slightly as he thought about the slithery, slimy reptiles. *Lawd, I hate a snake!* The very idea of a close encounter with his mortal enemy provided enough incentive to keep his speed at a persistent and steady rate.

The crack of a pistol quickly brought him back to the here and now. It caused his heart to skip a beat. Bullets were whizzing by, but they were hitting the trees to his left…way to the left. The shots didn't come near him. He relaxed a bit, knowing that he was undetected and that the shots were being fired at will.

He thought, *He must'a made it back to da wagon and got dat pistol I seen lyin' under de bench.*

After a few more steps, he continued to encourage himself. *He just shootin'. Prob'ly prayin' he can hit me somewhere. Anywhere.*

This wasn't a game and Anderson knew it. Being a runaway slave was bad for your health. Those white slave owners in Mississippi were notoriously evil and the man who'd just purchased him not two hours ago was plenty mad that Anderson was able to escape. Lord help him if he were caught.

If he were caught, there would be hell to pay and the balance would come from his hide. Weighing his options, he knew he'd either be beaten to within an inch of his life, sold to an even harsher master or even killed. Working in Anderson's favor was the top price, which had been paid to acquire him. That was the one and only thing that might keep him alive because no businessman wanted to lose his investment.

But, he had no intention of being caught. Catching him would be like trying to find a lost ball in high grass. He'd gotten a pretty decent head start. It also helped that the man who'd purchased him was old, made the mistake of being alone and he didn't have any dogs with him. Everything was working for his good.

He could still hear the voice of the angry white man, swearing and threatening when he first realized Anderson had escaped. He yelled out in white-hot anger, "Niggar, when I get my hands on you…!"

But you ain't gon' git yo hands on me, he had thought confidently. That was a good twenty minutes ago.

This was the fourth, no, the fifth time he had made a similar escape. And he hadn't been caught yet. *And this sho' ain't gon' be the first time either.*

But he hoped this would be the last time. Even though he was a young man, he felt he was getting too old for this. He'd grown tired of putting his life on the line. Mostly, what Anderson wanted was to work the fields like the other slaves. To do his work and be left alone. He wanted to jump the broom one day and have a normal life. Normal for a slave, that is.

It would be kinda nice to have a wife and some chirren one day, he often mused.

But first, he had to get out of this jam. As he continued the course, the voice of his pursuer was getting smaller and smaller. The man had run out of bullets in that six-shooter so the gunfire had ceased. All Anderson had to do was make it to the small clearing where there should have been a horse waiting for him, ready to whisk him to safety.

A couple hundred yards and he'd be home free. He was so close to freedom, he could taste it. Beads of perspiration were flowing down his cheeks like water from the pump of a well. His clothes were drenched in sweat. Some of the salty mixture dripped into his eyes. He quickly wiped his brow and kept his course. When he finally saw the head of a horse, tied to the big magnolia tree right where it was supposed to be he smiled and headed straight for it.

Almost der, he thought.

When he was less than forty paces away, a middle-aged white man carrying the biggest pistol Anderson had ever seen in his life stepped out from behind the bushes.

The sight of him stopped Anderson dead in his tracks.

* * * * *

'Scuse me y'all!

It's the Belle speaking, and I'm at it again. Starting my story in the middle of the tale like I don't have right good sense. If y'all don't know me, I have to tell you from the get-go, it's a real bad habit of mine. One of many, I'm afraid. It's a terrible way to start a book. You'd think I didn't go to writing school.

Well, truth be told, I didn't go to writing school. But that's just between the two of us.

Let me see if I can set this recollection up a little better.

Anderson was my great grandfather. If you ask me, that's a mighty strong name for a slave. A strong name for a strong man. He was born into slavery in 1855 in Mississippi. When I was trying to find out about him, I went to Pam, our family historian. She promptly produced a census report that said he lived at Beat 1. Whatever and where ever that is. I reckon that must have been before all the cities had names, but don't get me to lyin'.

What I know about him comes from stories handed down from generation to generation. For as long as I can remember, my momma, Beulah Mae, had been telling the story of her granddaddy and his escapades. She remembered him as a fun, playful, boisterous man who loved to talk. He loved gathering Momma and her three sisters and nine brothers around him at night before they went to bed to tell them about his life as a slave.

They would sit on the floor of the front porch of his house with him sitting in a big white rocker, weaving baskets, which was his hobby. He sold quite a few of those baskets as well, but that's neither here nor there. The story that I'm about to finish telling y'all is one that had been passed down through my family for years and years.

He was a deeply religious man who constantly spoke about how God kept him through this, that and the other. God brought him out of slavery too. From what I've been able to determine, he didn't have the Kunta Kinte experience of slavery which is probably why he was able to talk about it. Yes, he was the property of a white man and yes, he had to work the fields and do as he was told. He wasn't free, that's for sure, but he wasn't beat down like a dog either. I guess that's something.

Anderson had a different slavery experience. At least different from any that I've ever heard of. That was probably the result of having an owner who had a flair for the dramatic and a mind slanted towards mischief. Now, Momma couldn't remember the name of the man who owned her grandfather and I certainly don't know. Seems to me, his name ought to be something like Robert Cumberland because that sounds like somebody who would own slaves.

(Note to reader: If your name is Robert Cumberland…my apologies!)

Anyway, Robert Cumberland owned and operated a large farm in Mississippi. Grandpa Crowder used to tell my momma that his owner wasn't too harsh a man and that he and the other slaves never got a whippin'. Funny, when I think of slavery, that's the first thing that comes to mind; grown men and even women being treated like animals. I'm glad that didn't happen to him, but I still shed a tear for the tens of thousands who experienced the whip. Lord have mercy!

Trying to escape wasn't something he ever tried either.

He explained, "Where wuz I gone go? If I could'a made it up north, den what? I don't know nobody up der. Still, if my way had been hard, I might'a tried to escape."

His main motivation for staying was that the slaves knew how brutal some of the other owners could be. They actually knew what was going on at the other plantations. If they had an owner who treated them halfway decent, some deemed it worthwhile to just stay put and make the best of it.

But, this is not a story on the history of slavery. It's a story about my great grandpa Anderson.

So, back to it.

And this time, I reckon I'll start at the beginning...

* * * * *

Robert Cumberland was a landowner who had a decent size plot in Mississippi. It was a large piece of land, but I'm not sure it held plantation status.

He owned a few slaves and Anderson was one of them. Anderson had his usual duties of rising at the crack of dawn and working in the field till the sun went down. He did this without complaint. He didn't know any better because slavery was all he knew. I really don't know how Mr. Cumberland came to own him. Maybe he inherited him or maybe he bought him at some slave auction. Or, maybe he bought him from another plantation owner.

Anyway, Anderson really stood out from among the other slaves because he was exceedingly tall and strong, well over six feet. He was a medium brown-skinned man with thick black hair. His arms and legs were long and muscular because daily, backbreaking labor tends to buff you up. He was a fascinating specimen of masculinity. To let him tell it, he could do the work of ten men.

From time to time, Mr. Cumberland would have other plantation owners from outside of Mississippi over to buy whatever crops or animals he was selling. Mr. Cumberland would take special care to learn as much as he could about the people he was selling his crops to. Older, proud men traveling alone who owned smaller plantations were of particular interest to him. He would get as much information on them as he could before he had them come to his farm.

Mr. Cumberland would take the prospective buyers by the fields where the slaves were working and Anderson would always be right up front, working hard and barely breaking a sweat. Because of his height and build, he would usually attract the attention of the plantation owners who wanted to increase their herd.

Before long, someone would ask about Anderson and Mr. Cumberland would tell him what a good slave he was; how productive and obedient he was and how he'd never had a problem with him. The prospective buyer would ask if he would consider selling Anderson. Mr. Cumberland would ponder the proposition before finally saying that he would consider an offer. At that point, Anderson would be called over for a closer inspection.

Addressing him, Mr. Cumberland asked, "You're a good, strong, hard worker, ain't you boy?"

Anderson, a grown man, would respond like a good negro. "Yassuh. I loves hard work."

"Yes, Anderson works from sun up until sunset without hardly breaking a sweat. I really don't know if I could stand to part with him, he is one of my most productive niggers. I'd have to get two niggers to replace him. Still, I might be persuaded for the right price. How much you offering?"

From there, they would hem and haw until they could agree on a price. Once the deal had been made, papers would be signed. On the day the exchange was to take place, money would change hands, and Mr. Cumberland would surrender Anderson to his new owner.

Mr. Cumberland would go to the barn and get the waiting Anderson. He would place the shackles on his ankles and watch him struggle to get into the back of the wagon. He wouldn't even help him up…this was slavery after all. After surrendering the keys to the shackles to the new owner, he would bid his farewell to the new owner and return to the house. As the wagon pulled out of the plantation, the other slaves stopped their work in the fields and would come to the fence to watch Anderson as he left.

Some stood there in silence, some waved goodbye and some would shed tears at Anderson's departing. It was a very emotional scene, just like you see in the movies. They would stand there watching him go until Mr. Cumberland would yell at them from the house to get back to work and they would dutifully return to their unpaid labor.

* * * * *

On the journey to his new home, about ten miles or so into the trip, Anderson would tell his new owner that he had to relieve himself. This would irritate the new owner to no end and Anderson was very contrite and apologetic. The new owner had to comply because he didn't want a mess on his hands.

The new owner probably thought there would be no danger of escape since Anderson was shackled and the key was safely tucked away on his person. The wagon would ease to a stop and Anderson would struggle to get out and shuffle into the woods to do his business behind a tree or bush.

But, not the business you're thinking of.

You see, Robert Cumberland had slipped Anderson the keys to his shackles right before the new owner came to pick him up. Anderson walked a safe distance from the wagon and, when he was secured from view, freed himself and high tailed it back to the plantation following the usual route Mr. Cumberland had worked out years before.

By the time the duped new owner realized what had happened, Anderson would already have almost a mile head start on him. That's where the chase would begin. And that's where I rudely started my story a few pages back.

And that's where I'll pick it back up again…

* * * * *

A couple hundred yards and he'd be home free. He was so close. He could taste it. Finally, he saw the head of the horse tied to the tree right where it was supposed to be. Anderson headed straight for it. When he was less than forty paces away, a middle-aged white man carrying the biggest pistol Anderson had ever seen stepped out from the bushes.

Anderson stopped dead in his tracks.

In a hushed voice, Mr. Cumberland said, "What's wrong wid you, boy? Come on here."

Anderson ran and jumped on the horse parked right besides Mr. Cumberland's horse. Two of the fastest stallions he owned. The two of them rode back to the plantation on the main road while the former slave owner was still running and cussing in the woods.

Once they arrived back at the plantation, the other slaves jumped into action, opening the barn door so Mr. Cumberland and Anderson could ride right in. Once the animals were secure, the slaves would return to the field and work, like they hadn't seen a thing. You see, all the slaves were in on the charade as well.

Can you imagine the power they must have felt putting one over on a white man back in the day? I'll bet they laughed awhile at the many victims who fell for the trick.

16

Mr. Cumberland's secret was safe with them.

Mr. Cumberland returned to the house and Anderson rushed to a secret room in the attic. That would be his home for the next few weeks, until the coast was clear.

The duped owner returned to the plantation looking for Anderson. By this time, Mr. Cumberland would be in the living room with his feet propped up. I imagine his countenance would be beet red, huffing and puffing at the unexpected search mission he'd just been on. After being asking if Anderson had returned, Mr. Cumberland would put on an Oscar worthy performance on how he hadn't seen hide nor hair of Anderson since he left.

"Why in the world would he return here?" Mr. Cumberland would innocently ask.

And the former owner, realizing his loss, would hang his head and leave in defeat. In fact, he would usually be so embarrassed that he wouldn't report the incident to the authorities or anyone else. That's how he was able to get away with the thievery time and time again.

* * * * *

When telling the tale to his grandchildren, Anderson chuckled, "I would get a few weeks outta the fields 'cause Mr. Cumberland would have to hide me just in case people would come back lookin' for me."

It's hard to believe that this worked more than once, but they pulled the stunt time and time again. They never suspected Mr. Cumberland's duplicity. Anderson said he must have been sold about five or six times and was never caught. He said Robert Cumberland would laugh until he was red in the face at the gullible slave owners. It was like a game to him.

So, my great grandfather Anderson thanked and praised God all his life because as a slave, his way wasn't too hard. He escaped the physical degradation that was the everyday experience of other negro slaves. Better still, when Robert Cumberland died, he made sure Anderson and the other slaves were freed. That's how slavery ended for Momma's family.

I sometimes wonder if Mr. Cumberland financially provided for Anderson after his death. Momma said he always had some money in his pockets and, when she was a little girl, he told her when she got married he was going to make her a wedding dress out of dollar bills. Unfortunately, he died a few years before Momma married.

To this day Momma is still saying, "Shoot…..I never did get my dollar bill dress."

* * * * *

Anderson did wind up getting married to a pretty lady named Selena. They wed in 1879, bought a little farm in Mississippi, and settled down to a much quieter life. During the first sixteen years of marriage, they had eleven children, two sons and nine daughters.

There's one daughter that I'm particularly fond of. Her name is Sarah.

Chapter 2

THE DUTIFUL DAUGHTER

Sarah was born in 1887 in Grenada, Mississippi. It feels a bit odd calling her Sarah with out putting Big Mama in front of it. And, for the love of all that is sacred and holy, please don't ask me why black folks, and some white folks, call their grandmothers Big Mama. By the time I came along, that's what everyone else was calling her and I just got in line.

Big Mama Sarah married my grandfather, Papa George in 1906 when she was nineteen. He was born in 1874 so that would have put him at thirty-two. Go 'head Papa George! The babies started flowing a year later and didn't end until sixteen years and sixteen children later in 1931. Like I told you earlier, there were three children, all boys, who went to be with Jesus as children. Having large families wasn't uncommon back in the day, especially if they were farmers.

Papa George was a giant of a man and Big Mama Sarah had some height to her as well. Perhaps that's why all the children were on the tallish side. For the most part, all of the boys were six feet, or close to it. Momma, her own self is five-eleven in her stocking feet. To this day she believes the sheer number of boys in the family, as well as their height, is what protected them from the racist shenanigans that were going on back then.

Papa George made his living as a farmer and all the children provided free labor. The family was prosperous, considering the times. They lived at, or near a place called

Glenwild Plantation in Mississippi. It was a large piece of
land that had two houses on it. I'm told the manager's
house is still standing to this day, but I can't swear to it
because I haven't been back there for awhile.

Papa George grew some of everything on that farm.
Most of what the family ate, for sure. They grew peas,
peanuts, apples, peaches and nearly every vegetable you
can think of. But the biggest money maker for Papa
George was sugar cane. He grew acres of it and people
from around the county, both black and white, would come
from miles around to buy it from him.

They also grew cotton, which my momma hated to
pick. The thought of her picking cotton surprised me.

I asked her one day, "Did you actually have to pick
cotton?"

She answered, "Sho' I had to pick cotton. Cotton
didn't pick itself."

"But what about your brothers?"

"What about 'em?"

"How come they didn't take care of that? You're a
girl. You should have been in the house helping Big Mama
Sarah cook."

She laughed for about five minutes. "Child, you don't
know nothin'. There wasn't no difference 'tween me and
my brothers when it came to work back den. We girls was
just as strong as them. We all had to work the fields and
take care of the pigs, horses, and cows. That's how we
survived."

She continued, "I didn't mind the work of pickin'
cotton. That wasn't the problem. That cotton used to have
these big stinging worms on them that would bite the mess
outta you. You run up on one of those and you had a whole
heap of trouble. Used to hurt so bad it made you wanna to
cry. That's what I hated."

* * * * *

Big Mama Sarah was a dutiful daughter who cared for her father, Anderson in the years before he died. Now, I always thought Momma's grandmother, Selena died before Anderson, but I found out that wasn't the case. Selena was living with Big Mama's sister, Lillian when Anderson passed. I asked Momma about this and she said they were separated.

My mouth was wide open, "Separated?"

"Yeah."

The scandal! I wanted to know all the dirt. "What happened?"

"Didn't nothing happen"

"Well, why were they getting a divorce?"

"Child, shut yo' mouth. Wasn't nobody gettin' no divorce."

I was confused. I tried to confirm. "But you said they were separated."

"Uh huh," she confirmed. "They was separated. One was living over here and one was living over there. Separated."

Sometimes, when I talk to Momma, my head hurts. But not bad enough to let it go. I decided to take a simpler approach, "Why were they living apart?"

She peered at me over the top of her glasses, then said, "Cause they was old and nobody had room to take care of both of them and our big families too. So, one was livin' over here and the other was livin' over there. Separated."

I once was blind but now I see. "Oh, separated."

"Yeah." Shaking her head she continued, "Back then didn't nobody know nuthin' 'bout no divorce. That's what you people do."

And I ain't even married.

* * * * *

Turns out, Anderson was a handful towards the end of
his life. He always had money in his pocket and loved to
spend it on candy, sugar, and junk food...all stuff he wasn't
supposed to have. If Big Mama Sarah wouldn't cook a
cake for him or buy candy for him on the rare occasion
when she went shopping, he would get upset. She would
chastise him about eating so much sugar, but not too much
because that just made him want it more.

But, when he'd had enough of her restrictions, he
would fix her little red wagon by walking down to the main
road and hitching a ride from anybody who happened to be
going into town. It didn't matter if he knew them or not.
Once he made it to town, he would head straight to the
general store and buy all the sweets and fatty foods he
wanted and eat it all before he came home. He'd come
back to the house smelling of chocolate and all Big Mama
Sarah could do was shake her head.

Anderson had an unfortunate accident that took some
of the wind out of his sails. Seems he developed some type
of problem with his scalp. Back then, people didn't jump
up and run to the doctor when they were sick. They used
herbs and home remedies to cure themselves.

Someone told Anderson to make a salve using lard,
black pepper, and some other ingredients. He did this and
rubbed it over his scalp. Well, the problem was, it was the
middle of summer and when he began to walk around in
the heat, taking care of his business, he started to sweat.
Wouldn't you know that salve started to melt and ran into
his eyes? He was running around trying to get to the well
to wash his eyes out, but it was too late. He completely lost
his sight in one eye...never to return.

* * * * *

It was the last Saturday of his life.

Big Mama Sarah knew in her heart that her father wasn't long for this world. She had been taking care of Anderson for several years and knew his habits. When he started to slow down and experience one pain after the other she took notice. When he finally took to his bed she knew it was closer still. But, when he started calling on people who had long gone to glory, she knew his time was winding down...probably within the next few days. Because that's what people do when they're about to meet Jesus.

Big Mama Sarah loved her father and the thought of losing him was unbearable. But she knew people didn't live forever. Anderson had been blessed to live right at eighty-four years; that's a blessing. She was grateful for the time, but that didn't make losing him any easier.

On that last Saturday, she felt helpless. She heard his cries but was unable to go in to minister to him. For a long time, she didn't move a muscle. When she couldn't take it anymore, she sent a representative to the bedroom to see about him.

* * * * *

Anderson was in the bedroom calling out, "Cellie! Cellie!"

Big Mama Sarah sat in the living room wiping tears from her eyes. My momma, Beulah Mae, was sitting in the living room with her, feeling sad and trying to understand what was going on. At the age of thirteen, she knew her grandfather had been feeling poorly, but she didn't know the end was near.

She asked her mother, "Who he calling? Who is Cellie?"

23

Big Mama Sarah answered, "Cellie, his sister."

Momma responded, "I didn't know he had a sister name Cellie."

"Cause she's been dead for a long time."

"CELLIE!"

Each time he yelled out, it seemed to hurt Big Mama Sarah more. Finally she said, "Beulah Mae, go in dere and talk to him."

Years later, Momma said if she had known he was in the process of dying, she probably would have been scared. She should have taken a clue from the family cat that walked into the room with her and stopped dead in its tracks. The cat stood there, frozen, looking towards the corner of the room as if it saw something. Then, without warning, the cat turned and high tailed it out of there like someone was chasing it.

Crazy cat, she thought as she walked over to the bed and sat down next to her grandfather. She took his hand and began to massage it.

"Cellie, dat you?"

Momma answered, "Naw, Grandpaw, it's me. Beulah Mae."

He was confused, "Where Cellie?"

"She ain't here."

"Where she go? I just seen her."

Humoring him, she responded "She just stepped away for awhile. Tell me about her."

He managed a slight smile, "Cellie my baby sister. She beautiful and she can sang. She got a high-pitched voice. Keen. Sound like a whistle. She can hit dem high notes."

Momma smiled, "Dat's real nice Granpaw."

Looking around, he asked again, "You sho Cellie ain't here?"

"I'm sho."

He appeared to accept that because he said, "Oh, ok."

Momma patted his hand before she got up and left his bedside. She went back to the living room and just as soon as she sat down, she heard, "CELLIE!"

Grandpa Anderson finally met up with Cellie. He died a few days later.

* * * * *

But, back to Big Mama Sarah. She was something else. She loved Big Dip ice cream and Cracker Jacks. She always smelled like Lifeboy Soap. The one thing we remember was she always used to start her sentences with was the phrase, "Well, folkest..."

She was a sweet old lady who loved her children and grandchildren but, she was also a tough old broad if the spirit came upon her. Tough, but never mean. I guess growing up in rural Mississippi in the late 1800's and being the mother of so many children would put a bit of a rough edge on anybody.

She had all kinds of special powers. At least that's what it seemed like to us, her grandchildren. By special powers, I mean to say, she knew things. She knew things before they happened. It was eerie.

After all of her children were grown and married, the boys moved away to places like Chicago, West Memphis and Little Rock, Arkansas and Kansas City, Missouri. All the girls settled down in Memphis.

Those who stayed in Memphis would sometimes decide to surprise Big Mama Sarah with a visit. Everyone would promise not to tell her we were coming and no one ever did. We would get up early on Saturday morning, or a Sunday afternoon after church, pack up the cars and follow each other for the two hour drive to Grenada, Mississippi. We would be in utter shock and amazement when we would arrive to a huge meal already prepared and sitting on the table and Big Mama Sarah sitting in her white rocking chair with a big smile on her face saying, "It's about time y'all got here."

We could never surprise her!

Or, there was the distant cousin that none of us knew about. She lived in another state with her father and no one had ever met her, including Big Mama Sarah. When the child turned eighteen, she decided to introduce herself to the grandmother she'd never met. She found the address and set off on her journey, telling no one where she was going. She pulled up to that house on Cherry Street and got out of her car.

Big Mama Sarah was sitting on the porch quietly rocking away and looking at the lady over the top of her glasses as she approached. When the lady got to the front porch, Big Mama put a big smile on her face and said, "Hello dear, you must be Crystal."

The girl's jaw dropped. She said, "Excuse me, but how do you know my name."

Big Mama Sarah just smiled at her and said, "I know all of my grandchirren. Great grandchirren too. Come on in this house and get somethin' to eat." Of course, she already had dinner for two prepared.

She always had time to talk to us and share her wisdom or just words of encouragement to help someone along the way. My sister Mae's son, David was just telling me about a conversation he had with Big Mama Sarah at her home in the Westwood area of Memphis in the 1980's.

David is a bonafied genius who graduated high school at fifteen, college at nineteen and Harvard Law School at twenty-one. Big Mama Sarah said to him, "Boy, I hear you powerful smart, ain't you?"

David was a bit embarrassed at the attention, but honestly answered, "Yes ma'am. I do well in school."

She said, "Uh huh. Well, what you wanna be when you finish with all this learnin' you gettin?"

Without blinking an eye, he told her, "I want to be the

President of the United States."

She looked at him for awhile trying to see if he was serious. Then she excused herself and hobbled to her bedroom. David didn't know what to think about her hasty exit, but before long she came back with a dusty old box. Calling David over to sit right next to her, she slowly and lovingly wiped off the box and gave it to him. He opened it to see a beautiful ink pen. It was obviously very old and quite expensive for those days.

He didn't want to take it but she wouldn't hear of it.

David was honored to have it. "Thank you so much, Big Mama Sarah. What's this for?"

She said to him, in all seriousness "When you sign yo first bill, use this pen."

David still has that pen to this day.

As I said before, Big Mama Sarah was feisty too. There was another time when one of her grandson's was talking to her about black power and tracing our roots back to our native land. This grandson was all into African culture. He was telling Big Mama about the moles on her face.

He said, "You know, Big Mama, they say that people who have a lot of moles on their face come from the same tribe."

She looked at him and said, "Boy, don't call me no tribe."

* * * * *

It was about 1:00 in the afternoon on June 20, 1990 in sunny Los Angeles, California. I was sitting at my desk working hard because my boss was in the office that day. I answered the phone as soon as it rang. It was my sister Denise. She told me to brace myself. I really hate it when people say that. What does it mean anyway? How do you do it?

She said, "Big Mama Sarah died today."

Y'all, I cried awhile.

I cried right there in everyone's face and I didn't even care. I cried so hard my boss came out of the office and tried to comfort me, but I couldn't be comforted. My coworkers were all trying to help me but I just wanted to be left alone.

I loved that old lady.

All of us living in Los Angeles caught the first flight out and were in Memphis in a day or so. Family came from far and wide for the home going service. Not just from the cities I named earlier. Family had branched out to New York, Michigan, Texas, Georgia, and beyond. I have never, ever, ever in my whole entire life seen that many people at a funeral. I would put the number at two hundred, family members alone, more or less. There was some comfort in that.

Before we knew it, we were sitting in N.J. Ford Funeral Home on South Parkway listening to person after person share precious memories of Big Mama Sarah. My plan was to sit as far away from that coffin as humanly possible so I was hanging out at the end of the line when we marched in. Well, wouldn't you know the family filled up one entire side of the chapel and I would up on the third row of the new section. I was close enough to see her lying there...grey wig and all.

God blessed Big Mama Sarah to live over one hundred years. One hundred and two, if I'm not mistaken. I know I should be grateful for that...to have her around for so long. Another way to look at it is, when a person has been around for so long, it's harder to let go. It's hard to overcome the pain of not having them around to talk to when you need it. Y'all know what I'm talking about. It's hard to stop missing them.

It's been over twenty years now.

When I stop missing her, I'll let you know.

CHAPTER 3

MOMMA 'NEM

Momma, also known as Beulah Mae, was born in 1922. So that y'all can picture her in your mind, let me describe her to you. I already said she's got some height to her. She's also a firm size eighteen, been that way forever. She wears it well too. Her skin is ebony, which matches her hair. She has a pretty face. But it's also the kind of face that you can look at and know that she don't take much foolishness.

Now, Daddy's name is Matthew. He is the polar opposite of Momma, appearance wise, that is. He's biracial; half black, half other. When he was younger, you'd really have to look twice before you decided what race he was. His skin was just that white. He's about the same height as Momma and on the thin side. He's a handsome man.

Growing up, Momma went to school from the fall of the year to spring, almost like the school terms of today. And, it's true what the old folks say about traveling a great distance to school. Momma said she had to get up right early and walk several miles through the woods to get to the one room schoolhouse where she got her education. But, she didn't mind overly much, because it was at school where she met my daddy

Momma used to sit and watch Daddy out of the corner of her eyes because he was a handsome boy as well. She said the girls would be falling out over him, rubbing their hands through his thick, wavy hair and stroking his white looking skin. He loved the attention he received from the girls because he didn't get much love at home.

"Hussies!" is what she called them. "Those girls was fast. My momma would'a had my hide if I'd been acting like them."

She liked him just fine. But she wouldn't pay any attention to him, which worked in her favor because it made him like her more. That's a lesson for another day.

Each year, as soon as the school term ended, she had to go out and work the fields with her brothers and sisters. This was the schedule until she made it to the ninth grade and she became a full time laborer. It's sad to say, but there was no high school in their rural community. The nearest high school was in town and the family couldn't afford to send all the children into town every day, so her education ended with the eighth grade.

I asked her how she felt about not being able to go to high school and she said it didn't make her no never mind. She was happy for her eight years of schoolin'. Back then, people were happy with what they could get. But don't get me to preaching.

There was no shame in her, but she did say, "You don't have to go tellin' people 'bout my education."

I told her I wouldn't, but, y'all know I can't hold water.

Life in the country followed a usual routine. Momma, Papa George, and her brothers and sisters woke up early Monday through Saturday and worked in the fields, sowing and reaping. When the sugar cane was harvested, they would all work to grind the cane until it released its juice. Then, they had to cook the juice in a large cast iron kettle over an open fire until it made syrup. Funny thing, it seemed like as soon as they finished the process and would get ready to bottle the syrup to sell, people from the area would come by with their own bottles and jugs, asking for some syrup. Papa George would give away as much as he could spare because that's how he was.

Before they'd leave the house each morning, Big Mama Sarah would tell one of the kids to go and kill a couple of chickens in the yard or bring a ham in from their smokehouse. Now, that's a little too fresh for me, but that's how they ate back then. While they were working outside, Big Mama Sarah would be busy in the kitchen preparing the family meals. Cooking was her job all day every day. Once everyone left the house, she had to prepare two meals a day for her family, dinner (which was served at noon) and supper. She would rise early and as soon as the house was empty, she'd get started on dinner, the main meal of the day. Around noon, Big Mama Sarah would go out to the back porch and ring the bell to let everyone know dinner was ready.

Momma said, "Child, you could hear that bell for miles away. We'd drop them plows and hoes and take off runnin' to the house 'cause we'd be so hungry."

"For dinner we'd have cabbage, greens, squash, and onions and whatever meat she made. It was good!" Big Mama Sarah was a good cook and people knew it.

Momma told me that every Sunday after church, people would drop by their house for a visit and wind up eating like there was no tomorrow. Now, this wasn't a bad thing, there was always enough for everyone. The problem was the adults ate first. From what I hear, the guests would be talking, eating the food, and having a high time while the children had to wait until they were through before they could eat.

Momma said her mouth would be watering because you could smell all that good food but couldn't eat it until the last guest had had enough. Memories of having to suffer on a hungry stomach stayed with her, and when she started her own family, the children always ate first. And whoever didn't like it could go find somewhere else to eat.

There was one particular Sunday when people were taking an extraordinarily long time to eat and Momma couldn't take it anymore. She was the one with the sense of humor, always trying to get people to laugh so she decided to put on a little show while she and her siblings were all huddled up in the back of the house waiting to eat.

She got up and started acting crazy, ranting and raving and circling the bedroom like she was looking for food. Momma said to her siblings, "I'm so hungry, I'm gettin' out of my senses, now!"

Then she got up, went and got this man's hat, and threw it across the room. Everybody laughed awhile and it took their minds off their hunger. But, wouldn't you know it. After everyone had left and the kids had finally finished eating, somebody went and told Big Mama Sarah what she'd done.

Mournfully, Momma said, "Mama tore my behind up."

I was incensed. "Why would they rat you out like that? It was just a joke."

She chuckled and said, "Girl, we was in the country. Wasn't nuthin' else to do. We didn't have no TV or radio. Might as well see if you could make somebody get a whippin'. That's what we did for fun."

She continued, "Still, at the time, I was plenty mad about it. I'd did all that actin' and got all those laughs but I was the one to get a whippin'."

* * * * *

Momma wasn't the only one with a sense of humor, or an active imagination. Her brother Benny could also be counted on for a laugh.

Like I told you, Papa George was a farmer. The family ate most of the crops they grew, but a lot of the produce was sold to people in the community. Papa George left strict instruction for the children not to eat fruit from several of the trees in the yard because fruit from certain trees were to be sold. And they all knew to obey him or they'd get a whippin'.

Well, one fine day my Uncle Benny was walking around at the far end of the yard when he came across a peach tree with the most beautiful, ripe, juicy peaches he'd ever seen. He was so hungry he knew he had to have one in spite of Papa George's instruction. Slowly, he looked over his left shoulder and then his right to see if the coast was clear. He didn't see anyone. Two bad he didn't have another shoulder to look over, because Papa George was standing nearby looking right at him. He was shielded by some trees so Uncle Benny didn't see him.

Now, instead of simply picking a peach and eating it, Uncle Benny decided to have some fun. He walked up to the tree and knocked on it.

"Knock, Knock!" Uncle Benny said.

Changing his voice to sound strong and treelike he answered, "Come in."

Then the hospitable tree said, "Have a seat."

Uncle Benny responded, "I believe I will." And he climbed up the tree.

Papa George was watching the whole show, struggling to keep from laughing out loud.

The tree said, "Rest your hat."

Uncle Benny said, "I believe I will." He put his little straw hat on the limb.

The generous tree said, "Have some fruit."

Uncle Benny said, "I believe I will."

And with that he picked two of the largest peaches he could find. Go big or go home!

As soon as he put the first peach to his mouth and took a bite, Papa George bellowed, "Boy, didn't I tell you to leave those peaches be?"

Papa George scared the mess out of Uncle Benny, who promptly fell out of the tree. Thank the Good Lord he wasn't hurt...until after Papa George finished with him, that is.

* * * * *

Big Momma Sarah was a strict parent and didn't take much lip from her children. I guess that's where my momma gets it from.

When Momma was a young girl, she and her two older sisters, Pearl and Arlene had a gospel singing group called, "The Three Sisters." Original, huh? Momma was the lead soprano. Pearl was the tenor and Arlene was the alto. To let Momma tell it, they were really good and were starting to get invited to sing at churches all over Grenada County, Mississippi.

One Sunday, they had an engagement to sing at a large Methodist church. Since this was a pretty big event for them, Big Mama Sarah decided they should all get new dresses for the "gig." This excited Momma and her sisters to no end because it wasn't often that they got store bought clothes.

When they went to the dress shop, the girls each picked out the dress she wanted. Momma chose a yellow and white dress because she liked the way it looked on the hanger. None of the girls bothered to try on the dresses before they purchased them.

When they got home, they ran to their bedroom and tried on their new outfits. Pearl and Arlene came out modeling their garments and thought they were just fine. When Momma put hers on, it was long and loose fitting. As it tuned out, the dress was pinned up in a way that made it look prettier than it was. Off the rack, the dress was big and boxy. Like something a much older lady would wear. This was a major problem for Momma and she flat out refused to wear the dress to the performance that night.

When Big Mama Sarah heard about this she gave her what for. She said, "What are you talkin' about, young lady?"

Red Alert Y'all!

When Big Mama Sarah used the term 'young lady' it usually meant proceed with caution. The likelihood of a person being separated from their teeth was high. But Momma wasn't scared.

"Look at this" she said, with her hands spread out to her sides. To further emphasize the point, she spun around so that Big Mama could get the full effect of the ugliness of the tent-like ill-fitting garment.

"I ain't wearin' this old lady dress. It looks like it was made the year King Uzziah died. It's ugly, it don't fit right and I hate it. People gone laugh at me."

Big Mama Sarah shook her head. "So, I guess I can see what you singin' for. You ain't singin' for the Lord. You up there for show."

"Naw Mama, that ain't it. But, if I'm gonna be in front of all those people, I need to look good."

"Lookin' good ain't got nothin' to do with it. You suppose to be singin' for the Lord."

"It got a little to do with it. You don't want people laughin' at me do you Mama?"

"Well suh. If that's how you feel, then I'll tell you what. We ain't gonna give 'em no opportunity to laugh at you. You ain't singin' no mo'."

"Mama!"

"I don't wanna hear another word from you."

"But…"

"Not another word. I don't know why I ain't seen this before now. Beulah Mae, you ain't got the right spirit and the Lord ain't pleased. Now you march yo'self back to yo' room and take off that dress. We gon' take it back."

Mumbling to herself, Momma went to her room and took off the offensive garment.

And with that Big Mama Sarah sent word to one of Momma's cousins who replaced her in the group. The new group sang together a few times, but soon after, Pearl and Arlene decided it wasn't as much fun without Momma and they all went back to the church choir.

And that was the end of The Three Sisters.

Singing ran in the family, though. On lazy evenings after all the chores were done, the whole family, all fourteen of them, would gather on the wide front porch of the main house and have a good old-fashioned sing along. They'd sing one song and as soon as it was over, one of Momma's brother's would start another song and everyone would just fall in with their parts.

Momma said the white folks up and down the road would come out on their porches and listen to them. The next morning, one of the neighbors would ask Papa George, "Who was that leading, *I'll Fly Away* last night. They sho' sounded good."

I remember when Momma was telling me that story. She ended the tale with a comment on how strict Big Mama Sarah was. She said, "My momma was hard on us. We couldn't get away with much of nothin'. If we misbehaved, she'd tear our behinds up. Y'all better be glad I'm your momma. I'm easy on y'all."

I just looked at her.

CHAPTER 4

MAKE ROOM FOR DADDY

Up until this point, I've done a whole heap of talking about Momma and her family. But, I don't mean to slight my daddy. Let me start off by telling y'all, their early lives were vastly different. Polar opposites. Whereas, Momma grew up in the midst of a loving family, strong father, supportive mother, and respectful siblings. Daddy's early life was a whole 'nother story. He's been through a whole lot of stuff. Ironically, when I ask him about it, he says stuff like, "If it had not been for the Lord on my side, where would I be?"

He used his trials to make him stronger.

For those of you who don't know, let me take a minute and get y'all up to speed...

* * * * *

Daddy's momma died when he was five years old and his father was some man who was either white or an American Indian. I'm leaning towards the American Indian theory, but that's just me. Either way, he never had the pleasure of meeting the man because Daddy was the result of a liaison. That was not cool back then.

Over the years, he came to joke about his father's identity. If someone were to ask him who his father was, some days he would answer, "Chief Sitting Bull." Some days he would say, "Tonto." He would laugh and so would we. But, for him, I think he was just laughing on the outside.

After his momma died, Daddy, his two stepsisters, and his stepbrother lived with his grandmother, but raising four extra children, in addition to her children and other grandchildren, proved to be too much for her. After two years, she decided to give Daddy and his siblings away to anyone who would have them. People came from near and far. Sure enough, one by one, he watched his siblings leave with people he had never met before. Worse than that, by the time Daddy got old enough to look for them, they had all moved out of Mississippi. He never saw them again, even to this day.

Doggone shame if you ask me.

Grandmother was going to give him away too but, when the old couple came to take him, Daddy's young aunt grabbed hold of him and would not let him go. She begged and pleaded with Grandmother to let him stay, and she relented. Daddy got to stay in the family, but he went to live down the road with his aunt and uncle. That was when the real trouble began. Because his uncle, and mostly his aunt were some low down, nasty, evil people.

Just plain ugly, inside and out...

* * * * *

Hold on y'all.

I gotta stop right here.

Now, before I go on, I have to educate ya'll. See, in the south, we have at least five levels of ugly. There might be more depending on what part of the south you're from, but here are the most common. They are as follows: (1) They look like who shot John? (2) They look like who did it and what for. (3) They look like they'd fallen out of an ugly tree and hit every branch on the way down. (4) They look like the north end of a southbound mule, more commonly known as butt ugly. And, the ultimate level of ugliness is (5) they have a face that could scare the devil.

My daddy said his aunt was ALL five levels of ugly.
Hope that don't keep y'all up at night…

* * * * *

Seems to me, if these people didn't want my daddy,
they should have said so. But, from what I'm told, Daddy's
Grandmother was mean and usually got her way about
things. She made them take Daddy and they did, but they
didn't like it one bit and took their anger out on him instead
of confronting Grandmother. They beat my Daddy. They
abused him while pampering their children right in his face.
They barely fed him. They made him sleep on a cot in the
kitchen even though they had an extra bedroom. They
worked him like a dog.

He put up with it for years, stealing away to
Grandmother's house for a break every now and then.
Grandmother treated him well. She let him stay for a week
or so and during that time would dress him properly and
feed him and treat him right nice. But, then she would send
him back to Pharaoh's house and the trouble would start
back up.

Reckoning day finally came when he was a young
teenager, around fourteen or fifteen. He'd had it up to here
and decided enough was enough. That ugly aunt of his got
on his last good nerve and he got a fireplace poker and
went after her. Daddy had every intention of performing
the very first reconstructive surgery in Grenada County,
Mississippi.

Y'all, it took everyone in that house to keep him off of
that woman because he had had it. When they saw how
mad my daddy was they started sleeping in shifts. And that
was the last of his troubles with those people, I'm tellin'
you.

Now, going back to my anonymous grandfather.
Daddy never officially met the man. He saw him a total of

one time and then it was at a distance. He was not allowed
to speak to him. Everybody in their community knew who
Daddy was and who his father was as well. It was the talk
back then in their small community; a black woman and a
white/red man. Scandulous!

Well, to let Momma tell it, the man had a hand in
Daddy's life. Daddy would deny it until the cows came
home, but Momma presented a strong argument. She
remembered seeing Daddy's father once or twice back in
the day. Momma said Daddy looked just like his father.
Not only that, Momma said that, growing up, Daddy was
always very well dressed. He used to wear expensive cable
knit sweaters and thick wool coats in the winters. When he
went to church, he wore nice suits and shoes. He dressed
better than everyone else.

When Daddy would complain about not having a
father, Momma would say to him, "Matthew, where did
you get all of those nice clothes you used to wear?"

He'd answer, "When I'd go stay with Grandmother
she'd give 'em to me. You know that, Beulah Mae."

Momma would counter, "But your people were po'.
They didn't have much of nuthin'. Where you think they
got the money to buy that kinda stuff?"

"They had a little money coming in."

Momma was unconvinced. She said, "Uh-huh. But
Matthew, nobody else in yo' family dressed like that. You
was the only one."

She'd let it marinate for a minute and then come back
with, "And another thing, you always had a little money in
yo pocket. Where that money come from?"

"Grandmother gave it to me."

Momma just looked at him. You could tell he was
thinking about what she said, but in the end, he put the
thought out of his head. His father's rejection hurt him and
he wouldn't entertain a benevolent thought about the man.

* * * * *

It was a Saturday morning in the summer of 1955, long before my time. The phone rang bright and early. My oldest brother, Mark answered it and after a moment said, "Daddy, telephone."

Mark laid the phone down on the stand in the hallway and whispered to Daddy as he approached, "I think it's important. It's a white man and he asked for Mr. Matthew DeVault."

Daddy nodded his head and picked up the receiver, "Yes?"

Daddy stood there for a few moments answering the man's questions while the family listened to the one sided conversation. "Yeah, that's me."

"Uh, huh."

"Yeah, Grenada County, Mississippi."

"1920."

"Yeah"

"WHO?"

"I ain't got no Daddy."

Everyone's ears perked up when they overheard Daddy say that. Everybody with right good sense knew not to ask him about his daddy. That phone call was trouble.

As he began to understand the conversation, Daddy's tone was growing more agitated and louder with each response. He was turning red, a sure sign that he was angry.

"No."

"No."

"I don't want it."

"I said, I don't want it."

"Give it to somebody else."

"That's not my problem. I don't want it. And that's all I got to say about it." With that, he hung up the phone and walked out of the house and into the back yard. No one was brave enough to ask him about the call until much later in the day when Momma brought it up at the dinner table that evening.

Innocently, she asked "Who was that on the phone this mornin', Matthew?"

"Some lawyer in Mississippi."

"What did he want?"

"You ain't gon' believe this, but that man died and they called to tell me. He got my number from Uncle Percy. Imma talk to Percy 'bout givin' out my number."

"Forget Percy. Who died?"

Daddy waited a long time before he responded. Fourteen eyes were on him waiting to hear who died. Daddy finally answered in a round about way, talking like a white man, "The man said, I regret to inform you that your father is dead."

He paused and said with force, "I told him, I ain't got no Daddy."

"What did he say to that?"

"He said that man listed my name in his will as his son. He said that man knew about me, but under the circumstances thought it would be better for me if he kept his distance."

With disgust, Daddy added, "Called me his son."

Momma let that marinate for a while. She knew he was having trouble processing this information. Finally she said, "Oh."

Tina asked, "Well, what did the lawyer want with you Daddy? They havin' trouble buryin' Grandpa."

"DON'T call him that."

Tina flinched at his tone. Daddy wasn't one for yelling.

He lowered his voice and said, "Naw. He was callin' me 'cause my name was in the man's will."

Under his voice, Daddy repeated himself, "Callin' me his son."

This news perked up my siblings ears. Jean asked, "A will? Really, Daddy? What did he leave us?"

Notice how she slipped that in, "us." Trifling.

"Said he left me fifty acres of land in Mississippi."

Let the party begin!

My brothers and sisters all began to talk at once. They just knew they were rich.

Tina said, "Can I have a new pair of shoes?"

Earl chimed in, "Does this mean we don't have to sleep in the attic no more?

Mae asked, "We movin' to Mississippi?"

Hey, let me speak from beyond the womb while we're dreaming and put my request in, "Can we build a summer house in the Hamptons on Daddy's job at the warehouse?" These questions were foolishness and Daddy put a stop to it quick and in a hurry.

"I told him I didn't want the land."

My siblings were indignant. They all started talking at once. "What?!"

Mark said, "What do you mean you don't want it? Yes we do!"

Tina offered, "But Daddy, that land is probably worth a lot of money. We could be rich."

Daddy said, "We're getting by."

Mae said, "Yeah, barely. Don't you want better for your children?" If you ask me, she went a little too far with that one.

Momma thought so too 'cause she gave Mae the eye. She'd had enough of their foolishness. "Y'all hush now."

Then she spoke to Daddy. "Matthew, you told him you didn't want the land. You sho?"

Daddy took a moment to look at Momma and everyone at the table. Finally he said, "The man never owned me when he was alive. I been grown long enough for him to call me if he'd had a mind to. I ain't gonna let him own up to me now that he's dead and gone."

And with that he got up and went outside to sit under the cherry tree.

The hurt showing on his face and the pain in his voice settled it with Momma and with everyone else too. They all came to understand how deeply rooted his hurt was. No amount of money was worth seeing Daddy hurting. They let it go at that.

And wasn't nobody mad but the devil.

* * * * *

Now, that's some powerful recollecting, isn't it? Are you dazzled? Are you amazed? Well, you ain't seen nothing yet. We haven't even got to the meat of the story. Wait until I tell y'all about *MY OWN FAMILY.*

PART TWO

MY OWN FAMILY

REMEMBER WHEN

I am the eighth born of Matthew and Beulah Mae DeVault. My older siblings came along in the early to mid part of last century. They are old. Very old...all of them. Relics. But not me. As for me, I made my debut much, much later during the era after we were called colored and before we were African Americans.

I have three brothers. Now, considering my father's name is Matthew, and my oldest brother's name is Mark, it kind of surprised me that my parents didn't name my other brothers Luke and John. You know, in keeping with the whole apostle theme. But they didn't do that. My other brothers are Earl and Wayne. I have four sisters: Jean, Mae, Tina, and Denise. This is how everyone lines up: Jean, Mark, Mae, Tina, Earl, Wayne, Denise, and me.

We grew up on the south side of Memphis, right off Parkway near the I-40. Back in the day, my neighborhood was the place to live; for black folk that is. I'm talking nice brick homes and well manicured lawns. No crime to speak of. People got along pretty well back then because the fight was against racist white folk, and not each other.

Our neighbors were high muckity muck Negroes. In fact, one of our neighbors was one of the first black doctors in Memphis, if I'm not mistaken. He lived in the best house in the area and my brother, Mark, had the honor of mowing his lawn every week. That family stayed in our area until white folks eased up on where blacks were allowed to live and the good doctor and his family moved into a mansion across town. Everyone was proud of him!

Other than him, there were nurses, teachers, and a principal or two on our very street. You know the type; well educated black folk. I have to say, they weren't too happy about our large brood moving on up to their neighborhood and bringing their property value down, but that was their tough luck. Like it or lump it! We weren't stuttin' them.

When my family moved in, they were a family of seven; five children and my parents. For all intents and purposes, we were poor. The only reason we were able to buy the house in the first place was because the city of Memphis decided to buy the old, raggedy house we were living in so they could build a fire station. Look at God!

Daddy took that money and put it with the little bit he and Momma had already saved and we high tailed it across town. They were singing hallelujah on move in day, but Daddy had to work two and sometimes three jobs to keep the roof over our heads.

In the beginning, we didn't have much. No car or television or phone. Those things didn't come until later. Funny thing though; we didn't consider ourselves poor. I think that's because life was different back then. Times were simple and so were we. We didn't need as much to make us happy.

My older siblings grew up in the south in the middle of the civil rights movement, Jim Crow and segregation. They said it wasn't that bad. That just goes to show you, even though they were short on stuff, they did have the things that make for a pleasant childhood. Things like loving parents, siblings to play with and a huge yard to run around in.

It took a while for our neighbors to accept us into their cliques. I guess when they saw that we weren't swinging from the trees like Tarzan and Boy, or tearing up the neighborhood like a bunch of thugs, they deemed us acceptable. Momma's philosophy was this; we can do this the easy way or the hard way. She wasn't trying to be anyone's friend. Not only did she have a house full of kids but, she was from a large family herself. It's not like she was lonely.

When the other housewives in the neighborhood saw that Momma wasn't running after them, they warmed up to her. They started approaching her at the corner market or stopping to talk at the back fence when she was outside hanging the clothes out to dry. One of our neighbors even invited our family to dinner. Well, not exactly.

The neighbor lady asked Momma, "Mrs. DeVault. Why don't you and your husband come over for dinner tonight?"

Momma's ears perked up at the invitation. She knew the invitation didn't quite cover everyone. She clarified, "Me and Matthew?"

"Yes, we'd love to have you."

"Well, what about my chirren?"

The neighbor would stutter and explain, "Well, uh…I don't think we'll have enough to feed the two of y'all and all of those kids. Some of your children are old enough to baby sit, ain't they?"

"Yeah, Jean and Mark are old enough to baby sit. But Matthew and I don't go nowhere without the chirren. They gotta eat too, ya know. Thanks for askin' though."

That's how Momma was. If her kids weren't welcome, she didn't feel she and Daddy were either.

There was this one time a brave soul invited the whole family over to share a meal. Everyone was so excited to be eating at a table other than our own. Momma took all day pressing suits and dresses and combing hair, getting everyone ready for the event.

The evening was going well at first. The conversation flowed easily and my siblings were on their best behavior. It was a pleasant affair; that is until it was time to sit down and eat. That's when Momma's jaws got a little tight. See, there was a great difference in the food that was served to the adults and the host's children and what was served to my siblings.

You could practically see steam coming out of Momma's ears when she looked at her plate and saw baked chicken, greens, candied yams and cornbread. And then she looked at the table off to the side in the corner where her kids had to eat a glorified version of beanie weenies and rolls. Now, y'all know that ain't right.

It wouldn't have been so bad if all of the children had to eat the same thing. But for the hostess to serve her children one thing, and the rest of the kids something else was just flat out wrong. Momma felt really bad about the situation, but she knew it would make matters worse if she spoke out about it.

Two wrongs don't make a right.

Looking across the room, Momma's eyes met Mae's. She could tell her headstrong child was fit to be tied. Beads of sweat started popping out on Momma's forehead when she saw the disgusted look on her third-born daughter's face.

She said a silent prayer, "Lord, for once in her life, please let Mae keep quiet." She prayed that Mae would let an offense go and act like she had some home training.

But, Mae knew she was being slighted. She sat there with her nose up in the air and her arms crossed. She refused to eat.

The other kids ate like Vikings. See, they weren't as sensitive as Mae. It was a while before Mark noticed that Mae wasn't eating. He leaned over and said, "Mae, how come you ain't eatin'?"

Furious, she whispered, "I ain't eating this slop."

He didn't understand, "Slop? We eat this at home all the time. What's wrong with you?"

"Wrong with me? I'll tell you what's wrong with me. Why we gotta eat this cheap stuff and everybody else gets the good food?"

She broke it down to him, "I could see it if their kids got the same food as we did, but oh no, they got the same food as Momma, Daddy and everybody else. We're the only ones who got beans and franks."

He said, "And a roll. Don't forget the roll."

"It's beans and franks."

Ever the optimist, he said, "Yeah, but look how big the franks are."

She rolled her eyes at him, leaned back in her folding chair, re-crossed her arms and sat in that position for the rest of the evening. When Mark saw she wasn't going to eat, he reached over and took her plate saying, "I'll take that. More for me."

I'm telling you, that boy ain't got no pride.

So, in light of things like that happening, our parents were careful not to accept too many dinner invitations.

There was a couple who lived down the street that we trusted. This couple didn't have any children so they were always happy to see my family coming. They were well-to-do neighbors. When they got 'color' television, they invited our family over to help break it in.

They called us po' folks over since they knew our family didn't even have a television, let alone color. At that time, we couldn't afford such a luxury. My folks weren't proud though. Everyone rushed over to her house and parked ourselves in front of their television, Momma and Daddy too.

She turned on the set and everyone sat there in anticipation. Sure enough, there was color. The color was red. Everything was red because she had a piece of red cellophane attached to the front of the set. Don't laugh. That's what they called color television back then.

They tell me everyone was impressed.

* * * * *

Do you remember when mothers were also the family doctor? My momma's motto was, if you don't get sick in the first place, you won't ever need a doctor. I guess that was why Dr. Beulah Mae practiced preventative maintenance. Momma's preventative maintenance was the main reason why everyone in my family grew to hate Saturday nights.

Saturday night was the worse night of the week for us because it was the night we all had to line up and wait for our turn to take a big swig of cod liver oil, castor oil, or mineral oil. The "oil of the week," so to speak. Daddy had to take it too, and he complained more than us kids. I'm telling you the truth. Those were the most awful tasting concoctions known to mankind.

We would try to run and hide or beg and plead to get out of taking that stuff but nothing worked. Momma was like a tree planted by the rivers of waters on that subject. She would not be moved. At the time, we didn't know why we had to take medicine especially when we weren't sick. We thought it was a punishment, but it wasn't. Back then, parents did everything they could to keep their families healthy. A visit to the doctor was a luxury we couldn't afford.

But, if a family had to run up a bill at the doctor, or just plain fell on hard times the neighbors came to the rescue. The easiest way to raise money was for someone to throw a "Heaven or Hell" party. This is how it worked: someone would sell tickets to the event and people would volunteer to make the food, potluck style. When the guests arrived, they would tell the person at the door if they wanted to go to the heaven side of the room or the hell side.

On the heaven side, they'd serve light fare, like chicken salad, tuna fish on Ritz crackers, finger sandwiches, salad, angel food cake, vanilla ice cream and those pastel colored melt away mints.

On the hell side, they'd have hot and spicy food like the Memphis specialty, barbeque ribs or barbeque spaghetti, potato salad with the red potatoes, garlic bread and devil's food cake and chocolate syrup, maybe even chocolate ice cream.

I can still see my Bible totin' and quotin' Momma telling the person at the door, "I'd like to go to hell, please."

In fact, most people went to hell.

* * * * *

Back in the day, parents had a closer reign on their children. People had to create fun because money was tight. Sitting around watching television all day was unheard of. Even if you were blessed enough to have a television, no self-respecting mother would let you just lay around all day watching it and running up the electric bill. At least, not on our side of town.

But, it really wasn't a problem. Children couldn't wait to get outside, meet up with friends and run and play. They'd run around the neighborhood, having foot races, playing football in the middle of the street, trying to catch butterflies or fireflies, playing hopscotch, and four square. By the time night came, they'd be exhausted from so much physical activity. Once their heads hit the pillows they'd sleep like death.

Most kids created their own games or made their own dolls out of coke bottles, a cord or sea grass for the hair and a clothespin for the face. My sisters had paper dolls of Marilyn Monroe and Jane Mansfield because they didn't have black dolls back then. Before the time of easy bake ovens, they'd bake stuff in old cans by mixing up dirt and water, put the mixture in the can, and place it in the sun to bake. And it was so hot, it would bake the whole can, too.

If Daddy was getting paid, they'd ask Momma for a nickel or a dime to go to the store on the corner. And if she could spare the money, they'd walk there with our friends and get a whole bag of cookies or candy.

Everyone was totally safe too. Kids could play with other kids in the neighborhood from sunrise to sunset. But they were always mindful to be home before the streetlights came on. Getting home to our house late could have dire results. At best, you'd loose some of your freedom. At the worst, you lose the ability to sit down comfortably.

By the time I came along, my older siblings had already left the nest. Financially, things were a bit easier then, without so many people in the house. On Sunday evenings, Momma and Daddy would load Wayne, Denise, and me in the car. We'd stop by the Sundry, get an ice cream cone and head for the airport.

Once we arrived, we would get out of the car and sit on the hood for hours. I can remember being totally content to just sit there watching the planes landing and taking off and dreaming of one day being inside of those big jets going any place I good and well pleased. That was the best entertainment we could ask for.

That's how it was back in the day.

CHAPTER 6

JEAN, MARK, AND MAE

It just dawned on me that this might be the first time y'all have met us DeVaults. The way I figure it, it would be downright rude for me to just haul off recollecting stories about my siblings without even bothering to let you know anything about them. Un-neighborly, considering where I'm from and me being a Southern Belle and all. For shame!

Before I go one step further, I need to slow my roll and remember my manners. Let me introduce you to my own family. My brothers and sisters, that is. I'll keep it short and sweet. One story per person and then we can go back to talking about important stuff.

* * * * *

Jean was the oldest and the mother hen of the bunch, Momma's deputy so to speak. I said, "was" because she died in 1985, about a month after her 44th birthday. We had her funeral on April Fools Day and for Jean, that was about right. That girl was crazy. Crazy in the good way, though. I still have a few stories to tell about her even though she's gone on to glory. But for right now, let me move on and talk to y'all about living folks.

Mark was born two years after Jean. That boy loved to play practical jokes on everyone. Momma and Daddy included. During his early years, he developed his skill to an art form. I consider myself blessed that he was grown and out of the house before I came along.

Right off the top of my head, I'm remembering one of his jokes that didn't turn out too good. It was when Mark tricked Mae into drinking lye. In his defense, he wouldn't have done anything to hurt Mae. He didn't know it was like poison so he politely added a little bit of it to her milk. It was a good thing she didn't drink too much of it. Mae was as sick as a dog and missed a whole week of school with her gurgling stomach.

Not only was Mark a practical joker, he had a glib tongue that he used to snow all the teachers. It worked too. Those teachers at Carver High loved him and showed him all types of favoritism. Even the teachers who acted like they hated children, loved Mark.

Mark was a year older than Mae, but they were in the same grade and took some of the same classes. This was because when he was a young boy, he was hit by a drunk driver and the damage to his leg was so bad he missed a whole year of school. That's another story too. Anyway, the two of them were in the 11th grade and taking an English Literature class together. They had an assignment to write a story about anything they had observed about the world around them.

Mae agonized over the assignment. They were only given two weeks to finish the paper and it took her a whole week just to decide what she wanted to write about. After she finally chose a subject, she set about writing. Unfortunately, the words just wouldn't flow. It was torture. Meanwhile, Mark was moseying along, calm as you please like he didn't have a care in the world.

Two days before the assignment was due Mae asked him, "Mark, did you do your English assignment?"

Lazily, he said, "Nah. I ain't got around to it yet."

"What do you mean you ain't got around to it? We got that assignment almost two weeks ago."

"Time flies don't it, Sis?"

"Mark, this is no joking matter. We gotta write four

pages. Four whole pages, Mark. That was the assignment."

Still joking, he said, "You have an excellent memory. I've always said that about you."

"You know you're not gonna be able to do all that in two days.

"Don't worry about me, Mother." He called Mae "Mother" when she tried to boss him around, which was often.

"You play too much. Okay, I tried to tell you. Don't come cryin' to me when you fail this class. Then you'll have Momma to answer to." And with that she flounced out of the room.

Mark just shook his head and went back to doing what he was doing.

Nothing.

Two days passed and it was judgment day. Mark still hadn't written word one. Mae was sitting in class, busy putting the finishing touches on her masterpiece. The other classmates wrote on topics like the Civil Rights Movement, Voting and the Negro Baseball League. Heavy stuff like that.

When Mae's turn came, she walked to the front of the class and made her presentation on the importance of family. She considered herself blessed to receive a "B" from the teacher after reading her paper. While she was reading, Mark just sat there with both of his legs stretched out before him and his hand cupped behind his head. When Mae glanced in his direction, he winked at her. She rolled her eyes.

Finally, it was Mark's turn to make his presentation. He strolled up to the front of the class; he didn't even have any paper in his hands. Mae sat there with a smug look on her face just knowing he was gonna get what he deserved for his slothfulness.

Mark cleared his throat and said, "Well, I took the

liberty of memorizing my presentation so I wouldn't be bothered with having to hold a big wad of papers. I wanted the freedom to express myself with my hands if need be."

That lyin' demon, Mae thought. He didn't have any papers because he hadn't written anything. The teacher, believing him, smiled and nodded his approval.

He continued, "I would like to talk to you about a very important topic that is near and dear to our hearts. A topic of mystery and intrigue. A topic that receives jaw dropping reverence and awe. Ladies and Gentlemen of Mr. Woodrow's class, I would like to talk to you about women's hats."

Everyone in the room, except Mae, burst into laughter. Making such a big deal about hats. No one saw it coming.

He continued, "Women's hats are like the eyes and windows to their soul. You can tell a lot about a woman by the type of hat she wears. Women who wear small hats have small visions. Women who wear large hats have a large perception of life. Women who embellish their hats with flowers are earth people."

Now, I'm not gonna tell y'all the whole speech. But, can you believe that boy stood up there and talked for over ten minutes about women's hats. I don't know what's more unbelievable. That he spoke for so long, or that he did it all off the top of his head because he hadn't written a lick.

When he was finally done, he ended with this statement. "So, my fellow classmates, I would like to end with this thought. Don't judge. Don't judge that woman who sits in front of you in church with the big hat covered with flowers and bows. A hat so large it blocks your view of the preacher and the pulpit. Don't judge because there is no need to judge. These women are naturally selfish."

He received a standing ovation from the class. Once the teacher picked himself up off the floor, he gave my brother his grade. Mark got an "A."

Mae was mortified.

* * * * *

Speaking of Mae, she was the original strong willed child. Loud, opinionated and unafraid from the womb, she got more whippin's than all eight of us put together. That's how Momma got all those muscles in her arms. That's how she got her nicknames "Lash LaRue" and "Mighty Joe Young"…whippin' Mae. I'm telling you, either Mae's not right in the head or that girl's rear end must absorb pain because she had no fear of a whippin'.

None.

When Mae was a young girl, about seven or so, her class at Kansas Street Elementary School was planning a trip to the circus. When the teacher told the class about the trip, Mae was beside herself with excitement. She could barely concentrate on her schoolwork for thinking about the circus. At lunchtime, that's all everyone was talking about. This was a new experience for everyone.

When Mae got home, she ran into the house and told Momma, "Momma, guess what. I'm going to the circus next week. Here's the paper telling you all about it."

Momma frowned when she took the paper. After she read it, she gave Mae the bad news. "I'm so sorry baby, but you can't go. We ain't got no money to pay for this."

Mae couldn't believe her ears, "It ain't that much money, Momma. It's just a quarter."

"I know baby, but things are pretty tight this week and it's a quarter we don't have to spare Mae. I'm sorry."

"But Momma…"

"I don't wanna to hear no more about it. You cain't go and that's it."

Mae mumbled under her breath, "I'm gonna ask Daddy when he get home."

Momma grabbed Mae by the arm and whirled her around, "I heard that and you ain't gonna do no such'a thing. Yo Daddy got two jobs. He workin' hard enough as it is to provide for the six of us. Don't you go addin' to his burden and makin' him feel bad by askin' for somethin' I done told you, you cain't have. Now, go somewhere and sit down 'fore I get my belt."

Mae did as she was told, running to the room she shared with Jean and Tina. Dramatically throwing herself on the bed, she cried for most of the evening. She was so upset she refused to come out for dinner. Daddy asked what the matter was and Momma said she was just acting and not to pay her no never mind.

Mark, Earl, and Tina greedily ate her dinner.

The day of the circus came and sure enough, Mae didn't go. What was so bad about it was everyone in her grade went. Mae was the only one who was left behind. She had to stay in the library all day, which was bad because it gave her plenty of time to nurse her ever growing anger over the situation. By the time the librarian let her go, an hour early, Mae was livid.

Walking home, she thought to herself, *I'll show 'em. I'll show everybody.*

She walked into the house, right past Momma in the kitchen, and didn't say a mumbling word by way of a greeting. She walked into the bathroom, got a pair of scissors, and went into the backyard. She went past the towering cherry tree and to the far end of the yard behind the fig tree. That's where she did it. She got her revenge.

Mae proceeded to cut off all of her eyebrows.

Maybe I shouldn't say she cut "all" of her eyebrows off. I mean, there was only so much she could cut off with the rather dull pair of scissors pair we had. But, she put a good dent in them. She got most of them off. By the time she finished, she looked like she should have been traveling with that circus everyone went to see that day.

Now, I'm not really sure why Mae thought cutting off her eyebrows would "get" everybody. She was the one who looked a hot mess. But in her mind, she was getting people told. She was teaching people, namely Momma, not to mess with her.

All the while she was thinking, *That's what they get for not lettin' me go. Makin' me stay all by myself. This will get 'em good.* It never crossed her mind that she was the one looking a clown.

Reality started to set in a few minutes after the deed had been done and she started to come to her right mind. Ain't that the way? Mae realized that maybe, just maybe, this would be worse for her than for everyone else. That maybe she really didn't think this plan through. She knew she was facing imminent doom. Not only was Momma going to tan her hide, but Jean, Mark, Tina, and Earl were gonna laugh at her because she looked so stupid.

She started pacing and talking to herself, "I gotta fix this 'fore Momma finds out."

But she couldn't come up with a plan. So, she elevated her thoughts to prayer, "Lord, please help me. Gimme a sign, Lord."

That girl's a mess, ain't she? Doing her devilment and then asking the Lord to help her out of it.

She started pacing back and forth and then it hit her. She looked over at the barbeque pit. She ran over to it and lifted the lid on the barrel. *Praise the Lord*, she thought to herself when she saw the charcoal.

She got a piece of the ashy charcoal and ran over to try to see her reflection in the window of her bedroom. She was trying to use the window as a mirror but that wasn't working out to good.

She thought, *I can't see too good, but this is the best I can do for now.*

Mae began to draw her eyebrows back on with the messy charcoal. When she got through she couldn't really tell if she did a good job or not. I can tell you this. From what I've heard, that black charcoal against her fair skin made her look like a cross between Joan Crawford and

Groucho Marx.

Mae heard the back door slam so she knew her siblings had come home from school. She quickly washed her hands and strolled into the house like nobody's business.

When she walked into the living room everybody froze. Momma was the first to regain consciousness and said in an angry voice, "Child, what have you done?"

Her first thought was *I'm dead.*

Her second thought was, *Play dumb.*

"I ain't done nothin'. What y'all looking at?"

Earl started it. Laughing, that is. Then Jean, Tina, and even Momma joined in because she looked so ridiculous with that charcoal spread across her eyes and looking like an overgrown raccoon.

Momma wanted to get angry, but seeing Mae standing there took all of the edge off of her. All she could say was, "Girl, git to the bathroom and wash that mess offa yo face."

Momma turned and walked back into the kitchen. Glancing up to heaven she said under her breath, "Lord, you know."

Mae did as she was told and counted herself lucky she didn't get a whipping for that. But, everyone knows that if you make Momma laugh she won't whip you. It was punishment enough that she had to endure her family, people at church and at school laughing at her because Momma didn't even try to fix the mess Mae made.

It took a whole month for her eyebrows to grow back.

CHAPTER 7

TINA

I've been telling you, all of my siblings have their own identities. That is, some special quality that is totally unique to them. Jean was the mother hen, Mark is the prankster, and Mae is the bossy, outspoken one. That brings us to Tina. Tina is the pretty one.

Not that anyone was ugly, mind you. I'm just saying that she got a little extra in the "beauty" department. She has long, thick, wavy, brown hair, well below her shoulders, light brown eyes with thick curly lashes and cream colored skin. Back in the day, her 5'9" frame was the shape of a perfect hourglass. In her senior year in high school, she was voted "Girl with the Best Physique."

I guess you could say she was a little vain. She thought a lot about her appearance, so whenever she set foot outside the house she liked to have herself put together. She would hog the bathroom looking in the mirror making sure every hair was in place and her makeup was perfect. She was totally oblivious to those dancing on tiptoes in the hallway because they needed to use the facilities.

That's Tina for you.

* * * * *

When my older siblings were growing up in the 1950's, one of the highlights of the summer was the annual church picnic at T.O. Fuller State Park. It was a whole day of food, fun, and family. Not only that, it gave my siblings a chance to spend time with friends outside of school; church friends. Since we attended a good sized church, there would be hundreds of people at the event.

For Momma and Daddy, the picnic was a rare opportunity to sit back and relax and enjoy a day away from the stove and from work. The church provided all the food. All everyone had to do was show up and eat. It was standard picnic fare: hamburgers, hot dogs, chips, cookies, and sodas.

They would head out to the park bright and early to stake out a good location under a big oak tree. Momma would spread out an old blanket and she and Daddy would sit there catch up with some of the other church members while keeping a watchful eye on their brood.

* * * * *

It was church picnic Saturday in the middle of August. It was hot as all get out; not a day to be standing around outside for no good reason. But, that's what my family was doing. The whole family was outside in the front yard waiting to go to church to catch the bus to the picnic. All but Tina, who, at fifteen years old, was still getting ready for the event.

Daddy yelled into the front door, "Tina, you git out here rite now or you're gonna git left!"

Mae said, "Every time we try to go somewhere we always have to wait on Tina. She makes me sick, primpin' in front of the mirror all the time."

Jean joined in on the Tina bashing, "Yeah, we just going to the park. She acts like we goin' to The Peabody or somethin'."

Momma was sitting on the porch holding Denise, who was the baby at the time. Listening to all the badmouthing about Tina was starting to rile her up. She yelled into the house, "Tina, don't make me come in there, you hear?"

Hearing all of this negativity was starting to get to Earl, who was almost always on the edge anyway. He was beside himself with irritation, "Want me to go git her, Daddy?"

Daddy could just see Earl dragging Tina out of the house by her hair, "Never mind all that. I think I hear her comin' now."

When she made her appearance at the front door, she was wearing a pair of yellow and white shorts, a white t-shirt and white tennis shoes. She had yellow barrettes in her hair. Tina looked cute, but Earl was too angry to notice.

He yelled, "'Bout time."

Wayne added, "She took all that time and looks like THAT?"

Tina licked her tongue out at both of them and said to the others, "Y'all jealous."

The family made it to church just before the last bus pulled out of the gravel parking lot.

* * * * *

The first thing everyone did when they reached the park was to scatter in every conceivable direction, looking for their friends. Tina quickly found her friend Louise and they ran off towards the swings.

Tina said, "I'll pump, you swing."

"Okay."

Louise sat down on the wooden board and Tina hopped up putting one foot on the board on either side of Louise. Tina started pumping and Louise started swinging and pretty soon they were nearing a dangerous height.

Tina heard one of the adults say, "Y'all be careful. There's a bee hive on the top of that swing."

Tina managed to turn her head and sure enough, there was a hive with bees swarming all around it. Tina had a deadly fear of bees. She yelled down to Louise, "Let's stop. I don't wanna get stung."

Louise said, "Okay."

After they had slowed a little, Tina thought she would help the process by tapping her foot down. That was not a good idea. Unfortunately, she brought her foot down too hard. Her foot hit the ground and the force of it caused her to lose her balance and knocked her down. She fell hard and her head hit the ground with a scary thud.

Louise started yelling and people started running to see what the matter was. In a manner of moments, people were surrounding Tina as she lay there totally motionless and with her eyes closed. Her pretty yellow and white shorts were covered with dirt.

Momma, Daddy, and the rest of the family were nowhere to be found. Ain't that the way? It was a pretty large park, y'all.

Now, the good news is, Tina's feelings were more hurt than her body. She didn't feel any real pain. She was just embarrassed that all the people saw her fall. She decided to play unconscious.

Pretty soon, the lifeguard came over. He was a handsome, muscular fellow of about twenty or so. He saw himself as the authority figure so he decided to take charge of the situation but, truth be told, he didn't really know what he was doing.

He barked, "Everybody, get back. Let me handle this."

He was feeling for a pulse and put his head next to her chest to hear her heart beat. It was all Tina could do to keep from laughing and opening her eyes.

The lifeguard said, "Let's take her to the pavilion, out of the sun."

The pavilion was a covered area where there were tables, chairs, and a jukebox.

He proceeded to lift Tina into his arms and trot over to the pavilion, The lifeguard was doing okay for himself for awhile. But when they were about halfway to the pavilion, his strength started to give out. He wasn't such a big man now.

Tina heard him muttering under his breath, "Whew, you heavy."

"Man, I ain't gone make it."

Tina heard him saying this and she wanted to laugh in his face, but she knew she couldn't or she would blow her cover. She planned to let him get her to the pavilion and then make a miraculous recovery.

Much to the relief of the lifeguard, they finally made it. He gently laid her down on the ground. A large group of people gathered around Tina. Mae broke through the crowd and rushed to Tina's side.

She grabbed her hand and started patting it and said, "Tina. You okay? What happened?"

The lifeguard didn't pay Mae no never mind. Once he got his energy back, he started bossing people around again, "I need everyone to get back. Someone get me some water. Is there a doctor around?"

No one responded.

Just then, some idiot in the crowd said, "I know, let's take her shoes off."

Tina's heart skipped a beat. *U*h oh! *I just can't let him take off my shoes in front of all these people. I got a big fat hole in the toes of my socks. I told Momma I needed some new socks. This is all her fault. I'll just die if anyone sees me with holey socks.*

The lifeguard reached down and started trying to untie Tina's shoe. Tina did the only think she could think of. She balled up her foot inside of her shoe so it wouldn't come off.

It was like tug of war. This guy was pulling and jerking and trying to get that shoe off and Tina had her food balled up so tight it was about to burst through the rubber soles. It was a sight.

The lifeguard said, "Something is wrong with her foot.

It's knotted up."

Someone said, "I hope she didn't have a stroke."

Thank the Lord for Mae. She saw what was going on and she knew. She knew how vain her little sister was and guessed that her socks where holey. All the irritation she felt for her a few hours before vanished. She came to the rescue with one of the best performances of her life.

Mae said, "I think we should pray."

Some of the men jerked their hats off their head and put them over their hearts.

Mae began, "Father God in heaven, please, in your infinite power and mercy, stretch forth your mighty hand towards earth, right here in Memphis, Tennessee, in the pavilion at T.O. Fuller State Park and provide healing and deliverance to my sister Tina DeVault. In the name of Jesus, amen.

No soon as she got the "amen" out, Mae began patting Tina's face trying to bring her to. Then, Mae gave Tina her cue. She said, "Wait a minute, I think she's starting to come around."

Mae leaned over and spoke to Tina in her ear. "Tina, Tina can you hear me."

Miraculously, at that time Tina, eyes fluttering and head moving from side to side moaned a sickly, "Mae, is that you Mae?"

"Yes, it's me sister. Are you okay?"

"Imma be all right."

To the chorus of hallelujah's, praise the Lord's, and applause, Tina woozily rose to her feet, brushed herself off and started to walk slowly at first, like she was trying to get her strength back. She added a limp just to make it look good.

After they thanked the lifeguard, the crowd started to disburse. Mae and Tina started walking over to the pool area.

Tina, eyes straight in front of her, softly said, "Thanks

Sis."

Mae responded, "No problem. That's what I'm here for."

I wonder if that's what it means in the Bible when it talks about pride going before a fall?

Just a thought…

CHAPTER 8

EARL'S COMEUPPANCE

Out of all my siblings, Earl looked the most like Daddy. His skin was as white as wool and he had big black eyes and thick black curly hair to match. As a baby, he was a cute little thing, and when Momma took him out places, like to church or shopping, people would practically fall out over Earl playing with him and wanting to hold him. Momma wasn't having much of that though. She kept a death grip on Earl around people she didn't know because some people were just out for no good.

Perhaps his strong resemblance to Daddy is what made him Momma's favorite. Now, Momma would argue you up and down that she don't have any favorites among her children. She'd say that she loved us all the same. I'm sure in her mind that's what she thinks, but my elder brother and sisters would tell y'all it just ain't so. Earl had it a little easier than Jean, Mark, Mae, and Tina. If he misbehaved, he would get off with a warning while the other kids would have had to make the long trek to the cherry tree in the backyard to get a switch.

For example, when he was ten years old, he set Tina's hair on fire when she was standing near the stove. Only a little bit of it burned before she realized she was on fire and put it out. He thought stuff like that was funny but Tina sure didn't. She hit him right upside his head and ran into the living room and stood next to Momma. To emphasize her point, she stuck out her tongue at him. Earl, polite as you please, reached around Momma and hit Tina so hard that he knocked her into the closet. And Momma never said a mumbling word.

Or the time, when he was about six years old: he climbed up on the china cabinet. He was up there a good minute before he came crashing down. On his way down, he pulled down the china cabinet and all of Momma's good china. And I'm using the word "good" loosely because we couldn't afford much of nothing. Anyway, Momma came running into the room and picked up Earl, who wasn't even crying. She was petting him and rocking him back and forth. When my brothers and sisters came in the room and saw the mess on the floor and Momma holding Earl, they were in an uproar. They were all talking at once.

"Did Earl do this?"

Momma answered, "Yeah, but he ain't hurt."

"What you gon' do, Momma?"

"Ain't you gonna whip him?"

Momma looked at them and shook her head. She finally said, "What's wrong with y'all? Can't you see he's been through enough?"

To Earl she said, "Come on baby, let's go sit in the living room."

As she walked out of the dining room she said over her shoulder, "Y'all clean up this mess."

* * * * *

My brother Earl is a complicated person. His temper is legendary. We've got the holes in the walls of our house to prove it. But, I don't want y'all to think he's some kind of monster. There's another side to Earl. He's a good person with a good heart and he'll do whatever he can to help a person in need. The kind of person that would give you the shirt off his back if he thought it would help.

He has a weird sense of humor. He laughs at stuff no one else thinks it funny. Like the slapstick kind of humor, like people falling down or slipping on a banana. The

Three Stooges kind of humor where people looked like they're getting hurt. That kind of stuff would have Earl rolling on the floor while the rest of us barely broke a smile. Let me give you an example of what Earl found to be funny.

We had a one legged guy in our neighborhood named Thomas. Actually, I should say he was a one and a half legged guy because he had his whole left leg and most of the right. It was amputated a little above the right ankle. Our family didn't know him that well so don't even ask me how he came to be that way. I really couldn't tell you.

Thomas was the neighborhood criminal, which was a bold career choice considering his handicap. Theft was unusual in our neighborhood, but if something came up missing, Thomas was usually the one who took it. I don't know why he chose that line of work. Maybe he was bitter about loosing part of his leg and that was his way of getting back at society. Maybe he couldn't get a good job because of his handicap and stealing stuff what his only way of surviving. Then again, maybe it's none of those reasons.

It could be something like what Momma always says, "Some folks, to do right just ain't in 'em."

Only God knows why Thomas was the way he was.

Across the street from our church on Florida Street was Downing's Grocery Store. To us, Downing's looked like a Mega Market. It was a good size neighborhood store where you could find most anything you were looking for. There was no need to go anywhere else. Mr. Downing was an old white man who owned and operated the store for years. He was a good man who treated his negro customers with dignity and respect. There weren't a lot of men like Mr. Downing around Memphis.

He used to put his fruit and vegetables outside the store in big barrels. One day, Thomas got in his mind that he wanted an apple. Never mind the fact that he didn't have any money. He wanted an apple and he was going to get an apple. He walked right up to the bin and snatched one. Then, he took off running.

Mr. Downing saw him steal the apple and yelled, "Hey, put that back."

The bad news for Thomas was, the police just happened to be passing by and heard Mr. Downing yelling. The two white officers jumped out of their car and took off after Thomas. My family was just getting out of church at the time and saw the whole thing. Everyone held their breath because they knew when the police caught that brother there would be hell to pay.

Earl was the only one laughing and in his defense, I heard it was a sight.

Now, you might be asking yourself, how does a one legged man run? That's easy to explain. He ran with the short right leg on the curb and the normal leg on the street. Boy, that Thomas could move. He looked perfectly natural and was giving the police a run for their money. He was actually getting away for a while. In fact, he probably would have gotten away but the unforeseen happened. Unfortunately, Thomas ran out of curb. Y'all, that was it for his getaway. He hit the ground with an awful thud and rolled a few feet before coming to a stop.

You could hear Earl laughing all the way to Parkway Avenue.

The policemen were all over Thomas like white on rice. While everyone else was fearing for Thomas' life, Earl was laughing so hard tears were in his eyes. See, everyone else knew a black man in the hands of the Memphis Police Department wasn't funny. The police in Memphis were hard on black folk. Just the site of the officers grabbing Thomas by the seat of his pants and hauling him up to his feet put fear in everyone. Everyone but Earl.

As the police were hauling him off to their car, Thomas, trying to save face in front of the crowd of people who had gathered said, "Y'all never would'a caught me if I hadn't run outta curb."

That was more than my brother could take. Earl fell out on the ground laughing. As it turns out, Earl's laughing might have saved Thomas' hide. His laughter was infectious and he started the police to laughing. Pretty soon, my family and the other people who had gathered around felt it was safe to join in. I'm sure most people were hoping that Thomas wouldn't get a whippin' from the police if they stayed in a good mood.

The officers took Thomas back to Mr. Downing. All he had was one word for Thomas, "Why?"

"I was hungry."

Mr. Downing shook his head. "You could'a asked."

Thomas hung his head. "I'm sho' sorry, Downing."

His apology appeased Mr. Downing. He decided to let him slide that time. Now that the show was over, my family began the long walk back home. Earl didn't stop snickering until they made it to Arkansas Street.

* * * * *

Earl was a bit of a practical joker himself. The difference between his practical jokes and Mark's were that Mark's jokes were annoying. Earl's jokes could sometimes cause pain to others.

It was the beginning of summer and our house was as hot as fish grease. After a light dinner, my family usually retired to the back yard to sit under one of the many trees trying to get some relief from the heat. They would stay back there until the house cooled off because no one could sleep in the sultry summer heat.

This one particular summer evening Earl, about thirteen at the time, got an idea for a practical joke. As usual, everyone was lounging out back. Earl jumped up and said, "I'll be back in a minute."

He ran in the house and got Momma's sewing kit. He pulled out a stickpin and went over to the couch where he pulled up the cushion, bent the pen and stuck it in the cushion so that the point was sticking straight up. Then he put the cushion back in place and went back outside, like he hadn't done a thing.

When evening finally came, everyone decided to retire to the living room. Earl was the first one inside. He ran over and took a seat directly across from the couch so he could get a good look at his victim. He could barely keep a straight face as Mae came over to the couch and plopped down right on top of that pin.

"OUCH!" she yelled and she hopped back up.

Earl hit the ground laughing.

The commotion brought Momma and Daddy to the living room.

"What happened?" Momma asked, giving Earl the eye since he was the only one laughing.

Mae said, "Earl must have stuck a pin in this cushion. I sat on it."

Momma looked at Earl with a cold stare, "Is that right, boy?"

Earl was still laughing because this kind of stuff was really funny to him. He told Momma, "It was…. just… a joke."

Momma grabbed him by the arm and marched him off to the bathroom where he would pay for his crime. She said to him, "Boy that ain't funny. You could'a hurt her."

Throughout the house, you could hear Earl still laughing while he was getting a whipping.

Earl picked the wrong person to mess with. Mae could take a joke as well as the next person, but this was different. This time his prank inflicted bodily harm. He went too far and she was going to see to it that he paid for what he did. Her revenge would make the whippin' Earl got seem like a pat on the back.

She stayed up all night developing her terror technique. When she woke up the next morning she was waiting for Earl when he came to the breakfast table. He sat directly across from her and she stared at him coldly the whole time he ate. Her food sat in front of her uneaten. Earl wasn't paying her any real attention, glancing up at her every few minutes when he came up for air.

Daddy was at work and Momma was still in the kitchen but everyone else was at the table. They were looking back and forth from Earl to Mae and wondering how this was all going to end. Earl had a temper, but Mae had the psychological advantage. It could go either way.

Finally, Earl had enough. He said to Mae, "What's wrong with you?"

Her answer was soft and deadly, "I'm gonna git you."

"For that little stuff yesterday? Girl, cain't you take a joke?"

Mae didn't stray from her script, "I'm gonna git you."

"Well, you too late. Momma already got me." Trying to prove his toughness, he whispered, "It didn't hurt."

"I'm gonna git you."

"Oh yeah. You gonna git me, huh?" Earl wasn't taking this seriously.

Mae didn't let up. She repeated herself in the same voice, "I'm gonna git you."

Earl mockingly said, "Ohhh, I'm so scared." With that, he got up from the table and went outside to play.

No one left at the table said a word. They all knew Earl was as good as got.

After Earl left, Mae got up and went into the bedroom she shared with Jean and Tina. Wayne ate Mae's breakfast.

Mae's reign of terror against Earl went on for two months, practically the whole summer. She continued to stare at him for hours at a time. Whenever he came into the room, she would stop what she was doing and give him an evil look. After a while, he would turn and leave the room.

She moved like a cat. She would tip right up behind him and he wouldn't even know she was there until he felt her breathing heavily down his neck. He would jump and look back and see Mae staring at him. She would say the only four words she spoke to him for the whole summer, "I'm gonna git you."

Pretty soon Mae's tactics started to get to Earl. He would leave the room when she came in and if he saw her coming he would turn and go the other way. He got jumpy and would flinch if someone made a loud noise because he thought it might have been Mae extracting her revenge. By the end of the summer, Earl was a jittery mess. He went to Momma for mercy.

"Momma, make Mae leave me alone."

"What she doin' to you?"

"She all the time starin' at me and breathin' on me and sayin' she gon' git me. Make her stop."

Now, Momma knew good and well what Mae was doing. She had been watching her torment Earl all summer. She didn't do anything to stop it either. Momma had a dark side.

She said to Earl, "Why she doin' that to you?"

"I dunno."

"You sho' you don't know?"

"Naw." Earl decided to come clean. "It might have somethin' to do with me puttin' that pin in the cushion, but that was months ago and she still at it."

Momma asked him, "Is she touchin' you?"

"Naw."

"Then that's what you git. Y'all chirren work that out by yo'selves."

Earl knew he couldn't take one more minute of Mae's revenge. He went to her in the backyard and rolled up the sleeve on his right arm. He offered Mae his arm and said, "Here. Hit me as hard as you wanna. You can git me now and get it over with."

Mae's plan worked. She had taught her cocky little brother a valuable lesson. Brought him down a size or two. He hadn't played a joke on anyone in months and he was a nervous wreck. Most sensible people would have let it go at that. Well, y'all ain't never heard me say the words Mae and sensible in the same sentence.

Mae stood up and looked Earl dead in the eyes and said, "In my time brother, in my time." With that, she walked off.

That was pretty much that. Mae continued to torment Earl, but she never "got" him any more than that. She never planned to. She just wanted to see him suffer. And suffer, he did.

You know, come to think of it, sometimes, people in my family can be real trifling.

CHAPTER 9

STEAKMAN

I think Wayne might have been adopted.

There, I said it. Y'all are the first people I've ever shared that revelation with. You might be wondering why my parents would have adopted a child when they already had five at the time. Well, I haven't worked that out in my mind just yet, but they must have had their reasons. Wayne being adopted is the only solution I can think of. There's just no other way that boy came to be in our family.

Okay, I'm kidding, of course. Let's just say, Wayne and I grew up together so quite naturally we got on each other's nerves. I resented his superior attitude and he resented my perfection. He's eight years older than me. In his mind, I guess he thought he could tell me what to do. I wasn't having it.

I can still hear myself telling him, on more than one occasion, "You ain't the boss of me!"

Out of all my siblings, Wayne is the only one who got Momma's dark skin. When he was a young boy, he was tall for his age, with long skinny, pencil-like dark brown legs. He had short, tight, brown hair, big brown eyes, and perfect white teeth. We used to call him peanut head. To really make him mad, I used to tell him his head was so small he could see through a keyhole with both eyes.

Another thing, he was lazy as all get out.

When it was time to do chores, he'd run and hide. We would usually find him in the backyard behind the small tool shed Daddy built. Or, he'd be lying on the chaise lounge with the rake or shovel in his hand, using it hit the low branches of the cherry tree so the cherries would fall all around him. He'd pick them up off the ground or from his chest and eat them without even washing them. Nasty scoundrel! This was Wayne at the height of laziness.

Another way I can describe my brother is to say he's a gypsy. Always into something. Always moving around. Restless. A little bit of this, a little bit of that. That boy just couldn't seem to settle down and stick to one thing.

One year, Tina's husband, Ted, was going to help Wayne file his income taxes. He told Wayne to gather all of his paperwork and come to their house. At the appointed time, Wayne arrived with an envelope ready to get to work on the taxes.

Ted pulled out his pencil, papers, and a calculator and said to Wayne, "Okay, give me your W-2's."

Wayne said, "All right" and pulled out a stack of papers. He spread them out like a fan.

Ted said, "Naw man. I just wanna see your W-2's for right now."

Wayne said, "These are my W-2's."

Ted was confused, "Just the ones from last year."

"These are the ones from last year."

There were thirteen of them.

That's how Wayne was. He'd have a new minimum wage job just about every month and usually a new car to go along with it. New to him, that is. Just about every month when he got paid, he'd go to one of those "we tote the note" car lots and buy a new vehicle. It never failed. Sometime during that month, the car would sputter to a stop and break down in the middle of the road. Wayne would jump out, push it to the curb, and walk away, just leaving it by the side of the road. That's kind of what I meant when I said he was a gypsy. He lived day by day.

* * * * *

Long before that, when he was a little guy, around seven or so, he earned his nickname. My family used to call him "Steakman." Here's how he got that name.

Daddy worked two jobs just to keep a roof over our heads and food on the table. He would leave the house at 4:00 in the morning and come home at around 7:00 at night. Usually he would be dog tired, poor soul. Every now and again, Momma would try to give Daddy little treats to reward him for working so hard. (Not that she was a slouch in the work department with keeping house, cooking, cleaning, and taking care of a house full of kids.)

Well, one night, Momma had a very special treat cooking for Daddy when he came home from work. Steak. The meat, steak. Steak was actually cooking in our house. Not that we kids had any. Momma probably fixed hot dogs or spaghetti for the kids, something she could stretch a county mile. But she had been scrimping and saving and putting a few cents away out of her food allowance and she had finally saved enough. Daddy was having steak.

That steak was cooking on the stove and the aroma filled the whole house. She fried some onions and bell peppers for garnish and had a big baked potato to go with it. Everyone's mouth was watering that night. Especially Wayne's.

When Daddy walked through the back door he caught a whiff of that smell and said, "What's that cookin' Mae."

"I made somethin' special for you tonight."

"What's that?"

"You havin' steak with grilled onions and peppers, a big baked potato, and a salad."

You could light a small town with the brightness of Daddy's smile. He asked no questions about how she got the money for it. That was beside the point. Daddy usually bathed and changed his clothes before he ate dinner. Not this time. He washed his hands in the sink, went right to the table, and sat where his place was already set. Wayne followed him to the table.

Momma brought the plate loaded with all that good food and sat it in front of Daddy. Wayne's mouth was watering. He watched Daddy eat and savor every bite of that juicy steak, his eyes following the fork right up to Daddy's mouth. Daddy wasn't paying Wayne no never mind.

Daddy was about three quarters through eating his steak when he came up for air. That was the break Wayne was waiting for. As soon as Daddy put his fork down to rest, Wayne grabbed a fork he had been holding on his lap, jabbed it into Daddy's steak and said, "Daddy, you done?"

Daddy quickly grabbed his fork and stuck it in the steak saying, "No I ain't." I think that was the first time he noticed Wayne sitting there.

Wayne would not be denied. "You sho' you ain't through, Daddy? You look full." Wayne kept his fork in the steak, pulling it towards him.

Daddy was getting irritated. "Boy, I said I ain't through."

"Daddy, I'm hongry."

"Well, go ask yo' Momma for something outta the kitchen."

"I want summa yo' steak."

Wayne was really getting on Daddy's last nerve, "Boy, I said I ain't through. Let go."

Not deterred, Wayne persisted, "But, Daddy…"

"Boy, turn a'loose my plate."

All the while this banter is going on they are playing tug of war with the steak, moving it back and forth on the plate. It's starting to get messy. Eventually Earl came into the dining room and started laughing hysterically when he saw Wayne trying to hijack Daddy's dinner. That boy was doubled over with laughter. Momma heard the commotion and was in there lickity split.

Momma yelled at Wayne, "Boy, let yo' daddy's dinner go."

Wayne was not moved. It's like he was possessed by that steak. He said, "I just wanna taste it."

Momma went over and grabbed Wayne's arm and pried the fork out of his hand. My brothers and sisters were in hysterics. Wayne was escorted out of the room while Daddy quickly finished his steak…while the eating was still good!

That's how Wayne got the nickname, "Steakman."

If you don't count that, Wayne was, for the most part, a quiet sort. Kind of like Daddy. He didn't have too much to say, but when he did, it was usually the wrong thing and caused all kinds of problems.

Life wasn't always peaches and cream in our house. I remember the first time I saw Momma cry. Wayne did it. That was when Wayne was about sixteen, which would have made me about nine years old. He and Momma were having a heated discussion about something. I don't remember what the discussion was about because it had already started before I was aware that there was any trouble. Most likely about him cutting classes or getting into trouble at school.

By the time I had tipped over to the door and cracked it open to get a better view of what was going on it was over. The only thing I did hear was when Wayne said to Momma, "Oh, shut up."

I couldn't believe he did that, I had never heard anyone talk to her that way. We all valued our young lives too much to talk back to Momma.

I braced myself to hear the sound of a beating but the room was silent. She didn't lay a hand on Wayne. She didn't say anything either. Through the small crack in the door, I could see the back of her head as she turned, walked into the dining room and sat at the table.

I heard the front door open and close so I figured Wayne got out while the getting was good. Immediately, I came out of the room and walked over to where Momma was sitting. When I got to the table, I could see the tears rolling down her cheeks. She didn't make a sound but the tears spoke volumes to me.

I hated Wayne for that. I wanted him to pay and I knew who to enlist as the cashier. When Earl came home, I went and told him what Wayne did. Earl got so mad I knew he was going to kill Wayne for sure. Personally, I didn't care what he did to Wayne; he shouldn't have made Momma cry.

Wayne sauntered into the house about an hour later like he hadn't done anything wrong. Earl was waiting for him. Right before the murder, Daddy came home. He was just in time to grab Earl as he lunged for Wayne's puny body. I'm telling you, it's a good thing Mark came home about that time because it took both him and Daddy to hold Earl down.

I explained what happened to get Earl so riled up. Daddy was plenty mad, but he told Earl he would deal with Wayne and to "let it rest."

Earl didn't fight Wayne that day because even though he was about twenty years old, he still obeyed Daddy. He did leave the house because just looking at Wayne was fueling the flame. Before he left, Earl gave Wayne a look so cold that he was watching his back for a month. You know, I don't think Momma said a word during the whole scene.

There was another time Wayne opened his mouth when he shouldn't have. It was in the mid 70's when he was in his late teens. Wayne's best friend was a guy named Perry. Wayne and Perry used to get into more trouble than a little bit.

One day they were hanging out on the street corner, bored and trying to think up something to get into.

Perry said, "Man, it's boring around here. Too quiet. We need some excitement in this neighborhood."

Wayne thought about it for a while before snapping his fingers. "I got it. Let's make Earl mad."

Perry hesitated. Most people had the good sense to leave Earl alone if he wasn't' bothering them. Finally he said, "Well, I guess it's okay. As long as he's not mad at me."

It took them a few minutes to hatch up a plan. They saw a guy walking down the street minding his own business. That gave Wayne an idea.

Lord, the devil was a'loose that day.

Wayne ran in the house screaming for Earl. When he found him in the living room watching television, he said, "Earl, somebody's tryin' to break into your car."

"WHAT?!!" That was all it took to set my brother's blood to boiling. He jumped up and ran out the front door.

"There he is. That guy right there." Wayne pointed to the innocent man.

The guy must have heard all the commotion because he turned around and looked and saw Earl coming towards him in all his fury. He took off running with Earl in hot pursuit. Wayne and Perry followed.

Earl chased that guy for several blocks until he caught him in somebody's yard. That poor guy never knew what hit him. My brother gave him quite a beating. When he was done, he walked home and went back to watching television.

It shames me to say that Wayne and Perry had no remorse over what they did to that poor guy. Forget the fact that my brother could have been arrested for assault or the guy could have retaliated and got a group of people to attack my brother. They didn't even think of that. To them, it was just their idea of a fun way to spend an afternoon.

But, y'all know God don't like ugly. Over the years, the guilt of what he did to that innocent guy and Earl began to haunt him. He thought about it often. Wayne couldn't get any peace until he confessed to Earl some twenty years later.

For what it's worth, they both felt bad.

DENISE

My sister Denise put the "tom" in tomboy. Running, jumping, tackling, climbing trees, hurdling fences, and playing touch football with the guys of the neighborhood, that's her idea of a good day. And in the summer, everyday was a good day.

But, it wasn't just the obsession with sports that made her a tomboy. I'll tell you the truth, I don't think that child ever played with a doll in all her natural born life. If she did, I never saw it. And that's not all, she doesn't wear makeup or high heels. She only carries a purse one day a week and that's just because she needs something to hold her candy when she goes to church on Sunday. She wants no part of that girly stuff. It's not who she is.

Her existence is like a thorn in my flesh, because I can't, for the life of me, understand why she gets more dates that I do. Men are all over her like white on rice. They will climb over me to get to her. And me, with my make up, designer clothes, shoes and purses, I'm lucky if I get a second glance. That really gets on my nerves.

But I'm not bitter.

In the early days, her tomboy ways almost drove Momma to drink. I can still hear Momma lecturing her about trying to be more ladylike.

From the kitchen door you could hear Momma calling her, "Denise, git in this house."

"Aw Momma."

"I said git in here rite now! Don't make me come out

there."

The group of boys she was playing touch football with would mock Denise as she slunk towards the house.

"Ohhhhh Denise. Yo momma gon' get you."

"You in trouble, girl."

"Denise, you gonna get a whuppin'."

But Denise wasn't scared, "Nah…she just wants to make me cook or sew or something. I'll be back out a little later."

Momma would be waiting for Denise in the kitchen with her hands on her hips and an angry look on her face.

"Didn't I tell you 'bout rough housin' with them boys?"

"Momma, I ain't rough housin'. I'm just trying to get some exercise. Can't you see I have a weight problem?"

"There's ways to exercise without throwin' them boys around. It ain't ladylike."

"But my weight…"

"Weight problem or no, I want you to start actin' like a lady."

"Aw Mommma…"

"Don't aw Momma me. Now, go to your room and change. I'm gonna teach you how to make biscuits."

Denise would go to her room mumbling, "She's gotta be kiddin' me."

Did you notice that Momma didn't argue with Denise about her weight? She couldn't. From the day she was a born, Denise was a chubby girl and over the years, she just kept going that way. She's well over two hundred pounds, but y'all didn't hear that from me. The good thing is, her weight is solid. She ain't flopping all over the place. Probably from all that running around.

She's the only one in the family that's height challenged. The tape measure swears she's just a hair over 5'3" to which she responds, "You'ze a lie! I'm at least 5'5" in my stocking feet."

Nobody challenges her fantasy. Not that we're scared of her.

She's a pretty girl. She has long jet black hair that she pulls back into a ponytail each and everyday. It's good hair too, soft and wavy. So good that people are always coming over and rubbing her hair and telling her how pretty it looks, all the while checking to see if they can feel any weave tracks. On the other hand, my hair is so thick and coarse that I can hardly get a comb through it sometimes. I've actually broken combs trying to get my hair under submission. I'm not kidding either.

But I'm not bitter.

People are always saying to Denise, "You have such a pretty face."

That's the same thing people used to say to my sister Jean before she got so sick with the diabetes and got those black sores all over her body and her hair fell out. But don't mention Jean's name to Denise. Jean has been with Jesus for over twenty years, but Denise still cries about it like she passed away on yesterday.

The good thing about Denise is, in spite of her weight, she's always done just what she wanted to do. The extra pounds here and there never stopped her. She loves sports. If the NFL ever decides to draft women, I'm sure she'd be right there at the front of the line jumping up and down shouting, "Me! Me!" You name a sport and she's played it.

In high school she was on the volleyball team, but her main sport was tennis. No one taught her how to play. After my brother Mark moved to Los Angeles, he came home for a visit and brought a tennis racket with him. Denise asked him about it and before you knew it, they went over to Carver High School's tennis court and started playing. She loved it. Over the course of a summer, she had practically mastered the sport. When she started high school in the late 1970's she went to the tennis coach and told her she wanted to go out for the team.

Denise said the coach looked her up and down with a doubtful expression on her face.

Denise responded with, "Hey, don't let this flab fool ya. Gimme a chance to try out like everyone else."

The young white coach, who, by the way, looked just like Billie Jean King, quickly answered, "Oh yes, of course."

She sent Denise out to the court to play with the second string player on the team, a girl named Anne. My sister demolished her.

The coach was clearly impressed. She called the first string player, "Marjorie, come over here for a minute."

Then she turned to Denise and said, "Let's see what you can do with Marjorie. You're not tired are you, Denise?"

"Nah, I'm fine." She wasn't lying.

Marjorie came over twirling her racquet like she was all that. Tall, thin, and pretty, Marjorie looked at Denise like she smelled something. She probably misjudged Denise the same way the coach did.

The coach said to her, "Marjorie, this is Denise DeVault. She's trying out for the team. I want you to play a few sets, okay?"

"Sure Coach." She didn't even speak to Denise and didn't give her a second glance. Sounds like she had a touch of the big head to me.

Denise didn't beat her, doggone it. But, I'll tell you what, she sure gave that stuck up girl a run for her money. They were going tit for tat, smacking that ball around like they were mad at it. In fact, they were playing so good that all of the other players stopped practicing and came over to watch. By the time they finished playing, that skinny girl was huffing and puffing like she had emphysema.

Well, of course Denise made the team. And, by the time she was a senior in high school she was ranked number one in the city of Memphis and number two in state of Tennessee. Not only that, she received a tennis scholarship to a college in Middle Tennessee. She was the first member of the family to go to a for real, four-year university. Denise accomplished all of this despite the fact that she was overweight. She never let that stop her from reaching her goals.

But years later, there was a price to pay. For all of that running around and physical activity at two hundred pounds, there was a price to pay. For playing through pain and ignoring the doctor's advice to drop a few pounds or ease up on the physical activity there was a price to pay.

The price was two knees that cause so much pain that sometimes she can't even walk. The price was walking with a limp so bad people would sometimes stop and stare. The price was having one knee replacement surgery while in your mid 40's and knowing you'll have to replace the other knee before long. The price was having the doctor tell you that you should never play the sport you love more than anything else because your body just can't hold up to all that moving around.

She takes it all in stride though. You won't hear her complaining about how painful it is to move around. Denise keeps that kind of stuff to herself. Everyday, she's laughing and joking and trying to make people laugh so people won't know how much she's suffering. If you didn't know better, you'd call her the life of the party and think her life was just one big joy ride. That's how she is. Jean was a lot like that too.

If you ask me, I think it's better to moan and groan and get it out in the open so people will know what's going on with you. It just ain't natural to hold stuff on the inside. I think that after awhile, it's best to let it out so that your mind and spirit won't be clogged up with a bunch of pain. And if people think that you're complaining too much, then forget 'em.

But that's just me

* * * * *

So, by now y'all should have a handle on everything and everybody. You should also be aware that I use the words y'all and you interchangeably.

But, I digress….

There's one more person I need to tell y'all about. Me! The Southern Belle. Well, I hate to say it, but I haven't always acted Belle-like. I guess you can say I came into my Belle-ness late in life. You'll see what I mean after I recollect a story that doesn't show me in the best light. But, you know what they say…" tell the truth and shame the devil!"

CHAPTER 11

DON'T SHOOT!

When my older siblings were at home, Daddy worked two jobs so Momma could stay at home to take care of the family. It was a struggle most times, but we got by. By the time I came along and was halfway through elementary school, most of my brothers and sisters were married or out on their own. There were just three of us at home during this time, but Wayne and Denise were teenagers and could take care of themselves.

Since there were no more babies to take care of, Momma felt her work was done. She decided to get a job. She said she wanted to have her own money for a change. Daddy didn't oppose her. It wasn't long after she made the decision to work that she landed her first job working as a cook in the kitchen of Florida Elementary School, the same school I was attending at the time.

I imagine some kids would hate the fact that their mother was right there in school with them, but not me. Since I wasn't prone to getting into trouble, it didn't bother me in the least to have her there. In fact, I liked having her in the school kitchen because I knew all the cooks and sometimes they would give me extra food.

Another advantage to Momma working in the cafeteria was that I got to take a lot of breaks during the school day. My teachers knew Momma was in the kitchen so whenever they wanted something, like a cookie or some cold water, they would say to me, "Child, go to the cafeteria and ask your momma to send me a cup of ice."

They were always sending me down for something, but

I didn't mind. It was a great escape for me and I would always take the scenic route on the way back to the classroom.

After the sixth grade, I went to Riverview Junior High School. The first year went well; I made a lot of new friends and did well in my classes. Our family was doing well financially with two incomes. At the beginning of the school year, Momma and Daddy would give Denise and me $100.00 each and we would go to "The Treasury" and buy our own school clothes and Tom McAnn for our shoes. There was also plenty of money for lunch, class trips and going to the movies with friends. Life was beautiful.

Things changed for our family in the summer when I passed to the eighth grade. Momma got laid off from her job in the cafeteria. I will never forget that day because the letter came by certified mail. I thought it was a big wad of money but it was just the opposite. When Momma opened it and read it her face fell. She always tried to be so strong so it was rare for her to show any emotion, but this time, for one brief moment, she let her guard down and I saw her disappointment.

Momma had been enjoying her freedom outside the house. She was buying clothes for herself and big church hats and fancy handkerchiefs. She even had her own Goldsmith's credit card and helped Daddy pay a few bills. She tried not to show it, but I knew she was upset but you know how black women are. You can't keep us down for long.

Within the hour, she quickly recovered from her disappointment and called the Board of Education asking if there were any other jobs available. They told her they would put her name on the waiting list for open positions and would let her know when something became available. It was almost the end of the summer vacation when the call came informing her that a position was available at an elementary school near the Whitehaven section of

Memphis. She was very happy and I was glad for her.

She worked there for a year and was laid off again. This time they reassigned her immediately to a school that was closer to home.

I asked her, "What school will you be working at this time?"

She answered, "You ain't gonna believe this, but I'll be right at Riverview Junior High, with you."

At first, I was shocked. By this time, I was a teenager and had grown used to the freedom of going to a school where my mother wasn't right underfoot. Still, I reasoned, it wouldn't be too bad having Momma there. Might get me in good with the teachers. Jokingly, I asked her, "Will you be baking the bread again, or are they going to let you cook the real food?"

"I ain't workin' in the cafeteria. Imma be a maid."

"Say WHAT?"

I couldn't believe this was happening. I mean, to me, it was one thing for Momma to work in the kitchen, I could pretend she was a chef. It was quite another thing for her to be working as a maid, pushing a broom right there in front of all my new friends and scrubbing the toilets. I'll tell you what, I wasn't having it.

I said to her, "You gotta turn that job down Momma."

"I ain't turnin' nothin' down."

"Momma, this ain't right. You don't want to be a maid. We have overcome."

Momma looked at me for a long time before she said, "Child, good honest work ain't nothin' to be ashamed of. I'm takin' this job and thankin' the Lord for it."

With that our conversation was over. A few weeks later Momma started working at my school.

All my life I've heard the saying, "Tell the truth and shame the devil."

Well, the devil better get ready to be shamed because I have to tell y'all this. I was embarrassed that my mother was working that job at my school. I didn't want her there picking up other people's messes and mopping up the boy's locker room. It was humiliating for me and I was angry with her for invading my turf and putting me in an uncomfortable position in front of my new friends who were the daughters of teachers, nurses and bankers.

The only redeeming point was that Momma was assigned to work the night shift. She reported to work at 3:00, right when I would be going home. I breathed a sigh of relief. If I worked it just right, maybe we wouldn't even run into each other.

My plan worked at first. Momma would get to school a few moments before I left. She would be sitting, with the other maids, on the orange radiator in the school lobby, right by the front door. All I had to do was go out the back door and I wouldn't even see her.

When I wasn't with my friends, I would go ahead and walk out the front door, speaking to her and her co-workers while steadily moving towards the door. Sometimes, Momma had the audacity to call me over and ask me to stay and sweep the stairs for her because her knees were bad and it was hard on her going up and down so many flights.

Do you think I cared about that? No, I did not. My fourteen year old soul didn't care that this woman, who had sacrificed so much for me was in a little need of help. Stay and sweep the stairs? No way. I told her that I had homework to do. After a while, she stopped asking.

Well, one day, I looked in the lobby and she wasn't there so I thought it would be safe for me to walk out with my friends. I almost made it too, but right when I approached the door to exit, she was coming in. She was limping badly and I knew her knees were bothering her. I felt a tiny twinge of sympathy, but I pushed past it. She looked at me but didn't say a word and neither did I.

Y'all, I hate to say it, but I walked right past her like

she was a stranger on the street. I kept walking all the way down the staircase and down to the sidewalk. With every step, I was trying to reconcile the guilt that I felt over ignoring my mother and treating her like she didn't exist. I felt like the girl in that movie, *Imitation of Life*.

When I made it to the sidewalk, I turned and looked into the lobby and I saw Momma sitting there on the radiator. She looked so sad. She was just sitting there with her head bowed and a lonely look on her face. I knew I had hurt her. And sure, I felt remorse, but it didn't make me run back up those stairs and say, "Momma, I'm sorry."

Pride is an ugly thing, y'all.

Momma didn't say anything. She never mentioned the incident at home either and I was glad. That made the next time I walked past her a little easier. This went on for a month or so until one day I guess she got tired of my "high falutin'" ways.

She did the unthinkable. As I was walking out the front door, she actually spoke to me, right there in front of my friends. To make matters worse, she called me by my name, like she knew me. I started to keep walking but my friends all stopped and looked at me.

I didn't know what to. Part of me wanted to ignore her, but the other part of me knew I couldn't. The guilt was too much. My back was against the wall, but for the first time in a long while, the decent part of me won. I said, "Hi Momma." When I looked at her she bowed her head in response. The other girls spoke to her also.

When I got outside the school, one of my friends said, "I didn't know that was your mother."

I told them, "Yes, that's my mother."

She said, "She is very nice. She is not like the other maids; they act like they've been sucking lemons. Your mom always has a pleasant look on her face, like she's always happy. How come you didn't introduce us?"

I couldn't believe it. My mother was a maid and they

didn't care. They all thought Momma was nice. For a few moments I was elated. Now everything was fine. I had the approval of some girls whose name I don't even remember today. All that embarrassment, ignoring, and hiding was for nothing. It wasn't until I made it home that the shame started to set in.

After that I didn't wait for her to ask me for help. I walked right up to her in school and asked her if she needed help and she said yes. I was glad to do it. It was the only way I knew of to ease my conscience.

Today, I wish I could take it all back. Those times when I hurried past her or spoke softly so that no one else would notice, I wish I could take it back. Those times when she asked me to stay a few minutes and help her sweep the stupid stairs and I said no, I wish I could take it all back.

That's the thing though; you can't undo what you've done. Just like you can't unsay what you've said. It just don't work like that. Sure, you can say, "I'm sorry" but, sometimes that just don't cut it. That is why today, some blankety-blank years later, I still feel bad about what I did. I probably need to see a counselor about this because every now and then I feel the need to call Momma and apologize for what I did. And when I do Momma says she forgives me every time. So, we made up and now, there's no doubt in my mind that that old lady would take a bullet for me. Unless, of course, it was a bullet coming from her own gun.

Y'all ain't gonna believe this...

* * * * *

After I had been living in California for about a year, I decided to go home to Memphis for a visit. I didn't tell anyone I was coming but Tina, who was the only one who hadn't made the move to L.A.

Tina picked me up at the airport at 8:30 the night I

arrived and drove me home. I can still see the look on Daddy's face when he answered the door and saw me. He was so happy. We had an hour to ourselves to catch up before he had to drive over to Riverview to pick up Momma from her job at the school. I made him promise not to tell her I was home.

They arrived home fifteen minutes after Daddy left. When I heard the car pull into the driveway, I ran into the bedroom Momma and Daddy had shared since they moved into the house. I hid behind the dresser.

I could hear them talking as they came into the back door. I could hear Momma's footsteps coming down the hall. My heart was beating a mile a minute. I could hear the doorknob turn from where I was kneeling behind the dresser.

As soon as she stepped into the room and turned on the light, I jumped up and yelled, "Surprise Momma!"

No sooner had I gotten the words out of my mouth, did Momma reach into her bra and pulled out a small, gold plated pistol and assumed a position that would have made any one of Charlie's Angels proud. She pointed that gun right at the center of my chest. Her aim was steady. She was planning on shootin' to kill.

I screamed, "Momma NO! It's me, your daughter."

It looked like she was still trying to figure out if she wanted to shoot me. I wondered if she was remembering how I'd treated her years earlier. Then, slowly, wordlessly, she lowered the weapon and put it back in her bra.

I was furious. "Momma, you could have killed me. What, in Heaven's name, are you doing with a gun?"

She shrugged her shoulders like it wasn't a big deal. She said, "Child, it's bad over there where I work."

I was mortified. I said, "But, Momma, I don't think it's safe carrying a gun. It could go off accidentally. Besides, you wouldn't really shoot someone would you?"

She looked me dead in the eyes and said, "I would if

they pushed me."

I totally believed her.

* * * * *

So, I survived that frightening experience and lived to have many, many more. That's how it is when you're from a large family full of near crazy people. There's always somebody getting into something or the other. I'm telling you, I recollect some of the adventures my family has had over the years and it makes me shake my head in wonder. Now me, I call them shenanigans, but they would call them *GOOD TIMES!*

PART THREE

GOOD TIMES

CHAPTER 12

DADDY AND THE COTTON CARNIVAL

Now, let me recollect a little more about Daddy. Given his low opinion of his father, I sometimes wonder what Daddy thought about whenever he looked in the mirror. His skin was as white as any self-respecting Klan member. His hair was thick, black and wavy, not a nap in sight. When he was younger, Daddy looked more like a white man, than a black one. In fact, his looks got him into more than a little bit of trouble too.

After they were married, he worked a few odd jobs here and there in Mississippi. But, after Tina was born, Daddy decided the family could do a lot better if they moved from Mississippi to Chicago. Back then, Chicago was the promised-land for black folk. Everyone was moving up there. Daddy had more than one reason for wanting to go up north. He heard that his long lost siblings had settled up there. It was his dream of reuniting with them. His plan was to get a job and find his family. Then, in his mind, life would be perfect.

His thinking was, *Might as well kill two birds with one stone.*

His plans changed when he found a job his first night in Memphis. What happened was, his train had a longish layover in Memphis so he gave Momma's sister Pearl and her husband Percy a call from the station. Uncle Percy came right over and picked him up.

As soon as Daddy sat in the car, Uncle Percy started telling him how he could get him a job at the warehouse where he worked. Now, Daddy wasn't paying him no never mind at first because he really wanted to head for the Windy City. But his sense of responsibility for his family won out and he decided to give it a try. He went with Uncle Percy and before you could say "BOO," he had the job. So, Chicago went on the back burner for the time being.

He lived alone in Memphis at first, working and trying to find a place large enough for his ever growing family which was no small task. He found a small one bedroom apartment that would never be big enough for the whole family, but would do while he saved his money. It was a sad and lonely time but spending his down time working around the church helped.

Now, Daddy heard about the Cotton Carnival from his co-workers. For those of you who don't know, the Cotton Carnival is an annual event in Memphis. It was like the county fairs that you hear about today. Well, Daddy had never heard of the Cotton Carnival, much less been to one so he decided he would go and see what the hubbub was. He looked in the paper to get the location.

So, early Saturday morning, he put on his slacks, white shirt, black tie, grabbed his hat and caught the bus headed for Main Street. Y'all, people got dressed up for everything back in the day. When he got to the carnival, he was so excited with all the commotion that was going on that he wasn't paying close enough attention to his surroundings. His sense of self preservation was muted, so to say. There was talking, laughter, music and vendors were everywhere. It was a high time. He got in line, paid his entry fee and walked right in, taking in the sights, sounds and smells. It wasn't until he was well inside the carnival that he emerged from his dazed condition and took a look around at the people attending the carnival. He was properly horrified. They were all WHITE!

See, what his co-workers failed to tell him was that there were two Cotton Carnivals. Both were in the downtown area, but, the carnival on Beale Street was for black folks. The one on Main was for white folks. Y'all do know black and white folks didn't have much to do with each other back then.

Well, Daddy didn't know much about Memphis being a newcomer. He really didn't know about the carnival on Beale Street because, you know, they didn't advertise that one in the paper. He would have had to get the black newspaper to read about that one.

He was beside himself with fear. He thought, *Oh Lawd, look at all these white folk. I done gone to the wrong place.*

He tried to remain cool and not draw attention to himself but he was sweating and breathing hard. He had to put his hands in his pockets so people wouldn't see that they were shaking. He felt like he was going to pass out. I can't say I blame him though. If those white folks knew the truth, they never would have let him out of there alive. I told y'all already. White folks weren't no joke back then.

Not that he had anything to worry about. No one seemed to notice that he was black. They were looking at him but there was no disgust in their eyes. One white lady bumped into him. Daddy almost jumped out of his skin, but the lady looked him right in the eyes and said, "Excuse me sir."

She didn't see that he was a negro.

Daddy just nodded his head. He wouldn't dare speak for fear someone would recognize his race in his voice.

He could have easily stayed at the carnival and passed for white, but the notion never came to him. He knew who he was and he knew where he was supposed to be. And it wasn't on Main Street. He felt the distinct urge to turn tail and run for the exit, but he knew he couldn't do that without attracting unwanted attention to himself. He decided the best plan of action was to just slowly mosey over to the exit. All the while he was saying to himself, *If I can just make it to the gate and keep my mouth shut, maybe I'll make it outta here in one piece.*

Well, praise the Lord, he made it out alive and was thanking God for it. He practically ran to the bus stop, made his way to the back and started back home. The bus took him right by Beale Street and he could see crowds of people laughing, running, and having a fine time at the black carnival. But he didn't even think about setting foot outside of the bus.

By then, the carnival spirit had plumb left him.

CHAPTER 13

THE ADVENTURE AT PRESIDENT'S ISLAND

Growing up, Mark, Earl, and Wayne were very close, and I mean that in the literal sense of the word. The three of them shared a tiny bedroom, and when I say bedroom I'm being generous. They slept in the crowded, piping hot in the summer and freezing in the winter, attic of our South Memphis home. Y'all, that attic was so hot, we used to say it was the devil's winter home. But, they had to live up there because at the time, there were six children in a two bedroom house so something had to give. What gave was the rickety pull down steps to allow them access to the makeshift room.

I don't know if it was just positive thinking on their part, but to let them tell it, they loved it up there. To them, it was dark and mysterious. They bragged to my sisters about not being right under Momma's and Daddy's noses so they could get into more devilment. It was their safe haven to do whatever they good and well pleased. That turned out to be true when Earl got into trouble with Momma when he was about eight years old.

I don't rightly recall what my brother did, but whatever it was, Momma was fit to be tied. She went outside to get a switch off the cherry tree in the back yard when Earl had the bright idea to run to the hallway, pull down the attic stairs and climb up there. Earl knew that Momma, who was pregnant off and on over a twenty-three year period, wouldn't ever try to climb up those wobbly stairs. She was afraid of them. So there she stood, in the hallway at the bottom of the steps yelling at Earl and telling him he better come down right now and Earl looking down at her shaking his head.

The battle went on for a few minutes before Momma said, "Okay, just you wait until your Daddy comes home."

Momma walked into the living room with the switch still in her hand. Everyone who was in the room scattered just in case Momma remembered something they had done and starting swinging 'cause Momma wasn't one to let a good switch go to waste. She was outdone, but she was also amused. My brothers and sisters could hear her laughing from the front porch. And, when Daddy finally got home she told him what happened and he had a good laugh at her expense. It's hard to believe, but Earl didn't get a whippin' that time...lucky stiff.

Sometimes, when the weather was agreeable, the boys would invite my sisters to come up to the attic for a visit. This rare invitation was never refused. Jean, Mae, and Tina would climb up there remembering not to stand fully erect or they would bump their heads on the low ceiling that sloped downward on both sides of the room. They would spend the time telling jokes and making up stories. Sometimes they would play caveman by taking out some crayons and drawing on the plywood walls that Daddy put up to cover the insulation. They had no fear of writing on the walls because Momma couldn't make it up the steps. You know, those drawings are still up there today.

* * * * *

Most summer days, my brothers spent their time with the other boys who lived on our block. They would get together with three other boys in the neighborhood and go for long walks exploring the vacant fields around the area, go fishing or just picking blackberries. When they really wanted an adventure and they were feeling especially brave, they would walk over to President's Island.

I guess you can call President's Island the port of Memphis. It's located near downtown on the banks of the Mississippi River. It's a good three miles from our house. There were mostly trucking companies and factories over there with a lot of hustle and bustle going on all hours of the day and night.

Back then in the 1950's, the Island employed more than it's quota of unsavory, brutish characters, mostly white but a few blacks worked over there also. President's Island was definitely no place for black children. If somebody was up to no good, President's Island was the place to dispose of any incriminating evidence. As Momma used to say, "It's a good place to come up missin'."

All three of my brothers knew good and well that they weren't supposed to go nowhere near President's Island. Momma told them time and time again to keep their distance from that place. She would threaten them saying, "A hard head makes a soft behind."

But, you know how hardheaded little boys are. The threat of a whippin' was no deterrent to them. They made it their business to go there whenever they good and well pleased.

I can't say I blamed them. President's Island was a fascinating place to spend a lazy afternoon. They'd trot over there and have a fine time sitting on the banks of the Mississippi among the overgrown weeds, skipping rocks across the water, or just watching the steamboats and barges go by. The boys walked over there at least once a month without incident. That is, until that last time.

One hot summer afternoon, the group snuck away and walked over to the Island. Mark must have been about thirteen, which would have put Earl at nine and Wayne at seven. One of their friends brought an old football and they started tossing it around. Earl went out for a long pass, but he wasn't paying attention to where he was standing. When he jumped up to catch the ball he came down too close to the edge of the shore. He lost his balance and fell right into the mighty Mississippi. Earl couldn't swim. No one could. It was a bad situation.

The other boys stood there watching in horror, momentarily frozen in fear, as Earl fought to stay above water. Now, truth be told, the water probably wasn't all that deep, but my brother wasn't all that tall either and you gotta know he wasn't used to all that water either. That boy was struggling against the water, which of course made him sink even more and pushed him further into the river. He was grabbing at the overgrown shrubbery and limbs that lined the banks of the river, trying to pull his way closer to land but his wet hands couldn't get a firm grip on much of nothing. Y'all know how tragedies are, don't you? They happen very quickly.

After standing there, watching his brother about to get swept away, Mark finally snapped back to reality. He got an idea quick and in a hurry. He yelled out to Wayne and their three friends to run ahead of Earl in the direction he was floating. When they were a distance before him, they locked hands. Then, Mark got to the front of the human chain and walked to where Earl had managed to hold on to the frail limbs of a bush. Mark reached over and grabbed Earl. When he was sure his grip was secure, the other boys began to back up, pulling Mark and Earl out of the water. Reeling them in, so to speak. But, there was another problem.

The boys were yanking and pulling and trying to get him out, but Earl wasn't budging. As it turns out, his foot was caught on something under the surface of the water. To this day, they don't know what it was, probably a rusty piece of metal or a broken pipe. Whatever it was, it had a death grip on the leg of my brother's jeans. Ain't that the devil? Well, it took a bit of pulling and yanking before they were finally able to free Earl. The bad news is the object practically ripped the bottom of his foot wide open leaving a huge gash.

When they finally got him out of the water, Earl was in intense pain. Worse than that, his foot wouldn't stop bleeding. Mark told Wayne to pull off his tee-shirt and he ripped it into strips and wrapped it tightly around his foot. That seemed to slow the bleeding for the time being. Now, on to another problem. How were they going to get Earl home? He was in no condition to walk the three miles to our house. They knew better than to ask any of the white truckers for help. They also knew they were in for it when they got home because they shouldn't have been over there in the first place.

What they decided to do was to carry Earl piggyback. It was a slow and miserable journey being over ninety degrees and having to carry dead weight, but that was their only option. And if you ask me, that's what they get.

Each boy could only carry Earl a few blocks before they'd have to switch up. To be honest, Mark and Wayne didn't mind the extra time it took to get home because they were already envisioning the beating they were going to get when Momma found out what happened. Earl wasn't too worried. His thinking was that Momma probably wouldn't get him since he was already hurt. On the surface that made sense, but then again, with Momma, you never knew.

Mark, the one person who was always pulling a prank on someone, was desperately trying to scheme up a plan to get out of a whippin' but his mind failed him. God don't like ugly, y'all. That boy couldn't think up a good lie to save his life. And I do mean that in the literal sense.

It didn't help matters that the other boys were saying stuff like, "Oooooh, y'all gon' git it when you get home" and "Yo momma gon' whup you."

Everyone on the block knew our Momma didn't play.

When the group turned down our street, Mark and

Wayne felt like condemned men walking towards the executioner's chamber. If they'd walked any slower they would have been going backwards. When they finally made it to the house, Momma came running down the driveway. Momma was also the original neighborhood watch so she must have been peeking out the window.

She helped the boys carry Earl to the living room and sat him on the couch. Momma took over from there. She removed the makeshift bandages and poured some peroxide over the wound. Then she bound it up real tight with another old tee-shirt. The wound that at first looked like a crater wound up being a deep gash. Momma decided it wouldn't need any stitches. We didn't have any money for an unnecessary trip to the hospital. She propped his foot up on some pillows, gave Earl some aspirin and told him to stay on the couch for the rest of the day.

Now, it was time for the penalty phase. Momma dismissed my brother's friends who were sorely disappointed they wouldn't get to see Momma in action. Then she turned to Mark and asked, "What happened?"

Before he knew it, a lame little lie rolled out of his mouth. "Earl cut his food on a broken bottle." It must have sounded good to Wayne who eagerly nodded his head in agreement.

Momma looked at them. The kind of look that says, *I know this negro is lyin'*. She walked over to Mark and leaned over feeling the bottom of his jeans. "Why wasn't Earl wearing his shoes and why are your pants wet."

Now, Mark really hadn't thought that far ahead. Stammering, he said, "Okay...see, Momma. This is what happened. He took his shoes off...uh...because his feet were hurting. You know he's a growing boy and all. And...uh...his pants are damp because...uh...because we ran through Mr. Evers sprinkler to wash the blood off of Earl's foot."

"So, Mr. Evers had his sprinkler on in the middle of the

111

day?"

"Uh, yeah. His sprinklers were on, but he was turning 'em off when we left."

You know what? There was a miracle in Memphis that day because, by the grace of God, Momma let Mark and Wayne slide. Sure, she let them squirm for a while. Then she said, "Boy, take Wayne and go back outside so Earl can rest."

Mark and Wayne both grew a little closer to God that day because they knew they were recipients of unmerited favor. They knew Momma didn't believe their lie one bit. It's one of those unexplained phenomenon that happens when the moon is in just the right place. Maybe she was feeling generous or maybe it was too hot to whip kids that day. Whatever it was, they were thankful. They had learned their lesson.

In a few weeks, after Earl's foot had fully healed, Mark, Earl and Wayne went back to President's Island with their friends.

Because that's how hardheaded little boys are.

CHAPTER 14

THE BEST CHRISTMAS EVER

I gotta tell y'all, Christmas is my all time, number one favorite holiday. I love everything about it! When I was growing up, practically all of my older sibling were grown and out of the house. But they usually came home for Christmas and I experienced all the joy and rapture the holiday had to offer.

Back then, it wasn't ALL about the presents, but I'd be lying like Ananias and Sapphira if I said I didn't enjoy my share of dolls and that Easy Bake Oven. But, for real, it was all about family. This next story I'm gonna recollect is practically a legend in my family. Even though I wasn't born at the time, it's one of my favorites.

* * * * *

The gas floor heater in the hallway fought valiantly, doing the best it could to heat the whole six room house, not including the attic. But it was a loosing battle. Even with the flame turned up to high, it might as well have been a matchstick trying to heat Buckingham Palace… it wasn't doing much of nothing.

Normally, the house was warm and comfortable when the central heater was working. But, wouldn't you know, it broke down right after thanksgiving and Daddy didn't have the money to get it fixed right away. Thank the Lord, there was a backup heating system for the house. Normally, the gas floor heater did a respectable job keeping the tiny A-frame house warm; at least warmer than it was outside. But not on this cold, clear December morning.

December 25, 1956, to be exact.

Daddy had to be at church by 6:00am to light the fire and set up for the Christmas pageant that started at 6:30 so it was up and at 'em at 5:00. This wasn't a paying job and our family didn't live near the church. Daddy just volunteered to help out of the goodness of his heart. And, Daddy's big, good heart got on his children's last nerve because they had to get up and go to church with him.

It was time to wake the family.

Lord'a mercy, Daddy thought as he sat up in the bed, reaching for his red flannel robe. *Wonder if somebody left the window open? Must be five degrees in this house, let alone outside. Gotta get that wall heater fixed, but not now. Too many Christmas bills to pay.*

Well, cain't be helped. It's Christmas mornin'. Gotta lot to do.

He reached over and gave Momma a gently shake, "Mae, time to get up."

Momma didn't say a mumbling word.

Daddy tried again, "Mae, it's time…"

"I heard you Matthew," was her drowsy, yet crisp response.

Momma's not a morning person.

Shrugging into his robe and slipping his feet into the worn out slippers parked on the floor beside the bed, Daddy stood up and headed for the door. He turned to take another look at Momma still laying there under the mounds of covers. He decided to leave her be. She wouldn't be going to the Christmas Pageant anyway. Too much cooking to do.

Daddy left their bedroom and went down the hall stopping at the heater and giving it a gentle nudge…as if that would do any good. He went on to the girl's bedroom.

The soft knock on the open bedroom door was

answered by Jean with a groggy, "Huh"

Daddy answered, "Y'all git up."

Not waiting for another response he moved on. A few moments later, Jean, Mae, and Tina heard Daddy pulling down the cord to the half propped open attic door and yelling up to Mark, Earl, and Wayne, "Y'all git up."

"Aw right," answered Mark.

The attic door closed with a bang to make sure everyone knew he wasn't fooling around. He headed to the kitchen to put on the coffee and turn on the oven to get some heat going in the front of the house.

Tina waited until Daddy was safely down the hall before she started to complain, "Good Lord… it must be five degrees in here."

Shivering, Mae said "You reckon it's that warm?"

"Well, five degrees or not, we gotta get up 'fore Daddy comes back down that hall," said Jean.

Mae mused, "Y'all know I love the Christmas pageant, but why do we have to go every year? I mean, wouldn't it be nice to be able to sleep late and just open our presents like the rest of the heathens?"

Jean answered, "Girl, it's six of us, not including Denise. We are the Christmas pageant!"

Jean was right about that. This year's Greater Open Door Missionary Baptist Church Annual Christmas Pageant boasted almost all of the DeVault clan in the leading roles. Jean was Mary, Mark was the innkeeper, Mae was the narrator and Earl, Tina, and Wayne were in the choir.

It's not like there weren't other children in the church. There were… plenty. But whenever stuff like plays, pageants, and choir performance happened, my siblings were always at the head of the line, volunteering for roles. The little hams! Seemed like a good idea at the time. It was a different think when it was pitch black and twenty degrees outside.

"Still gotta get up," Tina said.

"First steps the hardest," was Mae's wise observation.
"Sho' is."

Jean, being the oldest at sixteen decided to take charge.
"Enough of this stalling. Stayin' here under the covers ain't
gonna make it no easier. We gotta get up or we gonna be
late and Daddy's gonna have our hides. So, at the count of
three we all gonna get up. Y'all gonna do it?"

"Yeah" and "Uh-huh," both sisters agreed.

"Okay then. Here we go. One...Two...Three."

Obediently, all three sisters sat up in the bed that they
shared, throwing off the covers.

Jean said, "JESUS it's cold!" and went back under the
covers.

Tina said, "Girl, you better not let Momma hear you
taking the Lord's name in vain. She's gonna get the oil to
you."

Jean responded from under the covers, "Honey child,
that wasn't in vain. I truly meant every word of it. I ain't
goin'."

Tina said, "Like you got a choice."

Mae took charge. "Naw, naw...get up, get up! It was
your bright idea."

Mae and Tina drug Jean up and they hurried out of the
bedroom and into the hall, huddling around the heater like
it was a campfire.

A few minutes later, the steps to the attic slowly
opened and Earl yelled down, "Look out
belowwwwwwwww."

The girls parted like the Red Sea so the boys could
come down.

Mark said, "Y'all look cold." He always had
something to say.

Mae retorted, "As if y'all ain't."

He responded, "Well, not as cold as y'all. Number
one, heat rises sister dear. Plus, it's only one small window
and all that insulation upstairs so it quite cozy. Number

two, we're men! We don't get cold like y'all girls."

Jean said, "Bet you ain't braggin' about heat rising to the attic in the summertime."

Mae, who's age was twelve but mouth was twenty-five said, "Men my foot! Mark, you only fourteen. Y'all ain't no men. And don't nobody want to live in that dark, musty attic anyway. Can't even stand upright."

The battle was about to begin when Daddy yelled from the kitchen, "Let me have that racket!"

Momma was now up and got to the heart of the matter, "Be a shame for me to have to come out there wid my belt on Christmas mornin'!"

Tina, who was nine at the time whispered, "Yep, that sho' would be a shame."

They all snickered under their breath and the debate was over.

Earl said, "Y'all girls gonna use the bathroom first so we can get ready. Quicker we go the quicker we can get back and open our presents."

Wayne chimed in, "Yeah!"

Earl was only seven, and Wayne was five so their minds were more on the boxes under the tree and less on the baby Jesus.

But those boxes under the tree would have to wait. Momma and Daddy insisted that first things should come first. And the first thing was to go to church and start the holiday off right then home to open the gifts.

Mark said, "Earl is right. You girls hurry up in the bathroom so we can get ready. Slyly looking at Mae, he said, "I got a feelin' this is gonna be the best Christmas yet."

Mae returned his look with a knowing nod and hurried towards the bathroom.

So y'all will know what that secret look was about, let me back up about ten hours or so and fill you in.

* * * * *

T'was the night before Christmas and it was raining cats and dogs. Plus, it was cold as the dickens, but not cold enough to ice over. The body heat, kitchen stove and floor heater had the house pretty comfy. Praise the Lord for that!

The kids were in the living room chatting and looking at the silver aluminum tree decorated with bright multicolored lights, gold tinsel and metallic gold and red ornaments. The color wheel was focused on the tree, gently spinning on each color and turning the room magical colors of red, green and yellow. Mahalia Jackson's "What Child Is This?" was playing softly on the radio. It was all very Norman Rockwell-ish.

Momma and Daddy, sitting a few feet away at the dining room table, were looking suspicious. At least that's what they looked like to Mark. He kept his eyes on them.

The whole house smelled of Christmas. Momma had already started her prep work for the massive meal that would grace the family table the next day. She was at the table dicing onions, peppers, and celery for the cornbread dressing that she would mix up later in the evening and more of the same for her famous spaghetti sauce that she would cook that evening.

A coconut pineapple cake, dripping with buttercream icing and a big three layer chocolate cake for Daddy had been made a few days earlier and allowed to sit so they could "come to themselves." Three potato pies had just come out of the oven and were cooling on the counter. She had already cooked the ham the family would devour for the traditional Christmas breakfast along with homemade biscuits, cheese eggs, and grits and hot chocolate. Momma had had a very busy week.

Come Christmas morning she would rise early and put the turkey in the oven and start the water boiling for the spaghetti. Rounding out the meal would be collard greens with ham hocks, creamed corn, and piping hot cornbread. And not that sweet cake-like stuff they call cornbread today. I'm talking the real deal savory cornbread made with cornmeal, no sugar and loads of melted butter slathered on top.

You would think she'd be tired of cooking, especially since she had to cook for the classroom parties each child had at school the previous week. Momma was hot stuff in the kitchen and everybody knew it. In fact, the teachers at Florida Elementary School and Carver High School used to fight over who would get Momma to fry the chicken or make the spaghetti for their parties. Things were getting out of hand until they developed a system of bidding to get her services. And that's the truth!

Adding to the wonderful aroma in that house on Christmas Eve were the six medium sized boxes, unwrapped but tied down with bright Christmas ribbon. There were only six boxes because Denise was just a baby and I hadn't made my arrival. The boxes were filled with treats and each child received one for Christmas. Each box contained the exact same amount of apples, oranges, nuts, raisins, red, white, and green ribbon candy, candied orange slices and chocolate drops, which was Daddy's favorite. It was like a box of heaven and a very big deal because it was one of the few times the kids received something of their own that they didn't have to share.

Growing up, my older siblings could never understand how they were able to receive such a bounty of gifts for Christmas considering the meager amount Daddy received working at the warehouse and various odd jobs he was able to get now and then. The presents appeared to be exploding from under the small tree. It was much later that they found out that Daddy was charging all the items he bought at Allen's Hardware store and working extra jobs to pay them off over time.

But, let me back up even more. I need to tell y'all

something else…

* * * * *

The Saturday before Christmas, Daddy and the kids bundled up and walked the two miles to the beautiful park located on the side of Florida Elementary School. Daddy put on his church suit, tie and hat while the girls would have on their school dresses and the boys in a pair of slacks and sweaters. He made sure the family got there nice and early because the line could be long and he didn't want the kids out all day in the cold. This year they lucked out and were the 10th family in line. It wasn't long before the line grew and grew until it stretched for blocks.

At five minutes to noon, the excitement grew to a fevered pitch. There had to be at least two hundred children in line waiting, not counting the fathers and a few mothers who braved the elements.

At straight up noon you could hear it coming. With Christmas music blaring out of the amplified speakers, the Coca-Cola Christmas truck turned off Florida Street and onto South Parkway and headed for the park. Pandemonium broke out among the crowd with children running, jumping and clapping their hands at the truck's arrival.

The truck came to a stop a few yards in front of the families and the whole side of the truck was gently lowered. The sea of children surged forward to see the man of the hour, Santa Claus, sitting on his throne. Santa was a sight with his velvety red suit, fluffy white beard and chocolate brown skin. The kids loved him!

One by one, the workers helped the children into the truck and onto Santa's lap so they could tell jolly Saint Nick what they wanted for Christmas. The best part was after the kids exited the truck and each girl was given a naked doll with a Coca-Cola bottle cap hat and the boys were given miniature Coca-Cola trucks. Each child also received a peppermint stick. You'd think they'd given the kids a block of gold.

Once all six DeVault children let their request be made known to Santa, the family started the journey home. They were still excited at seeing Santa, even the bigger kids like Mae and Tina who should have known better.

But, then again, maybe not. From what I'm told, childhood lasted a lot longer back in the day.

* * * * *

But, there I go digressing again.

Back to Christmas Eve and the cozy scene of peace, tranquility, and goodwill to all men. Mark decided to go to the kitchen to for a glass of milk and Mae, with her nosy self, followed him. Not that it was a long trip.

Daddy eyed them.

As Mark approached the refrigerator, a flash of something outside the window caught his eyes. He sauntered over to the window and eased the curtain open a quarter of an inch with his index finger ever so gently; something he'd seen Momma do countless times.

Mae asked in a voice full of concern, "What's out there?"

Mark answered, "Two men. One of 'em is Mr. Allen from the hardware store. Least that's his truck parked in the driveway. They're just getting out right now."

Mae was perplexed. "What's he doing here this time of night? And on Christmas Eve too? Should be over on the white side of town with his family."

Mark eased away from the front kitchen and tipped over to the window on the kitchen door to further his surveillance.

"Hey!" was his excited whisper. "They're getting something out the back of the truck. Something big and shiny, but I can't make out what it is. Bet they takin' it to the backyard."

Now Mae was totally confused. "Why would Mr. Allen be delivering stuff on Christmas Eve?"

She thought on it for a second and said, "Wait a minute. Fat, white man delivering stuff on Christmas Eve. Do you think Mr. Allen is Santa?"

Mark was outraged! "Stupid, it ain't no Santa! What's wrong with you? Twelve years old and still believing in Santa. Lord have mercy!"

It's hard to say if Mae were more crushed at finding out there was no Santa or angry at being called stupid. At any rate, she refused to show it. She's like Momma in that respect. She was just getting ready to launch a verbal grenade when Daddy yelled from the dining room, "What's goin' on in there?"

In unison they sweetly responded, "Nothing."

Forgetting about their milk, they hurried out of the kitchen.

Daddy eyed them.

They both returned to the couch where they were sitting but it was impossible to keep still. They were both fidgeting because they were dying to know what Mr. Allen was delivering in the back yard.

Mae jumped up and said, "I gotta go to the bathroom."

Jean looked up from her novel and said, "You asking for permission?"

Ignoring her Mae ran into the tiny room and opened the window. She could hear soft talking, even over the pounding rain, but it was too dark to see a thing.

Deflated she came back to the living room. She glanced at Mark, shook her head and whispered, "Can't see a thing. You try."

Mark barely nodded his head. He waited a minute and said, "Uh. I gotta go to the bathroom."

Earl said, "Y'all getting on my nerves. Just go already!"

Mark didn't have any luck at the window either. Mr. Allen and whoever was with him were busy working by the back door of Momma and Daddy's room on the far side of the house.

Just as he was getting ready to go back to the living room and admit defeat, he heard five knocks on the back door. Mr. Allen's signal.

Mark stepped from the hallway into the living room and said, "Anybody else hear that knocking?"

Daddy bolted straight up. He hadn't heard the pre-arranged signal over the music and chatter of the children.

"Naw boy. Go sit down."

"But Daddy, I heard..."

"I said sit. I'll go take a look."

He nodded to Momma and hotfooted it to the bedroom firmly closing the door behind him.

Momma chose the wrong time to go to the kitchen because when she did, Mark and Mae jumped up and ran to the door of the bedroom and Mark, eased it open... Dang, that boy is sneaky!

The one line they heard was enough.

Daddy was shaking Mr. Allen's hand and thanking him for delivering the two bicycles for Mark and Mae.

Delirium! Bliss! Joy unspeakable!

Mark and Mae had been asking for bicycles for years but our parents just weren't able. Until now, that is. The blessed Christmas of 1956!

* * * * *

The family finally left the house at 5:30 on Christmas morning.

Tina was thinking, *Thank God the rain stopped. It's miserable enough walking out here, pitch black and bitter cold. Would have been even worse if it had still been raining.*

Earl and Wayne led the bunch as the family headed down South Parkway to Florida Street. The same route the kids took each morning, as the church was directly across the street from the school.

The Christmas pageant went as pageants go. Jean with a pillow tied to her belly, performing her little heart out, and Mark belting out his only line, "There's no room at the inn."

Before long, the family made their way home, thankful that the house had finally warmed up with the heat from the oven and heater finally conquering the cold.

Mark and Mae did the best they could to act surprised when they stepped into the living room and saw the two shiny red and blue bicycles. The red for Mae and the blue for Mark. The kids were all happy for them because they knew that's what they wanted. They also knew they'd get to take turns riding the bikes so it was a win for all. They both wanted to take the bikes for a spin but Momma told them to open the rest of their presents.

Momma and Daddy took seats next to each other on the couch and watched the free for all with smiles on their faces. There wasn't a single thing under that tree with their names on it, but it was fine with them. Just seeing the joy on the faces of their children really was enough for them.

Mae got to her last present, which was in a dress box. She thought it was heavy for the dress or sweater she normally got and she was right. Tears practically came to her eyes when she pulled out a navy blue and white double-breasted tweed coat. The coat had navy blue velvet pockets and a velvet collar. It was the most beautiful thing she had ever seen in her life.

Mae was unable to control her self. She jumped up and cried, "Oh, thank you Momma! Thank you Daddy!"

Then she put on her new coat, grabbed her bike and bolted out of the door. Once she made it to the bottom of the steps, she jumped on the bike and took off riding up the street…price tags flying in the wind.

 Momma yelled at her, "Girl get back in this house!"

 Daddy just laughed and said, "Leave her be, Mae."

 Momma joined him laughing.

 It was the best Christmas ever!

CHAPTER 15

RADAR

Over the years, my brother Earl grew to look more and more like Daddy. By the time he reached high school, he was tall, slim, and handsome. On the outside, he looked like Daddy, but on the inside Earl developed something on his own. Earl had a bad temper. I'm talking bad, y'all. Earl was nobody to play with. To this day, nobody can figure out how he got to be like that. Momma must have been eating hot peppers when she was pregnant with him. But, that's just my two cents worth!

Now, I'm not saying he was a bully, 'cause he wasn't. I mean, he didn't go around acting like, "Y'all better not mess with me, 'cause I'm bad." He wasn't like that. I'm just saying that if you made the mistake of pushing him too far when he told you to leave him be, he'd rise up on you and pretty soon, you'd wind up looking for your upper and lower molars somewhere on South Parkway. And that's the truth.

As a matter of fact, Earl had plenty of friends. His best friend was this guy everyone called "Spicy." When they were in the eighth grade, Spicy decided to go out for the football team at Carver High School. Back then, high school started at the seventh grade. There wasn't such a thing as middle school. Anyway, Spicy went out for the team and tried to convince Earl, who had no desire to play football, to go with him to the tryouts.

When Momma heard about the tryouts, she wanted Earl to go. So did Tina. They were bewildered that Earl showed no interest in being on the team because running around, hitting people and knocking people down seemed to be right up his alley. I guess both of them figured it could have taken some of the edge off of his high strung personality. Convinced they were acting in Earl's best interests, Momma and Tina decided to talk to him about it one night after supper.

Momma spoke first. "Why don't you gon' over to the school and try out for the football team?"

Earl lazily answered, "I ain't interested."

"Why not?" Tina asked.

"'Cause."

"'Cause why?"

"'Cause I just don't wanna." He was starting to turn a little red around the ears so Tina decided to drop the subject. Momma didn't.

"What's the matter boy? You scared? Is that what it is? 'Cause you don't hafta be. Let me tell you what you can do. If somebody hits you too hard, you just go ahead and hit him back with your purse."

Momma's humor surprised her own self. She laughed until tears were rolling down her cheeks. Tina stifled a laugh for awhile, but was unable to keep it in and laughed right in Earl's face.

Now, as a general rule, Earl didn't take kindly to being laughed at. But, Momma is the one who started it, so what could he do? I told y'all he has a temper, I didn't say he was crazy. For maybe the first time in his life, Earl laughed at himself.

But a week later, there he was, out there on the field in the middle of the hot Memphis summer working out with all the other guys. Skin just as red as a beet, but it didn't make him no never mind. He wanted to lay aside any thoughts that he was afraid, because he wasn't. The truth of the matter was, he just wasn't the team sport kind of guy. He was more of a loner.

In his mind, he was just working out. He wasn't even trying to master the drills or impress the coach. In spite of his half-hearted attempt, he scored several touchdowns on his first day and everyone was real impressed. He kept going back with Spicy, but to tell the truth, it didn't matter much to him.

After the end of the month long tryout, Spicy heard that the team had been selected. He ran down the street to our house and interrupted Earl who was busy doing absolutely nothing. Practically dragging my brother out of the house, the two of them headed for the gym, but Spicy neglected to tell Earl why they were going. Now, Spicy ran most of the way, turning and beckoning to Earl to put some pep in his step. Earl was just lollygagging and taking his sweet time because, that's how he is.

Once they finally got to the school, Spicy rushed inside and over to the wall to read the list of the guys who had made the team. Earl, on the other hand didn't even bother to go inside the gym. He just waited, calm as you please on the steps outside.

Smiling, Spicy came running out the gym with exciting news. "We made it. We made it."

Earl answered, "Made what?"

"We made the team!"

Earl was confused. "What?"

"Man, what 'chu talkin' 'bout? The football team. We both made the team. What you think we've been doing over here for the past month?"

"Man, I was just there with you. I was just there with you. I wasn't even doin' my best. I told y'all, I ain't playin' on no football team. I was just workin' out with you."

"Well, like it or not, you on the team. And I am too. Man, I don't get you. Why don't you want to be on the team? It'll be fun. Think about the girls we'll meet 'cause we're athletes."

"I don't need to be on the team to get a girl. Look at me." Earl was joking. He didn't have the big head.

"Well some of us brothers need a little help. I'll be wearing the ol' red and white with one eye on the field and the other eye in the bleachers looking for any sister who'll look my way."

Earl's last word was, "Man, whatever."

When Earl came home, Momma was in the kitchen. He told her the news. Momma was excited. Earl wasn't. He told her he had no intention of playing on the team. They went back and forth about it and, to make a long story short, when time came for the first game, Earl was suited up in his red and white uniform sitting on the bench.

Earl did not disappoint. Y'all, my brother started playing in the eighth grade and by the time he reached the tenth grade he was the star of the team. As a matter of fact, he was so good, he earned the nickname "Radar." They called him that because if the quarterback threw the ball in his general direction, he would zone in and catch that sucker. It didn't matter where, he just had to be in the vicinity. He was just that quick. It was like that ball was made of metal and he was a magnet. He played hard and in his first season starting, scored eight touchdowns in seven games. That was a lot of touchdowns back then and it put him on the map. Earl became a neighborhood celebrity.

Y'all, it was pathetic. They tell me girls used to wait for him to come out of the locker room after football practice. They would fawn over him and flirt like there was no tomorrow. On Saturday mornings after a game, guys in the neighborhood would stand outside our house waiting for Earl to come outside so they could talk to him. Everyone knew where we lived. Even guys from other neighborhoods. They would come to our house to challenge him to a foot race. He never lost.

When Earl was in the eleventh grade, the team continued to thrive. They were playing better than ever and

were even traveling to play teams outside of Memphis.
Once, they had to play a black school in Little Rock,
Arkansas. Earl was excited about the game because he had
never set foot outside of Memphis, or our neighborhood for
that matter.

The team practiced hard for the game. Bless their
hearts! They wanted to represent the school and Memphis
well because they knew the game would be reported in the
black newspaper, The Tri-State Defender. The team was
meeting and discussing plays and strategies right up until
they went to the huge pep rally in the gym.

After the rally, the team boarded the nice bus the
school rented. Students, parents and more than a few
teachers gathered around the bus to see them off in style
before they set off for the two hour ride to Little Rock.
Everyone was so proud of them. Having that many people
putting their hopes on you can be a bit stressful, if you ask
me. Earl told me it didn't bother him one bit. He said that
his teammates weren't stressed at all. They were confident
they could pull out a win. They continued to strategize up
until the time they suited up to play.

Well, I'm sorry to tell y'all, they could have studied
and strategized until the cows came home and it wouldn't
have made one bit of difference. When they took the field
and took a look at the players from the other team, they had
to pick their chins up from off the ground. Those brothers
looked like they played for Arkansas State University, not
high school.

One of my brother's teammates said, under his breath,
"Man, what do people eat in Arkansas?"

Earl couldn't seem to find the right adjectives to
describe them so he started throwing out all the ones he
knew. They were huge. They were tall and wide as a wall.
They looked like men. Some of them had beards…in high
school…no joke!

And it gets worse. Not only were these guys large,

they were mean. They were yelling out what they were going to do to them on the field. Saying what they were gonna kick and what they were gonna break. Stuff like:

"We're gonna kill y'all!"

"Gonna send y'all home to yo momma's!"

"Y'all gonna be crying like girls!"

And I'm putting it nicely 'cause I'm saved. Well you can imagine, our team wasn't used to this type of barbaric behavior. We were city folk, for goodness sakes.

The game started slowly for the team, but as the first quarter came to a close, they started to find their rhythm. Carver really was the better team, and as they began to play their game the tide started to turn in their favor. But not for long. That was when things got ugly and the game reached the "hot mess" level.

The game was my brother's first incident of black on black crime. Not only was the Arkansas team bigger and meaner. The refs cheated. The referee's called back five of Carver's touchdowns. Five! How, you ask? Well, when a player on the Arkansas team fumbled the ball and Carver recovered and ran it in for a touchdown the ref said, "Y'all cain't do that."

Carver's coach was livid. "Why c'ain't we?"

The ref said, "Y'all can recover the ball, but you c'ain't move it forward."

"What? Since when?"

"Since now. That's how we play in Arkansas."

The devil is a liar, y'all!

But, wait! It gets worse. After a play was over, and the Carver players were trying to get up off the ground, the other team would stomp and kick them. The injuries were starting to mount up.

Once again, the coach complained to the head ref who said, "Well, don't be layin' on the ground and y'all won't get stomped."

Those refs know they're wrong for that!

When Earl heard this he shook his head, looked at Spicy and said, "It's gonna be a long game." He spoke the truth that time.

As more and more players hobbled over to the Carver sideline, the Coach was having trouble finding replacements to go in for injured players. In fact, when an injured player would come out of the game and the Coach would look down the line to call a replacement, all the players would lean back so that they were hiding behind the guy beside him. The guy on the very end is the one the coach would see and he'd get called in.

Earl later said, "That was on him. He should'a been paying attention."

The Arkansas crowd was all into the game even though they had to know it was wrong. They didn't really care how they won, as long as they won. And they did win. Arkansas beat Carver 13-7. The only redeeming point to this whole story is that the loss didn't go against Carver's record in Memphis.

In spite of their loss in Arkansas, Carver was on their way to having their best season but another obstacle stood in the way. A big obstacle named Manassas High School. Manassas was the league champs. This is the same school that Jean's boyfriend and future husband, Sam, used to attend.

That game was so big, it was broadcast live on the black radio station. High school football was so important to the black community that the games were usually sold out. I know Momma and Daddy and my family were at every game. Unfortunately, most people couldn't get tickets and had to listen to the game on the radio. Jean and Sam were listening to the game that night. Earl caught too many passes to count and scored two touchdowns.

That crazy Jean, whenever Earl caught a pass she'd get so excited, that she would bolt out the front door and run up and down the street yelling, "My brother caught a touchdown! That's my brother, Earl DeVault that just caught that touchdown!" Sam would have to run and catch her and drag her back into the house.

It was a good game, everyone said so. Earl had an exceptional night, scoring two touchdowns. Too bad they weren't enough to overcome the Manassas Tigers, though. The Cobras lost for the second time in the season.

But, at least it was a fair game…

CHAPTER 16

MARK SAVES MAE

Before the ink dried on his high school diploma, Mark found himself at Lackland Air Force Base in San Antonio, Texas. I guess he'd had enough of sharing that hot attic with Earl and Wayne. Maybe he knew there weren't any jobs for young, black men in Memphis in 1961. Or maybe he thought with him out of the picture, things would be much easier for our family with one less mouth to feed. Whatever the reason, he hot footed it out of there and didn't come back home for four long years.

When his time was up, he came back to Memphis a different man. Maybe that was it, he was a man. He was older, wiser, and a lot more mature. Although he was still good for a laugh or two, gone was the prankster who used to constantly pull tricks on everyone. You didn't have to watch your back so much with the new and improved Mark. I'm telling y'all, the household breathed a collective sigh of relief.

This new and improved Mark was what a big brother should be, a protector. Mae found that out the hard way, 'cause as big and bad as she could be, sometimes that girl was just downright stupid.

* * * * *

After he was discharged from the army, Mark was able to find a job pretty quickly working as a bartender at the Holiday Inn. It was a different story for Mae. After high school, she looked and looked but she wasn't able to find anything. Finally in desperation, she went down to Beale Street to try to find a job as a waitress in one of the juke joints. Like I told y'all, Beale Street was where black folks went to party. Needless to say, she didn't let Momma or Daddy know about her job search.

It was early one Saturday morning on a beautiful fall day when she caught the bus downtown to Beale Street. She could hardly believe her luck when, as soon as she got off the bus, she saw a Help Wanted sign in the window of the first club she saw. She made a bee line for the door just in case someone else on the bus was looking for a job.

Mae, at 5'11" was dressed to impress. She had on a powder blue slim skirt that accented her long legs, and matching blue sweater. She had on a pair of black pumps with Momma's black church purse to match. She also borrowed Momma's fake pearl necklace. Her thick shoulder length hair was styled in a bob and she even took the time to put on some make-up. She looked more like she was going for an interview in an office rather than a night club.

She walked inside the club and right up to the bar and asked to speak to the manager. The bartender gave her a long, hard look before turning to go fetch the man. While she was waiting, she took the time to survey her surroundings. What she could see of it, that is. The room was dark. So dark that she couldn't even tell the color of the walls. There was one small window that had a dirty dark blue curtain to keep out any light that dared to shine through. The furniture was blue pleather, which was cracked with some of the filling coming out of the sides. To her right, a broken down looking, older man sitting in the corner eating oatmeal was staring at her. To her left, a man was sweeping up broken glass from the floor. It smelled of smoke.

She wasn't scared.

The manager took his sweet time coming out of the back office. He was round all over, body, and face. He had a gruff appearance and a dark complexion with thick eyebrows that almost met in the center of his forehead. He looked like he didn't take no mess from nobody. I guess you'd have to be like that if you owned a business on Beale Street. Mae was not intimidated. She extended her hand to him and said in a strong clear voice, "Hello Sir, my name is Mae DeVault."

The man looked at her a moment before he answered, "Yeah?"

Mae said, "I'm looking for a job. I'll do anything. Well, not anything. What I mean is, I'd make a good waitress, or I can help keep the books. Maybe you have a position in the kitchen. I'm an excellent cook."

"We ain't got no openings."

"Yes you do. There's a big sign in your window that says, *Help Wanted*." For emphasis, she pointed towards the lone window.

"I'm telling ya, we ain't got no opening."

"But the sign…"

"No openings for you."

Her temperature was starting to rise. "What's that supposed to mean. I thought only white folk did that kind of stuff."

She was just going to walk out without another word when he spoke, "What are you doing here?"

"I told you. I'm looking for a job. I've been looking everywhere and I can't find anything. I can't just lie around living off my parents. I have to earn my keep."

His face softened a bit. You'd have had to look really hard to notice it, but it did. He said, "Listen, I'm not going to give you a job. You're a good girl. I can tell by looking at you. You don't belong in a place like this."

"I can take care of myself."

"That don't mean a hill of beans. Some of the stuff

that go on in this place ain't for you to see. This is not the place for you. I have a daughter your age. If she were trying to get a job in a place like this I hope and pray that someone would send her home like I'm sending you."

He smiled at her before he turned and walked away.

Dejected, she turned and made her way out the door. She walked up and down Beale Street looking in every store and restaurant but didn't have any luck. She wouldn't be finding a job on that day. She returned to the bus stop and took a seat.

She was sitting there wondering what she was going to do next when this long, green spanking brand new Cadillac pulled up in front of the bus stop. Through the open window, she saw a dark black man wearing a dark green suit with a beige hat. He appeared to be around forty-five years old. Mae was eighteen.

He asked her, "What are you doing sitting here on Beale Street?"

She looked up at the sign indicating that this was indeed a bus stop. Then she looked at him and answered, "Waiting for a bus."

That was her nice-nasty way of saying, "You are stupid."

He said, "It's not too safe down here, little lady. Are you headed home?"

Mae answered, "Yes."

"Let me give you a ride."

Mae looked at him like he was a crazy man. "I can't get in the car with you. I don't even know you."

Good for Mae. I'm so proud of her. I mean, I know it was the early 1960's, but you still can't go jumping in the car with just anyone, for goodness sakes. That would be just plain stupid.

He didn't miss a beat. "It's okay. I'm a preacher."

Mae said, "Oh…okay." Then she went and jumped into the passenger seat and away they went.

(Note to reader: disregard my comments made six lines earlier.)

She totally believed that he was a preacher. He had the car for it. In fact, she never thought to question him because, back then, preachers were respected and revered.

As soon as she got in the car and got settled he said to her, "Oh, would you mind if I stop by and see my sister? She's not well."

"No, not at all."

Next thing you know, this guy is pulling into a hotel off Beale Street.

He said, "Why don't you come on in and say hi to my sister."

Mae said "Okay," and got out of the car and followed him into the hotel. She never once questioned why his sick sister was staying in a hotel.

When they got to his floor, he pulled a key out of his pocket and opened the door. He then stepped aside and let Mae go in first. Mae entered the empty room, looking for the infamous "sick" sister only to find no one.

"Where is your sister?"

He turned from locking the door with a puzzled look on his face. "Huh?"

"Where is your sick sister?"

"You mean, you really thought there was a sick sister?"

"Yes. That's what you said."

He stood there shaking his head, as if he were trying to make up his mind about something. Finally he said, "Let me take you home."

They left the room immediately and returned to his big, green, Caddy. He took her home. By then, she was a little afraid of him.

When they pulled up in front of the house, Momma was standing at the side fence talking to a neighbor. When they saw that big, green car they both stopped their conversation. Momma leaned down because our house was on a small slope. When she saw Mae getting out the car she started walking towards her. Mae introduced Momma to the man.

When he left Momma said to Mae, "Nice car."

* * * * *

Mark is the only one she told. And why did she do that? That boy hit the roof. He spoke to Mae like he had never spoken before. I recollect the conversation went something like this.

"How could you be so stupid?"

"Well, I just…"

"Getting into a car with someone you don't know."

"But he said…"

"And to just go walking into a hotel room like that."

"I know, but…"

"I'll bet he wasn't a preacher."

"He said he…"

"Did you even ask yourself what a preacher would be doing riding around on Beale Street in the first place?"

"Now that you mention it…"

"He might'a been a jackleg preacher riding around picking up stupid people."

"But, see…"

This was the last thing Mark had to say on the subject, "All I know is this. He better not ever come on this side of town again. If he does, y'all better go looking for him in the Mississippi."

Mae didn't have a response to this. The only thing she was sure of was that he meant it.

* * * * *

Three days later, guess what pulled up in front of our house. That's right. Big green Caddy. Mae wasn't at home. Neither was Mark. Tina was walking to the corner store, she was about four houses up. The supposed preacher man saw her from behind and drove up to her and said, "Where are you going?"

Tina didn't know anything about this guy so she looked at him and said, "Why?"

It took a moment for it to register to him that this wasn't Mae because she and Tina did look alike…sorta.

When he came to his senses he said, "Oh, you're not Mae."

"No, I'm Tina."

"Where are you going?"

"To the store up on the corner."

"Let me give you a ride."

Without a word, she hopped in. I guess stupid runs in the family.

This forty-five year old man took my seventeen year old sister to the store and waited for her to come out. He then drove her home. As Tina was getting out of the car, Mark was coming from around the corner.

Uh-oh. Y'all, it was about to go down.

When Mark saw that big, green Caddy he knew who the driver was. He ran up to that guy opened the door and grabbed him by the throat and started choking him. He actually lifted that man from the ground. Tina was yelling and screaming and that brought Momma out of the house. It took both Momma and Tina to pry Mark's fingers from around that man's neck.

The preacher man was bent over and gasping for air.

Mark told him, "Don't you ever, and I mean ever, come back on this side of town again. Next time you won't have my momma and sister to keep me off of you. Now git!"

That man stumbled to his car and tore out of there like the Klan was after him. No one ever saw him again, and thank the good Lord for that because Mark told Earl what happened and they were both gunning for that so-called preacher.

CHAPTER 17

A POSITION OF POWER

I've said it before and I'll say it again and again. My Uncle Robert Lee was the coolest man on the planet. I recollect him as tall, thin and handsome, with flawless caramel colored skin and a thin moustache. He was dapper, walked with a swagger and carried himself like he was somebody.

He had a high level job in Kansas City that paid him loads of money and he spent it freely on his family. I'm referring to him in the past tense because he's gone to be with Jesus, God rest his soul. I'm telling you, he hadn't even made fifty years old when that cancer took him in 1979. It was a dark day in the life of my family when that doctor came out of his room shaking his head and we knew he was gone. We all still miss him but it helps to remember the good times. And there were many!

Like the time, when Uncle Robert Lee came to Memphis for the annual family reunion and decided to treat some of his older nephews and nieces to dinner at a high falutin' restaurant called, "Claybourn." This place was a black owned establishment that catered to upper class Negros. Now, my family had oodles of class, but little cash so I'm not sure we would have ever been able to afford to go there, but money wasn't an issue for Uncle Robert Lee.

He called our house the day before they were set to go in order to get a count of who was going so he could make the reservations. Jean, Mark, Mae, and Tina were representing the DeVault clan. The rest of us DeVault's were too young to appreciate the experience. Five other cousins were also going, so the final count was ten.

A few minutes before they were set to leave, Mark threw on his church suit and he was good to go, you know how boys are. Or maybe I should say "men" since he was twenty one at the time. But my sister's were another story. It took Jean, Mae, and Tina a whole day to get ready. I imagine the same debate was going on across town with my cousins. Several calls were made back and forth to confirm what everyone was wearing. You'd have thought they were going to the Peabody or something the way they were carrying on.

The group arrived at the restaurant a few minutes early. Uncle Robert Lee went to the desk and announced to the black maître d' "Williamson, party of 10. We have a reservation for 7:00."

The maître d' stuffily told him, "Since your party is so large, there will be a slight wait. We will call you when your table is ready."

Uncle Robert Lee raised an eyebrow at the news. I'm sure he must have been thinking to himself, *What's the point of a reservation if you still have to wait?* but, he didn't say anything.

The mood was celebratory so no one minded the wait. The girl cousins were busy trying to catch up with each other's lives and the boy cousins were busy trying to catch the eyes of any attractive girl who happened to glance their way. Be it customer or waitress.

Well, it was a full forty-five minutes before the group was seated at a table and given menus. The long wait had put a bit of a damper on the mood, but one look at the delectable items on the menu and the offense was forgotten.

But not for long.

It was another thirty minutes before the harried waitress came over to take their order. And, to tell the truth, she probably only came over because she saw the steam coming out of my cousin's ears. Everyone was getting plenty mad at the poor service, but, at this point, they remained cool and didn't complain about it outright. They were all trying to act like they had some home training. But, you do know home training goes out the door when people get hungry enough.

So, the diners all placed their orders, mostly chicken or pork chops, and the next waiting period began.

Thirty minutes passed.

Uncle Robert Lee asked when the food would arrive.

He was told, "It will be a little while longer."

Thirty more minutes passed.

Uncle Robert Lee asked when the food would arrive.

He was told, "I'll be with you in a minute."

It was now right at 9:30 and still no food. Y'all know good and well that black folks eat at 5:00. 6:00 at the latest. By this time, all thoughts of celebration were gone. Everybody's stomach was growling. The situation was getting critical!

Cousins were angry and mumbling under their breaths, "This is a dog gone shame!"

"If I had wanted to be treated like this I could'a went to Pauline's."

"Should'a known black people would be runnin' late."

"What did they have to do, go kill the chicken?"

"Let's just leave and go to Kentucky Fried Chicken."

Uncle Robert Lee hadn't said a word. He listened to everyone voice their frustrations, but you could tell the situation was not all right with him. I'm sure he knew that if he had joined in, it would have made everyone madder. But, finally, he'd had enough. His plan for treating his nephews and nieces to an elegant dining affair were completely ruined. He calmly rose from the table and said in a deathly quiet voice, "Excuse me for a moment."

All the complaining ceased. Uncle Robert Lee was one of those Negros that you have to watch when they get too quiet. No one had ever seen this side of him. I know they were thinking, "This is gonna be good."

Everyone was content to watch from the table as he gracefully strolled up to where the maître d' was standing. Everyone, that is, but nosey Mae. When he got up, she rose too and followed him. If there were going to be fireworks, Mae wanted to have a ringside seat so she wouldn't miss one word. That's how she is.

Uncle Robert Lee asked to see the Manager.

The maître d' didn't say a mumbling word. He just turned and went back towards the kitchen. No one knew if he were going to get the manager or not.

After five minutes, give or take, an older black man, around fifty years old, came hurrying out of the kitchen. He didn't look pleased.

He said, "Did you want to see me?"

Uncle Robert Lee answered, "Yes. We have a problem."

The Manager said, "Yes, what is it?"

He must have thought Uncle Robert Lee was stupid. There is no way that man didn't already know what the trouble was. If the maître d' hadn't told him, all he had to do was look around the crowded restaurant. My family wasn't the only family that hadn't been served. The service was slow for everyone and some people had gotten up and left.

Uncle Robert Lee explained, "We were on time for our 7:00 reservation, but we had to wait forty five minutes before we were seated. That's the first problem. The second problem is, we placed our order over an hour ago and we still don't have our food. We have been here for an hour and forty five minutes. I guess I should be asking you, what is the problem?"

The Manager looked at Uncle Robert Lee for a moment. Mae could tell he was angry, but he did a good job of keeping himself in check. He responded, "Sir, you

have to understand. We had a surprise party show up. It
was Dr. Abernathy. He has a large group with him. Of
course we have to take care of them first. You do
understand?"

If you don't know, Dr. Abernathy was very active in
the civil rights movement. He was right there alongside Dr.
King, fighting for justice for black folks. I commend him
for that. But it don't mean a hill of beans when a person is
hungry.

Now, I'm not trying to get sued, so let me say right
now, I'm sure Dr. Abernathy didn't know a thing about this
whole affair. He didn't know that his presence at the
restaurant was causing innocent and hungry people to go
unfed. The fault was totally on the restaurant.

The nerve! Well, suffice it to say, Dr. Abernathy and
his surprise party didn't mean a blessed thing to my family.
Mae couldn't believe the gall of the man. He was
practically telling them that they weren't important enough
to be served. She was so angry she couldn't speak. She
stood there and waited for Uncle Robert Lee to let him
have it.

Uncle Robert Lee calmly said, "I see. Thank you."

With that, he turned and walked back to the table. Mae
stood there, contemplating her next move.

She was thinking to herself, *Is that all?*

Such a letdown. She wanted to give the Manager a
piece of her mind. But, she decided against it. She
thought, *Uncle Robert Lee is a class act. I'm not gonna
show my colors this time.* And she meekly went to her seat
and sat down.

One of my cousins leaned over to him and said,
"What's up? Why didn't you say anything? This is
ridiculous."

Uncle Robert Lee was still on easy street. He said,
"Just wait."

And that's just what they did too. It was another thirty

minutes before things went down. But his words gave them hope that they would be vindicated.

While my relatives sat there stewing in anger and practically dying of hunger, it happened. Uncle Robert Lee had been biding his time, watching to see when the food would come. He sat there just as good until he saw the waiters bringing the food to their table and then announced to the group, "Okay, it's time to go."

And with that, he stood up and walked towards the door.

When he did that, everyone knew what he was doing and obediently got up and followed him. One of my cousin's said, under his breath, "Finally!"

The waiters stopped in their tracks with their mouths open. What was gonna happen to all that food?

They got as far as the parking lot before the Manager came barreling out of the restaurant yelling, "STOP! What do you think you're doing? You can't do this. I'm gonna call the police."

Uncle Robert Lee slowly turned to him. Obviously he had thought this through. He said, "Call them. We will wait. And I will tell them that we weren't important enough for you to serve us. Even though we had a reservation and waited patiently for about two and a half hours. And what will you tell them? We didn't eat any of your food."

They left the Manager stuttering in the parking lot.

Jean turned and rolled her eyes at him.

* * * * *

My family left the restaurant and went straight to the Harlem House of Florida Street a few blocks from our home. The celebratory mood had returned. They ate the best hamburger and french fries they ever had.

As they sat there relishing the moment, Mae said,

"Wow. I was wondering why you didn't say anything. But, now I see that was the best way to handle it."

Uncle Robert Lee looked at her and then at each person in the group. He finally said, "When you're in any kind of situation, you have to know if you have the power or not. Are you dealing from a position of power? In the restaurant, they were telling us what they thought of us. I began to think, what do we have to do to make us not feel bad in the morning? That is what you have to do."

When Mae was telling me this story, she said she took his words to mean, "Stop and think what you can legally do to destroy them."

Uh, I kinda think she missed the point.

* * * * *

Now, the lesson I learned from this story is this: no need to make a monkey out of yourself when someone does you wrong. Take the high road and act like you're somebody. Let them be the monkey.

After hearing this story about my Uncle Robert Lee, my respect for him grew. God rest his soul. It would have been nice if one of my brother's had followed in his classy footsteps. But, not so much. I'm not saying they're bad people, because they aren't. They're just...they're just...

Well, judge for yourself after I recollect on my brothers, *THOSE DeVAULT BOYS*.

PART FOUR

THOSE DEVAULT BOYS

THE PATTERNS

Mark loves him some music. Always has…practically from the womb. When he was a sophomore in high school, he played the French horn in the concert band, the trumpet in the marching band, and the string bass in a blues quartet. I'm telling you, that boy was forever blowing or plucking something. He couldn't get enough music. He was a music junkie; always walking around the house holding a transistor radio to his ear, spinning around and gyrating trying to mimic the latest dance steps.

Now, you would think my super spiritual parents would have had a problem with all that worldly music he was playing. Especially Momma who used to call any music not sung by either Mahalia Jackson or James Cleveland "the devil's music." Well, life is full of surprises because both Momma and Daddy were both okay with Mark's pastime. I guess they figured there were worse things he could have gotten into. It wasn't hurting nobody. In fact, they were hoping he would be getting a music scholarship because, Lord knows they didn't have enough money to send the boy to college.

In the summer of 1960, before Mark went to the eleventh grade, he and some of his buddies from the high school band formed a group called "The Patterns." The group consisted of Mark on lead vocals, with Freddie Smith and Owen Chaffey singing backup. Making up the band: Mark on the guitar, Mitchell McCoy on keyboard, Melvin Overstreet on sax, and Jimmy Pugh on drums.

Most afternoons, the group rehearsed in our tight living room. But sometimes, they would go to Freddie's house if Momma's ears

weren't pointing the right way and they needed to give her some space. If push came to shove and they weren't welcomed in one of the group member homes, they would go over to the high school parking lot and rehearse there. They had it bad!

Man, it would be hot, sultry hot as my aunt would say, but the group just kept plugging away. They were all in their element so the heat didn't make them no never mind. And their hard work paid off too. From what I understand, by the time school started in September, they sounded pretty good. Everybody said so.

* * * * *

Practically from the beginning of time, our high school had a sock hop for the students on the first Friday night of each month. For those of you who don't know, a sock hop is a school dance. They were wildly popular because it gave the kids something to look forward to during the long hot summer months. The gym would be packed with hot sweaty bodies trying to impress each other with the newest dance moves.

In July of 1960, the principal decided to make a change. Y'all know how it is when you've been doing something for so long and you feel the need to shake things up a bit. Well, that's what the principal decided needed to happen. So, instead of the monthly sock hop, he changed the format completely. The new plan was, the school was going to host a monthly talent show and the very first show was scheduled to be held the first Friday night in August.

The news spread like wildfire. When Mark and his friends heard about the talent show, they were all over it. They doubled up on their rehearsals. Since all of The

Patterns were members of the high school band, the director, Mr. Lucas, didn't have a problem with letting them use the school equipment to practice.

Y'all would have thought they were The Temptations getting ready to go before Berry Gordy with all the work they were putting in. Funny thing too, they wanted to be The Temptations. Back then, The Temptations were like gods to people my brother's age. I'm told that when a Temptations song came on the radio, the world stopped. Not just for my brother, but for everyone. They worshipped them, but don't let Momma know I said that or she'll get after me with her blessed oil. All I'm saying is, it was the smooth way they moved and their perfect harmony that just about drove black folk crazy. My brothers and his friends unashamedly copied everything about them.

Once they felt they had the gig down, they decided to move on to more important matters. What to wear? This was where my brother had his first problem.

"What we gon' wear, y'all?" That was Jimmy talking. He was an only child and both his parents were school teachers. He owned more clothes than Goldsmith's department store. Every time he stepped out of his house he'd be casket clean.

"Uh…let's keep it simple. We don't want to take away from our performance." That was Mark talking. He knew his wardrobe was pretty limited. The closest thing he had to decent were his brown church pants. And those were a little on the smallish side and so slick from Momma's weekly ironings, you could see your reflection in them.

Freddie spoke up. "How about a white shirt, black tie and black pants?"

Mark perked up, "That sounds good to me." He figured he could borrow Daddy's slick black pants. Momma was death with that iron, y'all.

"Naw man. That's too simple. Everybody'll be wearing that. We want to look different," said Jimmy.

Doggone clothes hog, Mark thought.

"Man, everybody ain't got a closet full'a clothes like you." Mark breathed a sigh of relief when Greg spoke up. Apparently, he wasn't the only one lacking in the garment department.

Jimmy was adamant. "I'm not saying we have to wear no expensive stuff. Though I could if I wanted to. I'm just saying lets look different. How about we wear dark suits, white shirts and neckties?"

"Man, what's so different 'bout that?" Melvin put his two cents worth in.

"If you'll let me finish." Jimmy gave him the eye and continued, "We could wear black sunglasses."

"At night? In the gym? We won't be able to see." That's what Melvin said 'cause he has no imagination.

"Uh...they'll have lights on. What do you guys think? I got the idea when I saw that new cat, young Stevie Wonder, on TV last week."

"But Stevie's blind. He don't need to see." Melvin again.

Mark got the gimmick. "Naw, I see what you mean. Man, that would be different and sunglasses don't cost too much. I say we do it. Is everybody in?"

The group agreed to the ensemble. Even Melvin got over his fear of the dark and voted with the rest of the group. After this was settled, the group called it a night and went home.

It was a long walk home for Mark. Where in the world was he going to get a dark suit? He knew there was no way in the world our parents would go out and buy him a new suit for the talent show. He knew better than to even ask such a thing with Daddy working three jobs to make ends meet. He revisited the idea of borrowing Daddy's black suit but quickly dismissed that idea since he wanted something that looked like it was made this century.

This was one of the things he hated about being from a

large family. There never was enough to go around and he frequently had to do without. By the time he got home, his mood was dark.

Jean and her boyfriend Sam were sitting in the living room when he walked in the house. They both saw the look on his face and looked at each other. Jean bravely asked, "Who died?"

"Huh?" He was so deep in thought he didn't even see them.

"Who died? Why are you looking like someone used up the last of the Royal Crown?"

"Oh. The group just decided to wear dark suits for the talent show and I ain't got nothing to wear."

Smiling, Jean said, "Why don't you ask Daddy if you can wear his black suit."

Mark rolled his eyes, "Yeah, right. Daddy's slick black suit."

"Well, the way you guys are sliding all over the stage, I would think that slick suit would be just the thing."

"That ain't funny." It was, but he was too depressed to laugh.

Sam spoke up. "I got a dark brown suit. You and me 'bout the same size, you wanna borrow it." Like Mark, Sam was nearly six feet tall and slim.

Mark's mood immediately brightened, "You mean it man? You got a dark brown suit?"

"Yeah man. It's my church suit. Just had it cleaned too. It's yours if you want it."

Sam puffed his chest out a little. He was always trying to impress Jean and he knew this display of sacrifice and generosity was winning him major brownie points.

"Shoot yeah, I wanna borrow it."

"When you need it by?"

"Next Friday."

"I'll drop by next Thursday."

So it was all set. Mark would wear Sam's suit. He

took the rickety stairs leading up to the attic two at a time. All was right with the world.

* * * * *

The excitement over the talent show reached a fevered pitch. Everyone in the neighborhood was talking about it. Judging by what Mark heard, practically everyone he knew was going.

In response, The Patterns rehearsed every day.

Thursday night came and Sam arrived for his weekly visit. In his arms was the prized possession Mark had been waiting for. It was still in the plastic bag from the cleaners. Sam proudly handed the suit over to Mark.

Mark took that suit and in his excitement, ripped the plastic bag off to get a good look at what he would be wearing in front of the group and the whole school. The horror! Mark's mouth fell open as he beheld a suit that was very nice looking. The problem was the suit was WOOL. Pure Wool!

Y'all, it was August in Memphis, Tennessee. The devil has a summer house in Memphis, that's how hot it is. It was 100 degrees in the shade, minimum. He'd faint dead away if he tried to put this suit on.

Mark looked at Sam who was smiling. Mark didn't want to hurt his feeling, but he had to say something. "Man, is this the only suit you got?"

"What's wrong? You don't like it?"

"Yeah Man, I like it. Uh…it's wool."

Sam's face fell. Mark backpedaled. "Naw, naw man. I love it. It's just that the suit is so clean and it's gonna be kinda hot and I don't want to ruin it by sweating in it. I think you should take it back and I'll see if I can borrow something from the guys in the group."

He said this praying it would work. He'd borrow something from that arrogant Jimmy Pugh if he had to.

Sam wouldn't hear of it. "Aw man, don't worry about that. I'll just get it cleaned again. Ain't nuthin' but a few bucks."

The more Mark refused the more adamant he got. Mark had no choice. If he didn't take the suit, Sam would know something was wrong. Mark took the suit, thanked Sam, and slunk up the stairs to the attic. When Earl and Wayne saw that wool suit, they fell over each other laughing. Mark failed to see the humor of the situation and told them so in language that would have made Momma pull out her blessed oil if she had heard it.

* * * * *

It was one of the hottest July's on record in Memphis and August wasn't any slouch either. The fans in the windows of the Carver High gym were going full blast because the room was filled to capacity. I'm telling you, every seat in the bleachers was filled and the folding chairs they set out on the basketball floor were all taken. My whole family showed up, including Sam.

The audience was filled with school kids, teachers, and people from the community. Even people from other rival schools like Melrose, Manassas, and Booker T. Washington ventured into enemy territory to see the show. Men and boys were dressed in their polo shirts, slacks, and Florsheims or Edwin Clapp shoes. Women and girls were wearing print sundresses and pumps. Folks knew how to dress back then!

The Patterns were the seventh group to perform out of the fifteen scheduled acts. Mark and the rest of the group nervously paced around behind the curtain until their number was called. When they walked onto the stage, they were greeted by cheers, mostly from the group's friends and family members. Even Momma jumped to her feet clapping and cheering exhibiting a rare display of emotion that was met with surprised looks from Daddy and my siblings.

When she noticed everyone looking at her, she shrugged her shoulders and said, "Shoot! That's my boy up there!"

The band began playing the first notes of the very familiar song that was all the rage at that time, "Cowboys and Girls." As the band played, people were rocking from side to side and slowly nodding their heads.

When my brother and the group sang the first call and response line of the song, "I remember, when we used to play shoot 'em up…" the whole gym stood up, including teachers and rushed the stage. People were going crazy! It was pandemonium!

Encouraged by the audience response, the group really began to put on a show. All the while, Mark was sweating so much under the bright lights that he was about to float away. He ignored it and kept with his passionate performance slyly smiling at the audience and winking at the pretty girls. Such a ham!

Well, he was really feeling his oats and made the mistake of whipping off his sunglasses and winking at the wrong girl. Now y'all, I'm not one to put down another sister; especially when it takes me a good thirty minutes to crank up my face in the morning. But, there was a sister standing at the base of the stage who had a face that could scare the devil (see note in chapter five).

And on top of that, she was a strong female. Mark winking at her gave her all the encouragement she needed because she responded by trying to jump on the stage and grab my poor brother. She almost made it to, but the stage was a bit too high for her to make it all the way up… Thank God for Jesus!

When she saw she couldn't make it, she did the next best thing. She grabbed the hem of Mark's suit. I mean the hem of Sam's suit. That sister had lost her mind. She had a death grip on that suit leg, jumping up and down and screaming like Mark was Michael Jackson or something. She was trying to pull him into the audience.

During the musical interlude of the song, Mark put the microphone behind his back and yelled, "Girl, let go."

But she wasn't listening 'cause she had it bad. He yelled again, "LET GO! This suit ain't mine. This is my sister's boyfriend's church suit and he'll kill me if I mess it up."

She didn't pay him no never mind.

Finally, someone from the audience grabbed her and said something that brought her back to her right mind. She quickly recovered the marbles she briefly lost and turned Mark's pant's a'loose. After the spell was broken, and Mark was free at last, free at last, he kept on singing and finished the song, but y'all know he kept his distance from the edge of the stage.

When the performance was over, Mark looked around at the audience as he and the group took their bows. He saw that people were impressed. Some had their mouths open in awe. He knew the group had gained their respect.

Mark and the group walked over to the wall of the gym and watched the remaining performers. They stood there with their arms folded across their chests, like they were big shots. And I gotta give it to them, they were. No one was surprised when "The Patterns" were announced as the winners of the talent show. The group took the $25.00 gift certificate they won to the Harlem House, on Florida and Parkway, and had a victory celebration.

Freddie said, "Man, we're rich. That's almost $5.00 each."

* * * * *

For the next year, the group kept practicing and continued to improve. Matter of fact, they were even good enough to get a gig at the Holiday Inn in Memphis and the Plantation Inn in West Memphis, Arkansas just across the bridge. Ironically, they played in hotel lounges but couldn't get a room at those same hotels because of segregation, but that's another story. That didn't bother them none. They were happy to be able to play anywhere and make some extra money.

The group stayed together throughout high school and even did contract work singing backup with Stax records. Their first check was $200.00. That was might good money back in the day. They were on their way down the yellow brick road. They were about to make something of themselves. That's why it's a doggone shame they couldn't keep it together. I'm sorry to say, their success proved to be their undoing. Some of them got the big head.

I'm not saying who did what, but let's just say they went wild with their success. They started spending money like it was water…didn't save one red cent of their earnings. They started shopping, buying flashy clothes, one of the guys promptly started drinking and showing up for gigs drunk. They began to fight and bicker about much of nothing. I'm telling you, not long after they graduated from high school the group broke up and went their separate ways.

Mark, not letting grass grow under his feet joined the Air Force. He was upset at the group's demise and wanted to do something completely different to get away from music. Well, guess where the Air Force placed him?

Where else? In the drum and bugle corp!

THE "N" WORD

In the summer before his senior year, Earl and his friends were horsing around and playing sandlot. Earl went out for a pass but something must have distracted him; maybe the sun was in his eyes or something. Y'all, that football came down and hit him dead in his left eye. The pain was excruciating but he tried to play it off because he was the big jock athlete.

When Earl got home his eye was swollen and dark. He downplayed the pain to Momma and Daddy saying that he had a black eye and that it was nothing. They believed him at first since he wasn't acting like he was in pain. Nobody knew how serious it was. If they did, maybe things would have turned out differently…but I'm getting ahead of myself.

Anyway, Earl was going around like it was nothing. He kept playing football and going about life as usual. He fooled everyone for a few weeks, but one morning, he woke up with a bad headache. The pain was so intense that he couldn't ignore it anymore. He told Momma about it and Daddy took off from work to take him to the doctor. It was there that he got the bad news. He had busted his retina. This, among other things, severely limited his peripheral vision.

Y'all, at first, he didn't know how serious the diagnosis was. He didn't really pay it no never mind. He just wanted the pain to stop and with the pills the doctor prescribed it did. So, the news did not destroy him. It made him work even harder at football. For a person who started out not even wanting to be on the team, football had become his life. Like Mark and his music, Earl was obsessed with football. His dream was to get a college scholarship and go to the NFL, like our brother-in-law Big Henry. Nothing was going to stop him. He played his senior year with no problem. In fact, he continued to excel. In fact, he became the first player in school history to make a diving catch. Show off....

He became so good that college scouts from some of the black schools were coming to the games just to recruit him. Our family was ecstatic. Earl DeVault, fifth child of Matthew and Beulah Mae DeVault was going to college. And then, the NFL if he was lucky.

Earl finally settled on the college he wanted to attend and to prepare and Daddy took him to have a complete physical as required by the school. Well, sorry to have to tell you this, but Earl failed the vision test.

Poor guy! Just like that his dream was over. No college scholarship. No NFL.

No nothing.

Earl acted like it didn't make him a bit of difference. But y'all know it did.

* * * * *

After Earl graduated from high school, he held a few odd jobs in Memphis before he moved to Chicago. By this time, Mae had married a guy named Henry and he was playing for the Chicago Bears. Earl stayed a couple of years and did well for himself. When Henry was traded to the Los Angeles Rams, Earl moved back to Memphis for a hot minute, got married and moved to Tinsel town the day after the wedding.

During this time, he developed a bad habit of driving too fast. I can't tell you the number of speeding tickets that boy racked up. Or how many times he tore the ticket up right in the policeman's face. It's like he really didn't care about getting arrested. He lived for the moment.

Things changed when his wife had their first child, a beautiful daughter. My brother loved that little girl. He changed his whole lifestyle. He kept his temper in check, stopped driving so fast, and started to come around family more often.

The Earl with the bad temper had been laid to rest. But, as it turns out that temper wasn't dead…it was just hibernating.

* * * * *

It was a warm, sunny Thanksgiving Eve in Los Angeles. The year was 1978.

Mae and Henry had invited a bunch of people over for an old-fashioned Thanksgiving dinner. Both Mae and Henry were excellent cooks. Earl was no slouch in the kitchen so he came over to Mae's house to see if he could lend a hand.

Mae had everything under control with just one thing missing. She forgot to get the ice cream to go with the sweet potato pie. Earl happily volunteered to drive Mae to a store in Santa Monica to get the ice cream. Now, Mae said they could just go to a store down the street, but Earl insisted on the trip to Santa Monica because the store he was going to was the only one that sold this particular brand of ice cream. Mae's son David, who was about thirteen at the time, went along for the ride.

The trio was driving down Wilshire Boulevard, chatting, laughing, and enjoying the trip. Even though it was November, it was pleasant outside so they rode with the windows down. Everything was fine at first. The trouble came when Earl failed to see a young white man and woman in the crosswalk.

Earl didn't see them until Mae yelled out, "STOP!"

The car skidded to a stop a few inches away from the terrified couple.

It was as if the Lord hit the pause button and life stopped for everyone involved. The group in the car sat in stunned silence and the couple stood in the crosswalk unable to move. Heart pounding, ears ringing, then silence. After about twenty seconds, the Lord pressed play and the young man ran over to the car and started talking through Earl's open window. In the interest of keeping this a clean book, I'll paraphrase the comments he made to my brother.

Yelling he said, "What's wrong with you? Are you crazy? Are you blind? You almost killed us."

Mae and David came to themselves before Earl. They were carefully monitoring him. They knew how he was.

Earl was just sitting there gripping the steering wheel in stunned silence.

So far so good, Mae thought as she watched Earl's catatonic state. He didn't say a word.

The guy was still yelling. "HEY! Can't you hear me talking to you? What are you stupid or something?" To emphasize his point, the man poked Earl in the shoulder and reached for the locked door handle trying to open the door.

This guy was just showing off in front of his girlfriend. Taking Earl's silence for meekness, he had no idea he was taking his life into his hands. See, Earl had a small car so the guy couldn't really tell who he was dealing with. Earl was 6'1" and 200 pounds of pure, mean muscle. Once he looses it, he looses it. There would be no turning back.

Earl continued to sit there gripping the steering wheel, with white knuckles. No one knows where Earl was mentally during those moments of silence, but Mae and David knew it was just a matter of time before things got ugly.

The man continued his tirade until he made his fatal

mistake. He said, "What's wrong with you? Can't you hear me, Nigger?"

Big mistake.

Big, big, big mistake.

Mistake of the century.

It was like, a hypnotist snapped his finger and brought Earl out of his trance. He flinched, blinked his eyes and slowly, slowly turned his head towards that white man and said, with eerie calmness, "What did you call me?"

Everything about my brother changed in an instant. He turned beet red and beads of perspiration popped up on his forehead. He was so angry he was vibrating.

If that white man didn't know he was in trouble before, he knew it now. He wasn't so big and bad now that Earl was riled up. He started recanting his remarks quick and in a hurry, "Look man, I'm willing to over look it this time. Just be careful."

Earl wasn't having it. He was trying to get out of the car, and the white man, who was trying so hard to open the door just moments before, was leaning against it trying to keep it closed.

All the while, Mae was pleading with Earl, "Just let it go."

Earl said, "Oh, Imma let it go alright."

David was pleading with Earl, "Uncle Earl, don't." David knew that white guy's rear-end was as good as kicked if Earl made it out of that car.

The white guy was saying, "Look, let's just forget the whole thing."

Earl still wasn't having it. He began to taunt the poor guy, "Oh no, I gotta be a nigger, huh. Well, let me get out of this car and show you how a nigger acts. I'm gonna kick your..."

The guy was nearly crying now. He said, "I believe you will, sir."

Earl was pushing on that door to open it and the white

guy along with his girlfriend was pushing it closed. This tug of war continued for a minute or two but the couple was fighting a losing battle. Mae and David couldn't keep Earl in the car. He broke free of them and got the door open. He headed toward the man.

Finally, the white lady spoke for the first time. She yelled at her companion, "Apologize!"

You didn't have to tell him twice. Backpedaling, he said, "You know what, I'm sorry. I apologize. I don't normally use that word, but you scared me."

Ain't that something? That guy went from Mr. Big Talk to practically begging for his life.

Well, thank God for Jesus! The Lord sho' nuff moved that day. He stepped right in and allowed that hasty apology to take the fire out of the situation. Earl abruptly stopped walking and just looked at the man. Then, he turned and got back in the car and drove off with Mae and David without saying a mumbling word.

If you ask me, that guy got off easy. Some people haven't been so lucky because Earl rarely walked away from a fight. Believe me, I know where the bodies are. Earl don't play. That's how he is.

They continued the drive to the grocery store to get the ice cream to go with the sweet potato pie for Thanksgiving. Earl finally regained his composure but it was a long time before anyone felt it was safe to speak. They all pretended it never happened. Mae knew from experience that was best.

I guess the moral of this story is: don't go messing with folks just because they aren't saying anything. The quiet ones are the worst of all.

All shut eyes ain't sleep, you know.

CHAPTER 20

IN DUE TIME

Wayne and I used to fight like cats and dogs when we were young. I had problems with him because he acted like he was the "baby" of the family and he wasn't. I am the baby of the family! Always was, always will be. Wayne had a spirit of entitlement that was, by all rights, mine because I was the last one born.

Wayne spent some time in the Army. He followed Mark's footsteps and enlisted right out of high school. Now if you ask me, I wouldn't have thought he was army material, but that's neither here nor there. He enlisted, they took him, he left, I rejoiced. I wondered how long the Army would last with him in it.

He came home for his first leave in the fall of that year in the mid-1970's. I think he had just finished basic training or something like that. Everybody was so happy to see him. He did look different to me. More mature and settled. I remember thinking that perhaps the Army was just what he needed. Momma did too.

She always used to say about Wayne, "Every little black pot has to stand on its own bottom."

The first night he was back, Wayne called Tina and suggested they go to the movies. Tina got the paper and called out all the films that were showing at the Malco. They finally decided on *The Exorcist*. When Momma and Daddy heard they were going to see that film, they wanted to go too. That was only the second movie they ever went to. The first was *Carmen Jones*.

They all got ready and headed for the movies. I was still in school at the time, but I suppose I could have gone if I wanted to, not that they asked me, mind you. Didn't make me no never mind. I had no desire to see that movie at all. I saw the advertisements for the movie with that girl's head spinning around and spitting up green stuff. It looked like a hot mess to me. Denise and I stayed home.

They were gone for a couple of hours and came back home at almost 10:00 that night. Momma and Daddy seemed to enjoy the movie. They were laughing and talking loudly and animated.

As soon as they came in I asked them, "How did you enjoy the movie?"

Daddy said, "Oh child, that girl in the movie was a wildfire."

I laughed at that. Daddy has his own way of describing things. I said, "Say she was?"

"Yeah. Head just a'spinnin' around. Eyes bugged out and walled back in her head."

Momma joined in. "Those priests sho' didn't know how to cast out the devil. Me and my prayer group could'a got him out."

Daddy added, "That priest caught it, didn't he Beulah Mae?"

"Sho' did."

I was enjoying their critique. "How'd he catch it, Daddy?"

"That child threw him up against a wall like he was a rag doll. I ain't never seen nothing like it."

Momma chimed in, "I'd like to see some demon try to throw me against a wall. I'd like to see it. He'd try to throw me and I'd pull out my blessed oil and get him right between the eyes. That'll stop 'em!"

Momma was all riled up at those demons.

It was late, but Momma asked Daddy and Wayne, "Y'all want a snack 'fore we go to bed?"

Wayne said his first words. "YES." He answered too quick and too loud for my liking.

I eyed him.

Momma and Daddy were just going on and on about the film, but Wayne was quiet. He didn't say two words the whole night. He was eating the tomato sandwich Momma prepared really slowly like he was trying to stretch out the time. Odd.

It was going on 11:00pm when Momma and Daddy finally decided to call it a night and went to their bedroom. I went to the room Denise and I shared. Wayne said he wasn't tired and that he'd sleep on the couch in the living room since he didn't feel like going up to the attic. I dropped off to sleep right away.

A terrible ruckus woke me and Denise up at 2:00 in the morning. There was a loud yell and stumbling sounds coming from my parent's bedroom. It was deafening. It's awful to be awakened out of a sound sleep with a noise like that. Gives the body a jolt!

Denise and I looked at each other and Denise said, "What the…?" before we both jumped up and ran towards the commotion. We threw open the door just as Daddy was turning the lights on. That's when we saw it. Wayne, laying on a pallet on the floor between Momma and Daddy's twin beds.

Denise asked, "What happened?"

Daddy answered, "I was just going to the bathroom and I stumbled over something. Boy, what you doing laying here on the floor?"

Wayne answered, "Nuthin'."

Everyone stared the answer out of him.

Wayne said, "Well, I thought y'all would'a got scared after seeing that movie so I came in here to keep y'all company."

Out of respect, no one said anything right off. Momma and Daddy just looked at each other. Then Daddy slowly shook his head. It took a minute before Denise started laughing. The kind of laugh that sounds like someone slowly letting the air out of a balloon. Pretty soon, we all joined her.

Did he think we were stupid? Did he think we'd believe that lame tale? That boy was scared. The movie really messed him up.

Momma was the first to gain her composure. She said, "Boy, this won't do. You can't be gettin' scared of no movie. You in the Army now."

Wayne didn't even try to deny it. "I can't help it. Remember when she looked dead in the camera and said '*In due time.*'"

He shivered just thinking about it.

Then he looked at me and said real spooky like, "In due time."

Denise shook her head and said, "Now that's a doggone shame."

I laughed and said, "Fraidy cat."

After uttering those words of wisdom, I turned and went back to bed.

If you ask me, that little black pot's gonna need some stronger legs.

* * * * *

My brother Wayne couldn't take much of nothing. He was scared of his own shadow. I'm glad he left the Army or we'd all be in trouble with him defending us. But, I know somebody who isn't scared of anything. He's been through a lot in his life, so maybe that's why. Y'all know what the old folks say don't you? "Whatever don't kill you makes you stronger." That is so true. And if you don't believe me, just ask my brother-in-law, *BIG HENRY.*

PART FIVE

BIG HENRY

CHAPTER 21

WELCOME TO THE NFL

Jean, Mae, and Tina all married when they were in their early twenties. Jean ended up marrying the wool suit guy, Sam and Tina married a young man named Ted. You'll meet him a little later. I love them both, but the brother-in-law I talk about the most is Mae's husband, Big Henry. His life fascinates me!

Everybody called him Big Henry when he was young because, by the time he was twelve, he was six feet tall and weighed almost two hundred pounds. And he wasn't done growing yet. He ended up being six feet six and two hundred eighty pounds. Lord knows that's big, ain't it?

Big Henry is as much a brother to me as Mark, Earl, and Wayne, so I'm gonna tell y'all about him right along with the rest of the family. To tell the truth though, I could write a whole book about the stuff that Big Henry had to go through but I don't have time for that right now. I'm gonna do my best to give y'all the short version.

Big Henry and his family lived on the other side of town in Dixie Homes. Dixie Homes were the projects, but don't think about the projects like they are today. Back then in the 40's and 50's, the projects weren't a bad place to live. They were nice, clean, and safe. Well, safe as far as how the neighbors treated each other. But, when the Memphis Police Department rolled through the projects, like they just loved to do, wasn't no black man or boy safe. Not from the police, they weren't.

Big Henry's momma was married, but his Daddy

wasn't, if you know what I mean. Not so you'd know it, anyhow. What I'm trying to say is, Big Henry's dad, Otis, had more girlfriends than a little. He didn't half take care of his family. That would have gotten in the way of his gallivanting around on Beale Street at the beer gardens with some hard up looking woman on his arms and a glass of beer in his hand. He didn't even try to hide his adulterous ways. But, I guess I better move on before I make y'all think I hate Otis. Y'all need to form your own opinion. I'm not here to judge, I'm just here to throw stones.

Anyway, Big Henry's momma was the glue that held the family together. She worked in the maintenance department at John Gaston Hospital, but that job barely kept enough food on the table for Big Henry, his older brother John, and three younger sisters, Olivia, Elaine, and the baby girl, Ruth. She separated from Otis often, but times were tough back then and it was hard raising five children by herself, so she usually wound up going back to him. Ain't that a shame?

Well, Big Henry's momma died in the summer of 1957 when he was thirteen years old. Her death was a severe blow to the family but it affected Big Henry worse than anyone else. Things went downhill faster than you can say Jack Spratt. First, John high-tailed it to the Marines. Big Henry's momma wasn't even cold in the grave when Otis kicked him out of the house and moved his young girlfriend, Felecia and her four children into the family home. He did y'all. I promise you he did. He let Olivia, Elaine, and Ruth stay, not because he wanted to, but because they were girls.

Mind you, I'm not judging. I'm just telling y'all what happened. You can make up your own mind.

So there Big Henry was. Homeless at the age of thirteen, just a week or so after his beloved Momma died. It was a desperate time for him. He lived in alleys, the laundromat, the school gym, and with family and friends who would take him in from time to time. But, for the most part, he tried to stay out of the way. His hatred for his father grew from day to day. He took that hatred and funneled it into high school football.

It wasn't long before Big Henry became a sports celebrity in Memphis. High school sports were a big deal in the black community back then because there wasn't a lot blacks could do for fun…legally. Big Henry excelled at the sport and was offered a scholarship to Tennessee State University.

So, those first fifteen, sixteen years were a mess, but thank the Lord they didn't define Big Henry. He went on to have a fabulous life. The only thing missing was a relationship with his family. You see, his sisters eventually bonded with Felecia and after awhile started calling her Momma. This sickened Big Henry and he didn't want to have anything to do with that situation.

Makes me a little nauseated too, but, like I said, it ain't none of my business.

* * * * *

Big Henry married Mae during his second year at TSU and she became pregnant a year later. The plan was for Mae to move to Nashville as soon as she gave birth, but an unfortunate mistake necessitated her staying in Memphis longer than planned.

The problem happened with baby David when he was three months old. He became constipated, as babies sometimes do. Mae, who was living with our parents at the time, was beside herself with worry for him. Poor little guy was in so much pain, crying and hollering something awful.

Mae went to the bathroom and got the Syrup of Black Draught from the medicine cabinet. That's what Momma used to give us when we were backed up. Now, Syrup of Black Draught was a laxative that was powerful on two levels. It was powerful strong and powerful nasty. I'd run the other way when Momma pulled it from the cabinets.

Well, Mae was so nervous that she misread the instructions. The dosage for children was one-quarter teaspoon. But Mae read it as 4 teaspoons. Girl, she tore that child's stomach up good. When Momma and Daddy returned home, David was screaming and Mae was crying. Momma and Daddy had to rush poor David to the hospital.

Thank the Lord, the doctors managed to plug David up. It was way into the night when my parents finally brought him home. Momma was fit to be tied. Her lips were tight when she walked in the house. She didn't say one word to Mae. She simply went to Mae's room, got the bassinette and drug it to the room she shared with Daddy.

She gently laid David in his bed, looked at Mae and said, "That's it for you!"

Momma wouldn't release David to Mae until Daddy stepped in. And that was a whole three months later. Mae took her son and got outta there while the getting was good.

* * * * *

After four years of playing college football, Big Henry received a bachelor's degree in history. Better than that, he was drafted by the Chicago Bears in 1965 and played his first season in 1966. Life was looking up for him and just about every black person in Memphis stuck their chest out when news of his achievement spread throughout the community. He was a local hero. Leading the praise parade were my parents and family who had long ago accepted him as son and brother.

After signing the contract, he received a signing bonus that made him stagger. It was the biggest paycheck he'd ever received in his life. He had never seen so many zeros. The amount was actually published in the Tri-State Defender so everyone knew his business. Big Henry didn't care. He knew folks were just proud of him.

Right before moving to Chicago, he went straight to the car dealership and purchased a spanking brand new, shiny Grand Prix. It was yellow on the bottom with a black vinyl top. Sounds like a mess to me, but y'all couldn't tell him nothing! After riding Mae and David around, they packed their belongings in the car and headed for the Windy City. After getting his family settled, Big Henry reported to the Bears training camp. Once he became a member of the Chicago Bears, the "Big" nickname was no longer applicable since several players were big.

In Chicago, he was just Henry.

Well, the trouble began when he rolled into training camp in that big, shiny new car. Seems that car didn't sit well with some of the players on the team. Let me tell you why. See, Henry signed his contract a year before the merger between the NFL and AFL. Before that merger, player contracts were on the rise because of the competition between the two leagues.

Henry made out like a bandit. It's not like he had a million dollar contract. At the time, the only players with the Bears making big money like that were Gayle Sayers and Dick Butkus. But, he entered the league making thousands more than some players who had been on the team for four or five years. Needless to say, he faced a lot of resentment.

They took it out on his car.

Everyday, Henry parked his car in a choice area on the lot, right in front of the dorm where he could see it from his second floor room. One morning, after practice, Henry came out of the dorm to find his car had been pushed over the embankment and into a ditch.

He knew how it happened. It was hot outside and he'd left his windows down. Like every other car in the lot. Someone came to his car, reached in, put it in neutral and pushed it until it went over the embankment. It would have been easy to do.

Henry was angered to the point of hatred. He had a pretty good idea who did the deed. There were three white players who took particular exception to him. They didn't even try to hide it. Henry knew what he had to do.

First, he enlisted the aid of three black players to get his car out of the ditch. He told them he knew who did it and what he planned to do. They looked at him like he was crazy.

"Man, you better be quiet" one player advised.

Another player agreed, "Yeah man, keep your mouth shut. Ain't no damage to your car. Let it go."

"LET IT GO?" Henry yelled. He was enraged and they were telling him to let it go?

"That right. Let it go. Man, if you come in here making waves, the coach could end your career with the stroke of a pen. Everything you've worked for could be flushed down the toilet."

"Yeah man, there are only, what, about twelve of us out of fifty on this team. They'll replace you and it would be like you were never here. Forget it."

"Man, you're young. Just getting started. Just let it pass and do what you come here to do. Play your game and forget it happened. That's what we all have to do."

Henry let them finish but he wasn't having it. He said, "Y'all talk like some of the old men back in Memphis. Y'all let the white man treat you like dirt and you just sit there and take it. And they just keep pushing and y'all just keep taking. And then what?"

They were all looking at him. They had no answers.

Henry said, "I can't do that, man. I won't do that."

Henry's response was final and the players knew it. They had been black all their lives. They knew where he was coming from. While they didn't agree with his tactics, they couldn't blame him for how he felt. The men shook their heads, hunched their shoulders and headed towards the room where the team met before going out to the practice field.

And Henry? He went to the trunk of his car and got one of his guns.

* * * * *

Hold up! Wait a minute!

This is the Southern Belle speaking.

I hate to interrupt this recollection just when it's getting good, but I gotta interject something. Because I know what you're thinking and it's not like that.

Let me tell y'all what Big Henry…uh, Henry told me about having guns in the trunk of his car.

Back in the day, the Chicago Bears training camp was located at Saint Joseph's College in Rensselaer, Indiana. It was smack dab in the middle of nowhere. They were surrounded by cornfields and little or nothing else. Most of the players brought fishing rods to get in a little fishing. Some players, like Henry would go out and shoot pheasants. They did this to amuse themselves while passing the time after practice.

So, Henry had the guns to shoot pheasants, not people. At least, that was the original plan. But after seeing his car in that ditch, anything was possible.

Now, back to my recollecting…

* * * * *

Henry walked into the assembly room (or whatever it was called) and sat in his normal seat. He calmly listened to all the instructions for the days practice. He made eye contact with no one. He waited good and well until they were about to break and move outside to the practice field before he said, "I got something to say."

The coach looked at him and said, "Yes, Henry?"

Henry rose from his seat and looked at the three guys, he thought might have been responsible for the incident. His expression went from blank to a flash of crazy as he began to speak.

He said, "Somebody in this room pushed my car into the ditch. I got a pretty good idea who did it but I won't accuse anyone right now."

Then, Henry reached under his shirt and pulled out his gun. He didn't point it at anyone, just held it in his hand pointed downward.

Then he continued, "If anything like this ever happens again, I will blow your *%$&ing head off."

It was as if a chill wind had blown through the room. No one said anything. No one looked around to see if the guilty person was squirming in their seat. No one reprimanded him. They knew he was a man who'd been pushed too doggone far.

After Henry had spoken his piece, he turned and walked out of the room without a word. The other players and coaches followed him out to the practice field and that was that. They heard him, absorbed what he said and moved on. No one ever mentioned the incident again.

They didn't understand who he was. Where he was from and what he'd been through. They didn't know about him being homeless since the age of thirteen. They didn't know about his run-ins with the Memphis Police Department. But Henry knew. He knew the thickness of racism. He knew he had to challenge it, to confront it. He wouldn't have been able to live with himself if he didn't.

And I'm telling you, Henry didn't have any other problems like that again.

* * * * *

But after that incident, Henry's eyes were opened. Before then, he'd been so happy to be on the team that he'd overlooked some things that didn't sit right with his spirit. But now, he questioned everything.

Like when they'd be at the line and the audible for the play would be called out, "Jigga, Jigga, Jigga." At first, he didn't get the connection, but now it seemed clear.

Henry asked one of the senior black players about the word, just to be sure.

The player said, "Come on man. Can't you figure out what he's saying?"

Henry said, "I want you to tell me."

The man looked at Henry and said, "Just drop the J and add a N."

Out of all the words in the English language, they had to use that word. Henry could feel the militant rising up in him again. He became more outspoken. Some of the players didn't like him, but he didn't care.

Henry's response to this was, "I didn't go there looking for love."

He was a man about his business.

BIG HENRY AND HIS BROTHER JOHN

By the time Henry had completed his first season with the Chicago Bears, his big brother John had moved back to Memphis after his enlistment in the Marines was over. John was in the service for a good ten years before he set foot in Memphis again.

While John was away, he'd gotten married and had two children, a girl and a boy. Life was looking up for Henry as his life was expanding. He was a husband, father, son-in-law, brother-in-law, and an uncle. He had family of his own. He could feel the wounds of his past starting to heal just by spending time with John. He felt like he was coming out of a long dark tunnel.

* * * * *

To say that John and Henry were close wouldn't give you a good description of their relationship. They clung to each other. They spent most of their time together during the NFL off season but, pretty soon it was time for Henry to report back to the Chicago Bears training camp. While Henry was preparing to leave, John got to thinking about what he wanted to do with the rest of his life. The Marines was all he knew as far as a job was concerned. He thought about re-enlisting. Before Henry left for camp, they talked about it.

John broached the subject. "Man, I got some papers here today. I'm thinking about re-enlisting."

Henry was dead set against the whole idea. "Don't do that. You did your time. Let it go. Do something else; something less dangerous."

"The Marines is all I know."

"Then learn something else. You're a smart man. Get a job. Or, come to Chicago with me. I'll see if I can help find you something."

"Naw, I don't want you to have to do that, little brother. I'm twenty six."

"Forget that stuff. You're only three years older than me anyway."

"Yeah, but I'm a man. Got a wife and two kids. I have to make some money to take care of them and they ain't giving good jobs to brothers here in Memphis."

"That's why I said let me help you."

John wasn't open for help. "I can do this. I gotta make money. Gotta take care of my family."

"You're just thinking about the money. But, your family is your wealth."

"I know man, I know. But I have to make my own way."

Henry said, "Man, forget that stuff. What you talking about anyway? Make your own way. You been in the Marines too long. You already made your own way when you enlisted and got away from Otis."

That slipped.

Neither John nor Henry had mentioned their father's name. It was like an unwritten pact. After John left for the Marines, one of his aunts wrote to him and told him about Otis kicking Henry out. John was incensed, but there wasn't a blessed thing he could do about it way over in Vietnam.

In a "Let's Hate Otis" contest, John and Henry would have tied for first place. They both despised him. Still, they never discussed what happened. But, John never went back to that house. He never saw Otis again. The pain was too great.

* * * * *

Just a minute…

It's me again. I promise y'all this is the last time I'm gonna interrupt but I gotta get this off my chest.

See, I think we all have stuff that happened to us that leaves little holes in us. Holes in our soul is what I call it.

You got holes.

I got holes.

All God's chir'ren got little holes.

Your hole might be a pinprick and mine might be the size of the Grand Canyon. The size don't matter much. Those holes hurts. It don't matter how the holes got there because in the end, the holes aren't the issue. What really matters is what you fill them with. And that's all I have to say about that.

Now, let me bring the little asterisks back and finish my story…

* * * * *

So, John was a nice, mild mannered, easy going man. You could get anything from him because he was freehearted and generous to a fault. He filled his hole with family. He loved his wife and kids. He felt a sense of responsibility to provide for them. That was the main thing weighing on his mind. That was why he was thinking about re-enlisting into the Marines even though Vietnam was raging.

Henry wouldn't let the situation die. He was practically begging John not to go back. "John, Vietnam ain't no joke."

"You think I don't know that? I already spent some time over there. But my squad is scheduled to go back.

I'm the leader. I have a responsibility."

"You're lucky you came back alive. I don't want to think about the people I know who came back mutilated, shell shocked, paralyzed or broken. On a slab. Man, think about it. I don't want to lose you. Think about it."

That was the end of the conversation. They left it at that.

Henry left for Chicago a week after that conversation and John continued to ask around for people's opinion on whether he should re-enlist or not. His wife was dead set against it and told him as much. He asked his aunts what they thought, but nobody wanted to give a yea or nay on the matter. Everyone felt that decision was something John would have to work out on his own.

The desire to do better for himself and his family overwhelmed any fears he might have had concerning his personal safety. He needed to do it. He only had to get through two years in order to be considered a career officer. Finally, he came to a conclusion. He thought, *I survived it once and I can do it again.*

John re-enlisted and was sent to Vietnam.

* * * * *

Henry reported to the Bears training camp while Mae and their son David quickly settled into their apartment in Chicago. It was a lovely place that they sublet from Henry's teammate, Gale Sayers. Before Henry knew it, training camp was over and the season was underway. Henry was glad to be back at work. He was so busy with traveling, practices, and the game that he didn't have time to worry about John. That suited him just fine.

That season came and went. During the off-season, Henry worked odd jobs to keep busy and to keep the money flowing in. After the break, Henry went back to Indiana for his third Bears training camp.

* * * * *

It was a Tuesday morning in the middle of the training season. Henry woke up earlier than usual that morning. He sat there on the side of the bed for a good ten minutes before he even attempted to stand up. He didn't feel right. He had an eerie, uneasy, uncomfortable feeling in the pit of his stomach. Like something didn't quite fit.

Finally, he stood and tipped over to the bathroom, careful not to wake his roommate. He bent over the sink and washed his face. When he finished, he reached over to the towel rack without even looking at it. After he dried his face, he stood up and looked at his reflection in the mirror.

He knew.

He was frozen. He leaned over the sink with both hands clutching the edge of the vanity and struggled to keep from throwing up. He was sick to his stomach and broke out in a cold sweat. It was thirty minutes before he was strong enough to leave the bathroom. He was dressed and out of the door on his way to practice in less than twenty minutes.

* * * * *

The phone ringing woke Mae up at 9:00 that same morning in their Chicago apartment. She was shocked that she had slept so late. She wondered if David was still in bed or if her independent four year old was awake and watching television in the living room. The phone's constant ringing brought her back to the present. She grabbed it like a hot sweet potato.

"Yes?" Mae rarely says hello. I get at her about that all the time because it's un-southern.

The man on the phone asked to speak to Henry. *Sounds official,* she thought.

"I'm sorry, but he's not here right now. He's at camp. Can I take a message?"

"Who am I speaking with?"

"This is Mae. Henry's wife."

The man proceeded to tell Mae why he called. By the time he finished and hung up, Mae did what Henry didn't. She ran to the bathroom and threw up.

After she composed herself, she went into the living room to find David sitting in front of the television watching cartoons. She said, "I'll get you something to eat baby, but first I have to make a phone call."

"Okay Mommie" was his cheerful response.

Mae found the address book and looked up the number for Henry's agent. She told him about the phone call and asked him to call Henry. She felt bad at not being able to deliver the news herself. The sports agent told her he would take care of everything.

* * * * *

It was a hot day but Henry didn't mind. His mind wasn't on the weather. Or the drills. Or his teammates. His mind wasn't on anything. He was numb on the inside so he wasn't thinking. His body was operating on its own. Just going through the motions of the practice.

Out of the corner of his eye, he saw someone coming onto the field. The man held a brief conversation with the coach, George Halas. Coach Halas, or "Papa Bear" as he was called, was the coach and owner of the Chicago Bears when Henry played. Henry considered it a privilege to play on his team.

Coach Halas and the man talked for a few minutes and Henry saw them look his way. He turned his head pretending he didn't know they were talking about him, but he knew. He huddled up for the next play. By the time the play was completed, Henry turned to the sideline and saw

Coach Halas walking off the field. After a few more plays, the defensive coordinator yelled from the sideline, "Hey, Henry!"

When Henry looked at him, he waved him over and said, "Come here for a minute."

Henry took the long walk over to him on the sidelines and answered, "Yeah?"

He said, "Coach wants to see you in his office."

Henry didn't respond, but turned and walked off the field.

Time stood still. It was as if Henry blinked and there he was, walking through the doors of the office. Coach Halas said, "Have a seat, Henry."

Wordlessly, Henry sat down in the brown folding chair in front of the coach's desk.

Henry spoke first. "You don't have to tell me. I know my brother is dead."

His words caught Coach Halas off guard. He responded, "What did you say?"

"I said I know my brother John is dead. I'm right ain't I?"

The two men looked at each other. Finally, Coach Halas said, "I'm afraid you are. But how did you know?"

Henry continued to look him in the eyes and said, "He's my brother."

Coach Halas was momentarily at a loss for words. Finally, he said, "I'm sorry for your loss. The Chicago Bears organization stands with you in your time of bereavement. If there is anything we can do for you, please let us know."

Henry asked, "Do you know what happened?"

Coach Halas said, "Uh...yes, I know a little, but we don't need to talk about this right now. We'll make arrangements to get you to...."

Henry interrupted him, "I want to know."

Coach Halas took a deep breath and said, "Your

brother was out leading his squad through a field and he stepped on a land mind."

He hesitated, took another deep breath and finished, "The bottom half of his body was blown away. His upper torso is in tact."

Henry flinched when he heard the news.

Coach Halas hurriedly continued, "He probably didn't know what hit him. He probably didn't feel a thing. It happened so quickly. I am very sorry."

Henry said, "How did you find out?"

"Your wife was called by some official this morning. She called your agent and he called us."

Looking directly into Henry's eyes, Coach Halas said, "Is there anything, anything at all we can do for you? Anything at all?"

Henry rose from his seat.

Evenly he said, "There is nothing anyone can do for me."

Coach said, "We'll make arrangements to get you back to Memphis immediately."

Henry responded, "Ain't no need to rush back. Ain't nothing I can do now. I'll finish practice and leave tomorrow. I'll miss Sunday's game, though."

"Of course."

When he got to the door, he didn't turn around. With his back to Coach he said, "If anyone had to tell me, I'm glad it was you."

He walked out of the office before Coach Halas could respond.

Henry finished the practice like nothing had changed. When practice was over, he headed to the locker room and changed. He was the first man out of the locker room.

* * * * *

John's body arrived in Memphis on a rainy, gray day.

Mae, Henry, and David arrived in Memphis a few days before the funeral. They stayed with Momma and Daddy. My parents tried to talk to Henry but he didn't have much to say. You know, some people are like that.

The Columbus Baptist Church was packed with John's family, including Otis, Felicia, and their ten children. My family was there along with John's classmates and high school friends. The sanctuary was filled to capacity. The ushers had to set out extra seats in the lobby. That's how much John was loved and respected.

It was a full military funeral and John was in a uniquely designed coffin. The top was glass from the waist up and wood from the waist down. Mae said it was like looking into a picture frame. John looked real peaceful. Like he was sleeping. She said by looking at him through the glass, you couldn't tell his bottom half was missing.

During the whole service, Henry sat there like a piece of stone. He was dead on the inside. No one could reach him.

Henry changed after that. He became withdrawn and uncommunicative. He always liked to spend time by himself. That's how he was. But after John died, his need to be alone was even more pronounced. John was Henry's only link to his family. Now that he was gone, Henry was adrift. Like, a part of him checked out of life.

I think I see how that can happen to a person. A body can only take so much heartache, you know.

Chapter 23

BIG BUSINESS

After John's funeral, Henry returned to the Bears and played with a vengeance. He was a terror. Just like when he was in high school, his anger served his career well, if nothing else.

Mae noticed that Henry was becoming more withdrawn as he struggled to deal with the death of his big brother. The only real link he had to his family. He didn't have much to say to Mae either on that subject. She tried to get him to talk about how he felt. The same way she had seen Momma talking to Daddy about his sorry upbringing. But Henry, much like Daddy, wasn't big on talking, especially since the pain of feeling alone wasn't something he felt Mae could understand. He was still a good husband and father, but the subject of his family was off limits.

Mae let the subject drop.

* * * * *

Mae loved everything about living in Chicago. She loved the social scene with the parties, the clubs, and the restaurants. She loved being the wife of an NFL player and the sisterhood she felt when hanging out with the other wives. She missed Momma, Daddy, and the rest of the family, but she loved living without rules and boundaries. She loved just about everything. Everything that is, except for one thing. The brutal Chicago winters.

Y'all it gets cold in Chicago. Not only that. It's cold

for a long time. Mae was used to the milder southern winters of Memphis. The harsh cold was too much for her and David was none too pleased either. She would stay indoors for days at a time because she felt like that Chicago hawk was going to snap her right in two. To tell you the truth, in Mae's mind, the fierce winters practically erased all of the good Chicago had to offer.

Henry felt bad for his family and after much discussion, the couple decided that they would open some sort of business in Memphis and Mae would return home and run the operation. But the question was, what type of business to open? Mae and Henry discussed it until Henry remembered a businessman he met when he went home for a visit. Henry gave him a call.

* * * * *

Dang it to heck!

Uh…it's me again, Baby Girl Belle.

For real, I thought the last interruption was the last interruption but it wasn't because this is the last interruption. For real!

Because I need to stop right here and explain things because, by now, y'all know how I am. I ain't trying to get sued so I'm gonna change the names of some of the people in this story.

See, some of the descendents of the people I'm about to talk about might still be high mucky muck in Memphis. The last thing I want is to go to my mailbox and see a letter from some attorney saying I'm being sued by some great, great, great nephew for blasphemy or liable or slander or what ever it's called. I'm not going down like that. The names are being changed to protect the innocent.

That's me, by the way.

Now, back to my story.

* * * * *

Joseph Masters was the brother of a very prominent Memphis businessman and politician. His brother, Harold practically ran Memphis during the 1960's. Harold didn't have any love for black folks and he didn't care who knew it. It wasn't something he was ashamed of, nor did he try to hide it because that's how things were back then. The only thing black folk could do for Harold Masters was shine his shoes or clean his toilets.

But Joseph was the complete opposite. He was a nice, peaceful man. Short and stocky, but not fat. He had a friendly, round face and wore black rimmed glasses. Not bad looking, but nothing to write home about either.

Perhaps it was the fact that Joseph was stricken with an illness that affected his walking. For Joseph, the process of walking was done with much effort. Henry thought his physical condition delivered him from pride and haughtiness. Joseph Masters was an honest, decent, and honorable man. How Joseph and Harold ended up in the same family was a mystery to everyone who knew them.

Now, Harold didn't want to have anything to do with black folks. But he sure didn't mind taking their money because he and Joseph owned businesses, restaurants and laundromats all over Memphis, including the black areas. Ain't that a mess?

Most black folks hated Harold, and their frustrations knew no boundaries. Blacks would boycott their businesses. The more rebellious would throw bricks through the windows of their businesses to try to drive away customers. Henry knew this was going on and that's what gave him the idea that would put money in his pockets and help the Masters Brothers at the same time.

Henry called Joseph and told him that he had a proposal for him. After briefly explaining the idea, Joseph agreed that it was a solid idea and invited Henry to his home in an exclusive, gated community in Memphis to discuss the details.

When Henry arrived at his home, Joseph was very courteous. He introduced him to his wife and children. The whole family was friendly. His wife was a handsome woman, taller than Joseph and slim. Impeccably dressed and she was just sitting in the house…a real Southern Belle. She remained in the room as they sat down and discussed the details of the proposal.

Henry planned to invest in the organization by taking over two fast food restaurants and three laundromats located in the black sections of Memphis. The organization would then market Henry as a co-owner in the establishment. Seeing that Henry was a local celebrity, sports star and well known and respected in the community, he would work to ease the attacks against the Masters Brother's businesses.

In essence, Henry was offering to be a liaison between the two brothers and the black community. It was a win-win situation. Joseph loved that idea and quickly made arrangements for Henry to present the proposal to his board of directors the following day.

As Henry was preparing to leave, Joseph did the unthinkable. He invited Henry out to dinner at Justine's, which was Joseph's favorite restaurant. Henry couldn't believe his ears and stood there dumbstruck. He was familiar with Justine's. Or maybe I should say, he had heard of Justine's. Justine's is where the white upper crust in Memphis dined. Blacks weren't allowed to eat there. The only blacks who were allowed inside the doors were the ones who washed the dishes and bused the tables. This was in the late 1960's you know.

Henry accepted the invitation, thinking *If he's bold enough to ask, I'm crazy enough to go.*

The way Henry saw it, Joseph had more to lose than he did. After all, white folk who befriended black folk could be ostracized by the white community. Back in the 60's, you would be called a nigger lover. That wasn't something to aspire to.

Joseph called for the limo and pretty soon Henry, Joseph, and his wife were on their way to forbidden territory.

On the way over, Joseph said, "Now Henry, let me tell you this before we get to the restaurant. One of two things might happen. They might welcome us with open arms or they might throw us all out. As far as I know, no negro has ever eaten in Justine's. You'd be the first. Do you still want to go?"

Henry loved it. He was always ready for a fight. It was all he could do to hold back his laughter. After all he'd been through in his life: fending for himself since the age of thirteen, dealing with the police in the Dixie Homes project he grew up in, and participating in sit-ins. So, getting thrown out of a high-falutin' restaurant was a cake walk for him.

Henry answered, "I don't care if you don't care. Hey, if they throw us out, we can get a bucket of Kentucky Fried Chicken and take it back to the house."

Laughing, Joseph said, "It's a deal."

Mrs. Master's said it didn't make her no never mind either.

Now that it was agreed that they would give Justine's a try, they changed the conversation to a more pleasant subject.

Moments later, the limo pulled in front of Justine's. Following Joseph and his wife, Henry walked in through the front door like it was something he did everyday. Upon seeing them, the black host lost his composure for a moment. Henry thought it was funny to watch his dumbfounded expression, all the while understanding his confusion. On the one hand, standing before him was Joseph Masters, one of the richest men in the city. On the other hand, he brought a black man into an eating establishment that only allows blacks to enter if they were servants. What do you do?

Joseph was cool. "Masters, party of three."

Henry could tell by the sound of his voice that Joseph was enjoying this.

The fellow bowed slightly and said, "Yes, of course Mr. Masters. Please follow me to your favorite table."

When the party stepped into the dining area, a hush fell over the room. People actually stopped eating, forks suspended in mid air. Conversations stopped. Even the music stopped for a moment. Every eye was on them as they walked to the choice table in the center of the room. After a moment, the white maître d' came over to the table.

Henry thought to himself, *Uh-oh, here it comes.*

But, to his amazement, nothing happened.

The two men greeted each other warmly. Joseph introduced Henry and the maître d' presented a bottle of wine for his approval. The maître d' raised his hand to summon the same waiter who seated them. He rushed over with the menus. By the time the group gave their orders, the room had returned to normal. Both Joseph and his wife ordered the creamed spinach. Henry had never heard of such, but at their insistence, ordered it. Henry had to admit that it was the best thing he had ever tasted. So, there were no fireworks that night. The evening turned out to be a night filled with good food, laughter, and hope.

When the dinner was over, Henry returned home to Mae. He told her all of the good things that had happened. She told him she was happy and proud of him. The last thing Henry remembered thinking as he fell asleep was, *Memphis has changed.*

* * * * *

The meeting with Harold Masters and the rest of his

board of directors was set for 2:00pm the next day. It was a Thursday. Henry was careful not to be late. He wore his best suit and walked into the boardroom with his head held high. The group of white men listened to him as he went through every point in his proposal.

They didn't say a mumbling word as he explained how he would invest his money in their business and help to establish a connection with the black community. They allowed him to talk for twenty minutes until he didn't have anything else to say. And then the board, led by Harold, told him what they thought of his proposal.

Harold Masters was a fat, triple chinned man with greasy hair. He was wearing an old tweed jacket in the middle of June and flooding pants. Mercy!

Harold addressed Henry. To tell the truth, as soon as Henry laid eyes on him he knew what the answer would be. When you see his kind, you know what they're about.

Harold said, "Thank you for your proposal, but we don't think this is the direction we want to go. We don't want you to leave empty handed though. What we can do is give you a laundry truck and help you establish a route."

Henry could feel the anger rising up in him. He said, "Do you mean to tell me that you want me to drive a truck and pick up dirty laundry and then take the clean laundry back to the people in the evening?"

He felt he had to spell it out to them so that they could hear how ridiculous it sounded.

Harold's answer was unapologetic. "Yes. We'll give you a route in an area that has a lot of restaurants. It could be very profitable."

Henry still couldn't believe his ears. He just couldn't let it go. "I come in here with a proposal to go into business with you. Financially, I can afford to take over four to six stores. Not only that. I can be a bridge in racial calamity. I can help turn your business around but you would rather give me a laundry truck?"

No response.

Henry glanced at Joseph. The crestfallen look on his face said everything. Henry could tell by his slumped shoulders that he was just as disappointed as he was.

That's the difference between the two brothers. Harold seemed to enjoy dismissing Henry. Putting him in his place, so to speak. But Joseph seemed as hurt as any black person would be. Joseph knew their business was suffering, but he was powerless to change things because his help came wrapped in the wrong skin.

This was the first time Henry understood the role of a board of directors. That they actually ran things and there wasn't a darn thing Joseph could do about it.

Henry folded up his notebook and said, "I thank you for your time."

And with that, he walked out of the office and straight to his car. A warmth hit him that felt like he had been released from prison. Before them he was calm and collected. By the time he made it to his car his legs were shaking and he could hardly get his breath. To release the tension, he said every cuss word he could think of and even invented a few to commemorate the occasion.

Henry went home and told Mae what happened. In his estimation, it was the worse conversation they'd had in their whole time together. He couldn't even look her in the eyes. Henry packed up just one more hurt to go along with all the others.

Being black sure was tough on a man.

Hey y'all.

I've got something important to say. Now, I've been recollecting and recollecting and it's been a real hoot, but it does start to wear on a body. But far be it from me to complain about it because this whole story was my idea in the first place. Anyhoo, I got to thinking about what I wanted to tell y'all next and it occurred to me that I'm missing something. Something really important.

Something of historical value, no less.

See, on April 4, 1968 an event happened in Memphis that touched the whole wide world. For those of you who don't know, that's the day Martin Luther King was assassinated. Well, lo and behold, I have three family members who were a mile or two away from the Lorraine Motel. Sure did! Henry, Mark and my brother-in-law Ted were right there in the thick of things and saw first-hand everything that happened on that awful day.

So, If y'all don't mind, instead of hogging the spotlight, I'm gonna turn the recollecting over to the men for a spell so they can give account of everything they saw with their own eyes. But don't worry yourself none 'cause I'll be right back when they're done. See, this is too important for me to put my two cents in 'cause I want you to get an eyewitness account of what happened in Memphis, THE DAY MARTIN DIED.

PART SIX

THE DAY MARTIN DIED

WHAT BIG HENRY SAW

Listen up…on March 28, 1968, I was a few months into the off-season. I had just completed my third year with the Chicago Bears and was looking forward to getting back to work. Training camp for the bears was several months away, so I passed the time picking up odd jobs just to keep from dying of boredom.

I knew that Dr. King was in town and there was going to be a march in support of the sanitation workers. It was all everyone talked about. I had participated in a few sit-ins before. Nothing highly organized. Just me and some friends would head downtown to main street and go to the cafeterias at either of the major department stores: Goldsmiths, Lowenstein's or Black and White. We'd sit our black behinds down at the counters and watch the white folk turn beet red.

They'd be yelling, screaming and pushing us but we were like trees planted by the rivers of waters… We couldn't be moved. The women were just as bad as the men with their insults and vulgarities. Downright nasty, it was.

Of course, the manager would wind up calling the police and we'd turn tail and make our escape before they got there. We usually got away, except that one last time when the cops caught me and beat me like they were Pharaoh and I was one of the Hebrews. After spending three days in jail with no food, water, or phone calls, they finally let me go and I hobbled back to the place where I was staying. That was my last sit-in.

So, I was happy to participate in the march.

Being a member of the Chicago Bears gave me a certain amount of celebrity around Memphis. At the time, there were very few Memphians, black or white, who were professional athletes; I reckon three of four at the most. So most people knew who I was. It was nice to be recognized everywhere I went and there were a few perks too. In the black community, I rarely had to stand in line when I went out to eat or to the movies. Someone would always recognize me and the people would part like the Red Sea and let Mae and me move to the front of the line.

I was just twenty-four years old at the time, but the attention didn't give me the big head 'cause I knew where I came from. But, thank the Lord, it was a different day for me. I knew I couldn't mess up. Black people were depending on me to keep it together. I felt like I was representing a whole race of people. I knew this so it was no struggle to stay humble. I still called black men "sir" and older black women "ma'am." Everyone was so proud of me.

I said all that to say that it wasn't surprising to me that, when I reported to the location they announced where everyone was supposed to meet, someone recognized me and asked me to be a section leader. I think they called the position a "Marshall." It was an honor and I gladly accepted.

A lot of planning went into those marches, you know. Some people from the SCLC (Southern Christian Leaderships Conference) were working hard to get things organized. They were organizing the march and the strike so they were plenty busy. They were doing a good job of it too. It was my job to go out with groups of people and keep things moving. People were ready to go this time because the march had originally been scheduled for March 22nd, but a massive snowstorm changed all that. A snowstorm in Memphis that late in the season was very rare. It caught everyone by surprise. But the show had to go on, so they postponed the rally until the 28th.

There were people everywhere, tens of thousands, I would say. Afterwards, I read that over twenty thousand students didn't report to school that day so that they could participate in the march. I ran into relatives I hadn't seen in years. Since my mother died and my father promptly put me out of the house at the ripe age of twelve, I had lost contact with the majority of her people. It was good seeing them as well as the other black folk of every age there waiting for their time to protest.

I have to say, I was surprised to see quite a few whites out as well. Way more than I would have expected. I mean, I knew that some white folks were out protesting the treatment of black folks just as hard and strong as we were. I had seen it on television and in the newspapers. I have to say, I was shocked to actually see it in Memphis. I had met very few nice white people in Memphis. And that's all I have to say about that.

After I accepted the Marshall assignment, I was given an arm band. People in my group were given signs to carry and I was issued a bullhorn. That was supposed to help keep down the confusion, and it did, for a little while.

Well, if y'all know your history, you'll know that this was the march that turned violent. To tell you the truth, it was like that from the get-go. The people in charge called it off quickly as people started to act up. I'm telling you, they high tailed King and the big name people outta there quick and in a hurry.

Y'all know how things can get out of hand sometimes. One unruly person throws a rock into a store window and someone else thinks that's a good idea and does the same. Next thing you know, there's a near riot and the police are called in and before long, a black boy is lying dead in the street. It was a doggone shame. If I'm not mistaken, that was the only march that ended with black folk acting like they didn't have right good sense. There may have been others, but I'm not aware of them.

I knew a few old high school classmates were some of the troublemakers. I didn't see them do it, but their names were in the papers the next day. When I knew them, they were just ordinary guys who never got into trouble. I was shocked to learn they had become militant. But then again, you can only beat a person down for so long before they will start to beat their way back up.

Less than a week later, King came back to Memphis to see about leading another march. That night he gave his speech, "I've Been to the Mountaintop" at Martin Temple. I didn't go to hear him speak because the weather was acting up again. But Mae and I listened to it on the radio.

That man knew how to talk!

On the next day, April 4th, I made up in my mind that I wanted Mae and David to meet King. I was just sitting there, minding my business and the thought just sort of come to me out of nowhere.... I wanted Mae and David to meet him.

If I'm not mistaken, I believe there was supposed to be a rally that night. I remember thinking, *Before he goes to the rally, I'm going to take my family to meet him.*

I told Mae to get ready because we were going down to the Lorraine Motel. She didn't ask any questions. She just got up and started throwing on her clothes. She probably thought I knew what I was doing but the truth of the matter is, I didn't. As soon as David was dressed, we headed towards downtown. I didn't have an appointment and I didn't try to get one. My hope was that someone would recognize me and let us in for a hot minute.

It was about 5:45 when we left the house.

The radio was tuned to WDIA.

It was about ten minutes after six.

Might have been twenty after, I don't know.

The news traveled fast.

A black voice assaulted me over the radio lines.

"MARTIN LUTHER KING HAS BEEN SHOT!"

To tell the truth, it didn't register with me. I mean, I heard the words, but I didn't get it. I turned to Mae, who had her hand covering her mouth, which was wide open. She had turned as white as a sheet. That's when I knew what the DJ had said.

Still, I asked her, "What did they say?"

She didn't get a chance to respond because the DJ did. "MARTIN LUTHER KING HAS BEEN SHOT AT THE LORRAINE MOTEL."

Y'all, I saw Memphis change in the twinkling of an eye, right before my eyes.

It was like everyone was being born at the same time. It was sudden. It was instantaneous.

It was...

We were only a few blocks from the Lorraine, but before I could go another block, the streets flooded with people. I saw concern in people's faces. At first, it was just worry and fear that I saw. I saw young people and old people heading toward the Lorraine. As if just being there could make everything alright. As if being there would take that bullet back.

'MARTIN LUTHER KING HAS BEEN SHOT AT THE LORRAINE MOTEL."

The reporter kept saying the same thing over and over and over again like he thought we had forgotten or something. Over and over again, he kept saying those words. I was dying on the inside. The worst part was not knowing what was going on.

"DR. KING HAS BEEN TAKEN TO SAINT JOSEPH'S HOSPITAL."

For the life of me, I couldn't turn the car around and head back home. I should have, and I regretted it later, but something kept me moving forward. Drawing me to the hotel. Maybe, it was a need to be there with other black people. Maybe I wanted to share this tragedy with everyone else. I don't know.

Finally, Mae came to her right mind and said, "Henry, this might get ugly. You think we should go back home?"

Her voice broke the hypnotic spell luring me downtown.

I said, "Yeah, maybe you're right" and turned the car around.

It wasn't long after 7:00 when it was announced, "Dr. King is dead."

To me, they shouted everything else, but this revelation came as a whisper.

Chaos had been all around us, but when they said he was dead, it was eerily quiet.

It was as if everybody heard it at the same time.

It brought silence...when they finally said it.

The next word, was no word.

And like a collective gasp, it started up again.

Memphis burned!

The violence escalated by one thousand percent.

It was as if people said, "Since he's dead, we don't have anything to live for."

Life became loud.

Spontaneous chaos erupted in the street.

People were throwing garbage cans, rocks, and bricks...anything they could get their hands on. It was like driving in hell. It was tight. Every car that had white folks in it was being stoned.

They were dragging white people out of their cars and beating them in the streets. I saw white people driving on the sidewalks trying to escape the mob. Some made it out but many didn't. In fact, I saw them pull one white guy out of his car and beat him mercilessly. They were tearing him up....over and over again, blow after blow after blow. The sidewalk was splattered with his blood.

Mae covered her eyes, but I didn't.

And you know what? I wanted to help him. In spite of all the beatings I've endured at the hands of white police officers. In spite of all the indignities I've suffered from white people; being called nigger, being spat on, being pushed around, sitting at the back of the bus, and not being able to walk through white neighborhoods. In spite of all that, I hated to see it happening to someone else.

But, the Memphis police wasn't taking this lying down. The police were riding herd on anybody black. They were driving their cars straight into crowds of black people. They were shooting and asking questions later. If people had the nerve to be out during the riot, they needed to be prepared to run.

It was taking forever to get home. Some of those guys with rocks were about to throw them at me but then they stopped. I couldn't understand it because a riot is a riot. It was sheer frenzy. People don't see color. I believe it was by the grace of God that I got through. I'm telling you, I got the heck outta there.

And these weren't just young people protesting either. There were some older men too. Looked to me to be in their 50's and even 60's. I don't think they were throwing for the purpose of damaging someone's business. I imagine every rock they threw represented an indignity they had suffered. For every time they had to sit in the back of the bus, drink water at a separate fountain, enter a place of business through the back door. For every time they had called a white man "sir" and were addressed as "boy" in response. For every whipping they got from the police. For being denied justice, a good education, any opportunity.

Yes, every one of those rocks and every one of those bricks had a meaning.

I was as scared as anybody. I'm not shame to admit it either. I was in that gray zone between fear and rage. Part of me wanted to get out of the car and throw rocks just like everyone else. My rocks would have been thrown at my father who put me out of the house when I was thirteen years old. At the police who used to drive through Dixie Homes and harass me and my friends for no reason other than the color of our skin. For the many officers who beat me for no reason other than the sport of it.

Yeah, I wanted to throw rocks. But I looked at my wife and my son and I knew I had to keep driving. I put my anger aside and focused on protecting my family. The world was exploding all around me. I felt vulnerable and helpless. But I knew I had to protect my family.

While we made that long hard journey home, our ears were glued to the car radio.

You could hear the chaos. Cars speeding, sirens squealing, glass shattering, people yelling, and screaming. There were explosions that sounded like sonic booms. Every noise that could be associated with a riot was heard in Memphis that day.

And the smoke…

You could smell the smoke in Memphis for days.

* * * * *

We finally made it home. I told Mae to spread blankets on the floor, turn off the lights, and turn on the radio. We didn't dare turn on the television because I didn't want anyone to see the reflection of the light and throw a rock.

We listened well into the morning hours. WDIA had black preachers and other known people in town begging people to stop rioting. James Brown was on the radio telling people to calm down. I'm not sure if that did any good, since the people who were listening to the radio weren't the ones out rioting.

WDIA was reporting that the area around the hotel

took the worst hit. We got up the next morning and went for a ride to see what happened while we slept. Beale Street, the heart of the black community, was a disaster area. We kept driving and almost every barbeque restaurant and Laundromat that had the name of Memphis' racist Mayor "Loeb" on it was torched and still smoldering.

* * * * *

Black folks lost a lot.
We lost King.
We lost our community.
We lost our businesses.
We lost hope.
After King's death, it seems like black people in Memphis became more militant. It seemed white people mellowed out a bit. For both groups, it was like a wake up call with a very loud alarm.

For me, I felt like I had a lump in my throat that I couldn't swallow or cough out. I figured it had to dissolve in its own time.

CHAPTER 25

WHAT MARK SAW

I hate to say it, because people say it all the time, but I really do remember it just like it happened yesterday. The memories are still just as vivid as they were the day it happened. To tell you the truth, I kinda wish they would fade a bit. It's been almost fifty years. I've forgotten plenty of stuff since then, but the day Martin Luther King died will live with me forever.

I was working in downtown Memphis at the Post Office. The one, right there near Madison and Front. I had just finished serving in the Air Force and had only been working there for about three or four months. Back then, the Post Office was THE place to work if you were black. They had great benefits and the pay was pretty good. But, I was just a casual employee so I knew I wouldn't be there for long.

I was working the swing shift on that day. It was a little before 6:00 pm on April 4th. The sun had just started to go down but it was still plenty light outside. Two of my co-workers and I were going to get some lunch at our usual spot, a restaurant that sold burgers on Beale Street. You know back then, Black folks couldn't just walk into any place and get served so Beale Street was one of our few options.

Back in the day, Memphis used to roll up the sidewalks after 6:00pm, so there wasn't much going on. It was quiet that night.

So, we're walking down Front Street minding our own

business and were just about to turn onto Beale Street when I heard this loud bang. Like I told you, I had only been out of the Air Force for a couple of months so the sound wasn't unfamiliar to me.

One of the guys with me said, "Somebody's having car trouble...did you hear that backfire?"

I looked at him and said, "Man, that wasn't no car. That was a gunshot."

Both of those guys were younger than me so they looked concerned. In fact, one of them suggested we go back to work.

To be honest, I didn't think much of it.

I told them, "Come on, y'all. It's probably some loud partygoers getting an early start in one of the juke joints. Don't worry. I'll protect y'all."

So we kept on walking and went into the restaurant and got our burgers. It really didn't take long for us to get our order and head back to work. It's hard to describe it, but by the time we started to walk back, the mood on Beale Street had changed. Mind you, when we came out of the restaurant, it was around 6:20, 6:30 at the latest. That's pretty early for the Beale street crowd. But there was an excitement, or maybe I should say an energy that wasn't there when we went in. Black people were running around. I could see folks headed up Beale Street turning left and heading south on Second Street.

I was trying to figure it out. *Must be some sort of giveaway*, I thought.

Going that direction you'd run into the Arcade Restaurant, but blacks couldn't eat there so that wasn't it. The only other places were Ernestine and Hazel's (a black owned restaurant) and the Lorraine Motel.

I didn't know what to make of it. I was still marinating on it when I heard a loud screeching sound.

The cops came from nowhere. There were two big, ugly red-faced white guys. If you have ever seen a movie where there's a racist white policeman, they must have used those guys as the models. They both jumped out the car and threw all three of us against the wall. My coworker's head slammed against the wall.

The cops were screaming and barking out orders to us, but I couldn't make heads or tails out of what they were saying. It was every black man's nightmare.

The two guys with me were terrified so I knew it was up to me to handle the situation. I struggled to remain calm because I didn't want to give the officers any reason to start swinging or shooting. The Memphis Police Department was no joke back then.

When I could finally get a word in edgewise, I said in my most calm voice, "Officer, what's the problem?"

One of them yelled, "Turn around and keep y'alls hands up."

We obeyed and slowly turned around.

I was looking him dead in the eyes when I saw his eyes go down to my chest. He saw that all three of us were wearing our Post Office badges. Back then, when you worked for the post office, you were issued a bronze badge that helped you gain access to the building.

I don't know who they were looking for, but judging from the look on his face, I saw it register that he had the wrong people. I felt a little bolder.

"Officer, can we put our hands down? What is the problem?"

He answered, "Yeah. Y'all can put your hands down."

For the third time I asked, "What is going on?"

"Y'all ain't heard? They shot that coon King."

And with that being said, the officers jumped into their black and white and sped off.

At that point in time, I felt like the only person in the universe.

The earth was still rotating around the sun. Time was still ticking. Gravity still held my feet to the ground. Jesus hadn't cracked the sky. Technically, the earth hadn't changed. Life was moving forward, but not for me.

I was aware that there was activity going on all around me, but I didn't have the power to participate. My whole body went limp. I felt like I was seeing life from the bottom of a very deep and narrow hole. That is what my world had become. A very deep and very narrow hole.

I heard the shot.

Tears began to well up in my eyes but I pushed them back.

I was too old to cry.

I awoke as if out of a trance and saw the growing chaos of Beale Street. People were pouring onto the streets....coming from everywhere. At that moment, the only emotions I could see were worry and concern on everyone's faces.

And fear.

But I knew that that could change in an instant. Since I'd heard the shot, I knew I was close to where King had been shot. I quickly realized that I was at the wrong place at the wrong time. The situation could turn volatile.

I looked at my coworkers and said, "We need to get outta here."

Wasn't nothing but a word. We ran, flat out ran all the way back to the Post Office.

I took comfort in the fact that he had only been shot. Maybe he could pull through.

* * * * *

By the time we got back to work, every white worker was booking it. That is to say, there was a line of them clocking out and running to their cars heading to their safe, white neighborhoods.

The black people were standing around in a state of shock. Finally, one of the supervisors, who was also black, asked us if we wanted to continue working.

Me and a lot of others said, "Yeah."

I wanted to work so I wouldn't have to think about it.

But I couldn't escape.

The people who stayed had no intention of working. Someone pulled out a transistor radio and we all hovered around it like a campfire. We were flipping the stations to either WLOK or WDIA…they were all saying the same thing.

They kept saying, "King has been shot."

"King has been taken to Saint Joseph's Hospital."

They were giving updates on what was happening across Memphis. The police were blocking off streets. People were throwing rocks and bricks and starting fires. But they weren't saying anything different about King. That was all I wanted to know. *How was King?*

At a little after 7:00, I found out.

"Martin Luther King is dead."

After that, things got worse.

I cried.

And I didn't care who saw me either.

* * * * *

The night before he'd been shot, me and some of the guys from "The Patterns" decided to go down to Mason Temple to see if we could see King. The weather was bad that night so we thought the crowd would be smaller and we'd have a chance at getting in. When we got there, there was a crowd, but not as thick as when he usually speaks.

He was already up speaking when we got there and some of the guys wanted to go home. I wasn't having it.

"I didn't come all this way for nothing. I want to see him."

I muscled my way through the crowd and finally made it to where I could see. People were looking at me, but I didn't care. I wanted to see him.

His voice was magnetic.

When he got to the part that said, "He's allowed me to go up to the mountain. And I've looked over, and I've seen the Promised Land..." I got chills all over my body. I felt like I couldn't breathe.

He had an aura around him. To me, it looked like he was glowing.

When it was over, people were cheering and yelling.

Little did we know...less than one day later....

WHAT TED SAW

I was working the second half of a split shift that day. I had one eye on the road and the other on the clock, 'cause I only had one hour to go. I came on at 3:00pm and was scheduled to get off at 7:00pm.

It had been a good day until then. Nothing out of the ordinary and I was glad of it. Let me just say that sometimes the bus could be an interesting place. The black passengers were alright. I never had any problems with them. It was the white passengers who taxed my nerves.

They would get on the bus with their noses turned up like they smelled something sour. Most of them wouldn't even look me in the eyes or acknowledge me at all. It was like I was invisible to them. I remember thinking, *If you so uppity, why you on the bus?* Still, it was no skin off my knees. After living in Memphis for so long, you get used to that sort of thing. As long as I still got my check at the end of the week....

I started driving the bus in January of 1968, so by April, I was still relatively new to the job. I'd had a month of training and by February I was driving on my own. At the time, there were only a handful of black drivers, about fifty out of four hundred more or less, so I considered myself blessed to have the job. Back then, driving the bus was just as good as working for the Post Office.

At 6:01pm on April 4, 1968, I was about a mile away from the Lorraine Motel. I didn't hear the shot because of the chatter on the bus, but I could tell something had happened because of the crowds of people. It didn't take me long to find out what was going on. I didn't have to ask, I heard the people on the bus talking about it as they got on the bus. Someone had shot Dr. King and he had been taken to Saint Joseph's. Blacks usually had to go to John Gaston hospital, but by this time, Saint Joseph's was also accepting blacks.

The news made my heart break. It was a good thing I had just pulled off from the curb and was driving slow. Otherwise, I probably would have wrecked my bus. I was trying to be cool and just do my job, but a thousand thoughts were in my head and a thousand emotions were in my heart. I felt bad. Like I had lost a member of my family. But I didn't want the people on the bus to see how the news had affected me.

Was it true?

I was hoping against hope that it was a vile rumor that needed to be put down like a crippled horse. I didn't have that fantasy for long. After awhile I knew it was true. I would have done anything to change it, but I knew it was true. All I had to do was look out the window of the bus to know that.

It looked like all of Memphis was trying to get downtown. People were flocking to the Lorraine like it was Mecca. I saw people running from the Foote Homes and Claiborne Homes headed that way. Cars were headed that way. I didn't know there were that many cars in Memphis! There was a constant flow of people and I saw everything from concern to anger on their faces. It wasn't long before there was total gridlock. I made it as far as Main Street when traffic stopped completely in every direction. It was like a sea of cars and black people.

I did the only thing I could. I shut off the engine and said to the passengers, "Sorry folks, looks like we're stuck."

I got off the bus and the rest of the passengers did as

well. I knew it would be a long time before I went anywhere. To tell you the truth, I was glad to get off that bus for a minute. I wanted to get away from the chatter or hearing people saying the same thing over and over.

"They shot King" was all I heard. I thought a breath of fresh air would do me good.

All around me, the people were talking about it. I never saw so many transistor radios in all my life. People were hanging on every word coming over the airwaves. Some people were angry, but most of the people I talked to were hurt, especially the older ones. Seeing the older ones so sad made me want to cry.

Two men who looked to be in their thirties were talking. I heard one of them ask, "Who did it?"

His friend answered, "You know who did it. It was the police."

"You reckon he gonna make it?"

"Man, I dunno."

"What are we gone do now?"

"He ain't dead yet."

Yet.

I looked around, taking in the crowd, when I saw an older, black lady sitting at the bus stop. I guessed that she was on her way to the Lorraine and had stopped to take a rest. She looked like a church mother. I'd put her at about seventy years old, give or take, and she had a head full of unruly, gray hair that was pulled back into a shoulder length, stiff pony tail. Her blue and red floral print housedress had seen better days and her swollen feet were stuffed into black shoes that, by all rights, should have been a size larger. Her right hand rested on an ornate wooden cane that looked like it came from Africa, but she probably bought it at A.Schwab's down on Beale Street.

She seemed to be in distress, so I went over to her to see if I could help. If she had been my mother, that's what I would have wanted someone to do.

I sat down next to her and asked, "Ma'am, do you need some help?"

"Son, we all gon' need some help after this day is over."

She was speaking prophetically, but I'm not sure she knew it.

She kept shaking her head and saying, under her breath, "Lawd, have mercy," "Jesus," and "Uh, uh, uh."

To me, that just about summed up the situation perfectly.

I said, "I wish we could get an update. All they keep saying is 'King has been shot'. It's been over an hour. Why can't they tell us something new?"

I hadn't meant to say all that, it just came out.

Shaking her head, she responded, "Maybe it's not too bad. He might pull through. Maybe he was shot in the shoulder or in the leg."

She said it like a prayer.

I confirmed, "Maybe. We just don't know."

She continued, "He gotta live. We need him. He's the only one that's gettin' things done."

I added, "He's like Moses to us. The only true voice we have."

"He gotta live. He just gotta…." That was all she could get out before she broke down.

I could see the tears streaming down her cheeks as she released the pain and tension that had been building up for the past hour. I really didn't have any words for her so I just nodded my head. To give her some privacy, I glanced at my watch. It was 6:50.

Maybe the new hour will bring new news, I thought.

As the next few minutes passed, and more and more people flooded downtown, I could sense the crowd was getting more restless. They weren't bad people. Not at first. Everyone was just concerned. But, I was starting to get an uneasy feeling. I thought it might be safer on the bus, but I didn't want to leave the church mother alone. I invited her to go with me and I was happy when she accepted. We walked together, against the crowd, in silence, and I helped her into the seat right behind me.

Some other people must have had the same uneasy feeling because they got on the bus with us. I didn't know if they were my original riders and I didn't much care. This wasn't the time or the place to be worrying about that.

Someone on the bus had a radio

It wasn't too long after 7:00 when the word got out. He didn't make it.

Dr. Martin Luther King was dead.

I turned around and looked at the church mother because she had cried out. She didn't see me at first, but eventually she looked back at me, shook her head and said, "Lawd have mercy... This is a terrible, terrible thing."

I will never forget the look on her face and how she said that.

Things got real ugly, real fast. The anger went into overdrive. All of the rage that was just on the surface came pouring out of people. People were tired of being treated like they were less than. People were tired of black folks dying.

I saw it all.

I have never been an eyewitness to anything like it in all my life and I watched in amazement. It was like the announcement came over the radio and BAM...everybody blew up at the same time. People didn't know what to do with themselves but they soon figured it out. They started rioting.

It was mass hysteria.

Oddly, I wasn't afraid.

People were throwing bricks at store windows and buses. It got so bad that the dispatchers called all buses back to the bus barn. Lot of good that did me. I was stuck. It was a good hour or so before I could get moving again.

That's how bad the traffic was backed up.

When I got back to the bus barn, I was amazed at the destruction I saw. I sat and watched the buses as they came in. The buses that were driven by white drivers had all the windows smashed out. The buses that were driven by the black drivers looked like they had just come from the car wash. Not a scratch on them. I felt kinda bad about it.

I have to say, the bus barn was segregated but integrated. The blacks were with the blacks and the whites were with the whites. There wasn't any real animosity that I could see and I didn't have any problems with any of the white drivers. Not to say some of the drivers weren't racist. There were a few. I remember there was this one white driver who, when a black driver came to relieve him, would exit out the rear door of the bus to keep from coming in contact with him.

Most of us just shook our heads about stuff like that. We didn't pay it no never mind. We considered it minor. This was the south in the 1960's. It was the atmosphere during that time.

* * * * *

Memphis burned all night long. I don't think I got a minute of sleep between watching the news, smelling the smoke, hearing sirens, and the sound of breaking glass all night long. On the news, I saw that black folks in the big cities like Chicago and Los Angeles were rioting too. And it was worse there than in Memphis. Somebody got a hold of James Brown and he was on the radio telling people to calm down. I don't know if people listened to him. Tina was crying off and on and I was trying to comfort her but, to be honest, I needed comforting myself. That church mother was right. It was a terrible, terrible thing.

In spite of the civil unrest, I still had to go to work the next morning. Everybody in the service industry had to work. The first leg of my split shift was from 6:00am until 10:00am. I got up extra early to give myself ample time to make it to the bus barn.

There had been no bus service during the night so we got a new start the morning after King died. Even though the National Guard had been called in and there was a curfew starting at 6:00pm, there was still plenty rioting going on during the day. For awhile, people simply weren't afraid of the police. They didn't care.

I started my route and I wasn't afraid. This was the first time some of the white drivers came over to the black drivers and started a conversation. Some of the white drivers were afraid to go out. I had no fear going through the black or white neighborhoods because I was wearing my uniform.

I drove my route and after three or four stops, my bus was full of blacks and whites. And guess what? The white passengers actually spoke to me now. I didn't get it at first until I met a bus going the opposite direction. The bus was driven by a white driver. All of the windows had either been bricked or splattered with eggs. The driver was the only one on the bus. My bus, and the buses of the other black drivers, was so full it was leaning. At one point, I had to ask some passengers to look and see if I could make a right turn. There were so many passengers, I couldn't see out the side mirrors.

I found out later that the passengers were getting off the buses with the white drivers and waiting for buses with black drivers. Worse than that, when a white driver came to a bus stop, the passengers, both blacks and whites would say, "Naw, go on. I'll wait."

I saw people with bricks and rocks, but when they saw that I was black, they let me through with no incident. As the sun began to set, I turned the light on over my head just so people could see a brother was coming through.

I'm telling you, that was the first time in my life my

black skin was right!

I was driving and listening to the passengers. Gone was the raw anger I witnessed the day before. Today, black people were numb with pain, sadness, or embarrassesment. Take your pick.

More than once, I heard someone say, "Why did it have to happen here? Of all places, why Memphis?"

Someone else said, "This man has traveled all over the world but look what happens when he comes here."

I also heard, "He has been in some bad situations. In and out of jail all over the south, but he gets killed in Memphis."

Yeah, mostly people were embarrassed.

I also heard, "Memphis killed Martin Luther King."

* * * * *

The curfew was on for several days and it did what it did.

It calmed the people down and helped the city to regain a sense of normalcy. After a few days, black people started to pick up, clean up, and start over.

Because that's what we do.

* * * * *

I'm back!

I sure do hope y'all enjoyed that little history lesson. I know I did 'cause it gave me time to get my second wind. Now that I've had a bit of a breather, I want to move on and do a bit more recollecting my own self. Let's talk about someone who needs no introduction. Why, they'd drum me out of the Southern Belle society if I didn't have a little talk about JESUS!

PART SEVEN

ALL ABOUT JESUS

UNCLE OSCAR

"MATHEWWWWWWW."

Daddy's sleepy response was, "Aw, the devil."

"MATHEWWWWWWW."

Momma turned over and drowsily said to Daddy, "Matthew, you better go git him 'fore he wakes up the whole blasted neighborhood."

Daddy struggled to get up out of bed. He was at that blessed moment when your mind empties, your body relaxes, and you're just about to slip into your nightly coma. He laid there for a moment hoping the sound he had heard was a dream. But he knew it wasn't. Finally, he sat up and threw his legs over the side of the bed, sitting there for a minute to come to himself.

Once he got up, he quickly found his robe, house shoes, and hurried out of the bedroom. Opening his bedroom door, he saw the attic ladder had been lowered and the light was on in the girl's room. He knew everyone in the house was awake.

"Lawd have mercy," he muttered under his breath.

When he stepped into the living room he was met by his three sons and three daughters, all rudely awakened by the worst alarm clock possible.

Wayne, who was lazily wiping sleep out of his eyes said, "There goes Uncle Oscar again."

Jean sarcastically added, "Yeah, again."

Ignoring them, Daddy looked at the clock on the living room wall. It was 1:30 in the morning. He wasn't surprised. This was about the time Uncle Oscar usually showed up. Daddy opened the front door and stepped out onto the porch. He saw his uncle staggering down the middle of our street.

Shaking his head, he assigned the unpleasant task to his two oldest sons. "Mark, Earl, y'all gon' up the street and git him 'fore he gets any louder."

My brothers knew the drill. Without saying a word, they hurried out of the kitchen door and started up the street.

Uncle Oscar was Grandmother's youngest son. He was Daddy's uncle, but Daddy just called him Oscar because he wasn't that much older. At forty-five, he was a hopeless drunk. He got like that most Saturday nights and since we lived kinda close to Beale Street, he'd come stumbling to our house, yelling at the top of his voice and embarrassing us in front of our high fluting neighbors.

He moved to Memphis in 1950, three years after my family made the move. For the most part, he was a pretty nice guy. Even when he was drunk he wasn't prone to meanness like some people are. He wasn't a bad looking man, either. About 5'9", 200 pounds give or take a few, dark skinned, with a thick, coarse, black afro, and medium brown eyes. Nothing to write home about, nothing to run from.

His dark brown polyester suit and orange shirt was a bold combination for back then, but he was working it. He probably started out the evening looking pretty snappy. But that's just conjecture on my part. I couldn't tell you much about that. From what I'm told, my family only knew the "last call for alcohol" looking Uncle Oscar. His suit was rumpled, tie twisted to the side, and when he took off his jacket you can bet there'd be two big sweat stains under each armpit. No, we rarely saw the good looking Uncle Oscar because when he came to our house, he was usually tore up.

No one understood why he got drunk almost every weekend. His life wasn't that bad; the beer and wine he consumed in mass quantities wasn't that good. He was a single man, had a decent job and made good money. Chopping in tall cotton as Daddy used to say. He had his health and wasn't wanted by the police. He should have been living the good life. But should'a don't mean a doggone thing some time. Should'a don't make no never mind.

For whatever reason, Uncle Oscar couldn't get away from the bottle. And when he imbibed, it was on. And more often than not, these were the times he felt the need to come on our side of town yelling for his escorts to our house. Praise the Lord our uppity neighbors never complained about him. They probably have drunk relatives stuffed in a closet somewhere themselves.

Mark and Earl came in the living room huffing, puffing, and practically dragging Uncle Oscar who had one arm draped over each of their shoulders. He reeked of alcohol.

"Hey Matthewwwww."

That man could stretch a "w," I'll say that for him.

Daddy looked at him and told Mark and Earl to sit Uncle Oscar on the couch.

"Hello Oscar."

Daddy acknowledged his greeting before he turned and went into the kitchen to help Momma bring out the hot coffee they were going to pump into him to start the sobering up process.

When Uncle Oscar came for his visits, my siblings knew to stay close by. They were all just standing in the living room waiting for what they knew was coming next.

Uncle Oscar looked at them and, yelling towards the kitchen door said, "Matthewwwwwww, you sho' got some pretty chir'ren. And so well behaved, too. Y'all come here and let me give y'all some money."

They surrounded him like vultures.

If my memory serves me proper, I believe Uncle Oscar was a truck driver. Or he worked at a trucking company. It was something like that. What I can tell you is this: he was loaded. When his hand came up out of his pants pocket, his fist was stuffed with a big fat wad of money. And I'm not talking all ones either. He was dishing out five dollar bills this time.

Uncle Oscar had just finished dolling out the last gift to my six siblings. Outstretched, waiting hands when Daddy returned to the room. When he saw what was going on he put a stop to it right then and there.

"No! Stop that right now. Give it back. I mean every bit of it. Give it all back, and I mean right now!"

They withheld their groans as they grudgingly returned the money to Uncle Oscar's hands.

You see, if my brothers and sisters had been half as nice as Uncle Oscar thought they were, they wouldn't have tried to take advantage of him when they knew he was drunk. They ought to have been ashamed, but they weren't. I can't say that I blame them though. I probably would have had my hand out too if I had been around. Money was hard to come by in those days.

Daddy wasn't going to let his children take advantage of Uncle Oscar in his inebriated state. See, Daddy has what they call "character." My brothers and sisters have what they call "greed." As soon as they saw their chance for financial gain was over, they each returned to their bedrooms and went to bed. So did Momma. Y'all know how Momma is... She doesn't have time for much foolishness.

They left Daddy to deal with his Uncle. Daddy handed him a cup of black coffee. "Oscar, why you keep doin' this?"

Sorrowfully shaking his head he said, "I don't know Matthewwwww. I just don't know."

"This is the second time this month. What's the matter?"

"I don't know Matthewwwwww. I just don't know." In psychological terms, this is called the "Broken Record Effect."

"Your life don't have to be like this."

It's usually around this time that Uncle Oscar would start crying, real tears too. He answered, "I know Matthewwww... I know."

"You need to be saved."

Wiping his eyes he said, "I'm trying Matthew, really I am."

"You ain't no such'a thing. You don't even go to church. Looka here. Why don't you go to church with me and my family in the mornin'? Jesus can help you but you gotta take the first step. You gotta put yo' trust in Him."

"You is so right Matthew. That's what I gotta do. I gotta go to church. I'm gonna do better. For real this time. This is what I'm gon' do; let me sleep on yo couch tonight and I'll be ready for church first thing in the mornin'."

Sighing Daddy said, "You promise?"

"Sho."

"Okay Oscar. 'Cause you gotta try. You gotta try 'cause nothin' beats a failure but a try."

"Okay Matthew. I'm gon' try. Don't let me oversleep now."

Daddy helped him to get settled on the couch before he went back to bed. When he got settled Momma asked him, "So, what was it this time?"

"Same thing it always is. Much of nothin'."

"That's the second time this month."

"Yeah, I know. Told him that too."

"Seems like it's getting' worse."

"Yeah."

"Did he act like somethin' botherin' 'em? Did he say anythin'?"

Imitating him, Daddy said, "All he said was 'I don't know Matthewwww. I just don't know'."

"He need a wife. That what he need. He need to settle down. Maybe if he settled down and started a family he could do better."

"I don't think it's a wife he needs. Somethin's missing. Somethin's missin' on the inside. Like he's empty and he's trying to fill it up with drinkin'. But drinkin' ain't the answer. I think he need Jesus."

"Well, of course he need Jesus. That goes without sayin'."

Momma waited a moment and added, "He need Jesus and a wife." Momma likes to be right.

"Well, he said he's gonna go to church with us in the mornin'."

Momma said, "Humph…"

Neither Momma nor Daddy were surprised when they walked into the living room the next morning to see an empty couch and $10.00 on the coffee table.

* * * * *

Those Friday or Saturday night visits from Uncle Oscar went on for a few years. Sometimes as little as once a month, sometimes as much as every weekend. He would stagger down the street, yelling Daddy's name, stumble into the house, and try to give the kids a boatload of money. He'd usually end up crying and saying he was going to church the next morning and wind up sneaking out of the house by dawn's early light.

To Daddy's credit, he never gave up on him. No matter how many times he came, Daddy would open our home to him. Daddy never yelled at him or looked at him in disgust. He would witness to him and tell him about Jesus and that he should go to church. Uncle Oscar would listen to him that night and then be gone in the morning before everyone woke up. It was a vicious cycle.

In the early 1960's, out of the blue, Uncle Oscar stopped coming by our house on Saturday nights. In fact, a few months went by and we didn't hear from him. Daddy called him but there was no answer. This went on for quite a while. Momma was relieved. In fact, everyone was. I can't say I'm mad at them either. I don't know how kindly I would have taken it if I were in this disrupting and embarrassing situation.

But Uncle Oscar was Daddy's blood. He felt the situation deeper than everyone else did. He felt responsible for him because they didn't have many relatives in Memphis. They had to look out for one another. Daddy was beside himself with worry, so he caught the bus over to Uncle Oscar's side of town early one Saturday morning. We didn't have a car at that time. From the bus stop, Daddy walked to his house and rang the doorbell.

Uncle Oscar answered the door. Daddy's jaw dropped. Uncle Oscar looked like a different man. He was neatly attired and his eyes were clear and focused. He hadn't looked this good in a long time.

They exchanged pleasantries but Daddy couldn't wait to ask him, "Oscar, why haven't we heard from you in a while?"

In a strong, steady voice Uncle Oscar answered, "Matthew, I can't get over there on Saturday nights no more."

"Say you c'ain't?"

"Naw."

"Why is that?"

"Well, I have to get to bed early so I can get to church on time."

Look at God, y'all.

Through all those years, Daddy didn't think Uncle Oscar was paying him no never mind, but he was. I'll say it again. All shut eyes ain't sleep.

Uncle Oscar told Daddy, "Matthew, I heard you.

Every time you told me I needed Jesus I heard you. I just didn't care. When I'd get up early in the morning and sneak outta yo house I could hear your voice ringin' in my ears. At first, it made me mad, you preachin' to me all the time, but then I came to see that you was right.

"Sho nuf?"

"Yeah. But, I didn't feel like I had the power to do anythin' about it. It wasn't until I got sick of myself that I understood what you were sayin'. It's like one day I just woke up. It was that easy."

Grinning from ear to ear Daddy asked, "Say it was?"

"Yep. I was tired of feeling empty. I was tired of drinkin'. I was tired of being tired. So, I got up early one Sunday mornin', about a couple of months ago give or take, and I walked into that church down on the corner. They were jumpin' around and praisin' God like their britches was on fire or somethin'. It looked kinda funny and it was all I could do to keep from laughing. I started to leave but somethin' kept tellin' me to stay. So, I sat there and listened. You know what happened next?

Daddy was practically sitting on the edge of his seat. He said, "Yeah, man. What happened?"

"Well, they went through the whole service and then they got to the end and had the...uh...what's it called? When the people come down and sit at the front?"

"The altar call?"

Yeah, that's it. The altar call. Well, they had the altar call. Next thing I know, I'm walking down to the front of the church. I hadn't planned to do that but my body started walking down there on it's own. It's like I was in a trance. Next thing I knew, I had gave my life to Jesus."

"Sho nuf?"

"Yeah. And let me tell you this. Now, I can jump around and praise the Lord with the best of them."

Uncle Oscar ended his story with this declaration, "I'm saved now. And I ain't never going back to the bottle."

After he finished testifying, Daddy jumped up from his seat and ran over to Uncle Oscar, pumping his hand like he was getting water from a well. He said, "Well Praise the Lord! That is good news and I sho' am glad to hear it!"

And Uncle Oscar didn't lie either. He never went back to the bottle. Uncle Oscar became a deacon at his church and was a faithful servant of the Lord until the day he died in 1978.

Chapter 28

COUGHING OUT THE SPIRIT

Jesus and I haven't always seen eye to eye on things. I mean, I like Him just fine, but I really can't say I always agree on how things should be run. But, we can talk about that stuff later. To tell the truth, my trouble with Jesus started early in life. I guess you could say we got off on the wrong foot because I didn't even get baptized right...at least that's what I was told.

It all started when I was in the third grade, so that would put me at about seven years old. I had already told Momma and Daddy I wanted to join the church on the upcoming Sunday. They were happy about that.

Anyway, my little knees were knocking as I walked up the center aisle on that blood red carpet at our church, The Greater Open Door Missionary Baptist Church. Our church was a pretty good size back in the day with about three hundred members. I'm telling you the truth, I could feel all six hundred eyeballs on me as I made my way up front to the altar.

When I finally arrived, the church clerk directed me to one of the folding chairs lined up across the front of the church. I quickly walked over and sat with my back to the audience. The choir was singing and the Pastor was trying to get more people to give their lives to Jesus. It was taking forever. After I had been sitting there for what felt like five hours but was actually only a few minutes, the clerk came over to me and asked why I had come down.

I stammered, "'Cause I wanna be saved."

She smiled and wrote my name on a white piece of paper. Then she went over to the next person who had come forward.

I sat there looking around at the Pastor, waiting for the choir to finish singing so I could get this over with. Finally, it was time. The Pastor came to me first, I guess since I was the youngest. They went to the older people last. I think they did that so the church could get happy and start praising God when a big old sinner was saved from hell. To them, my joining at eight years old was cute.

The pastor held his hand out to me. I stood up and walked to him. He said, "Well, I know who this is. Ain't you Brother and Sister DeVault's baby girl."

He put the big microphone in front of my mouth.

I nodded my reply.

"Child, what did you come down here for?"

He put the microphone to me again and I knew he was praying for something audible. My voice was shaking and my heart was beating in my eardrums but I managed to croak out, "I wanna be saved."

I could feel the people smiling.

The pastor pulled me next to him and gave me a hug. Then he said to the congregation, "That's good ain't it, y'all. It's good to come to the Lord when you're young."

Then he asked me, "Do you want to be baptized?" He put that big microphone in front of me again.

I nodded my head because I was done talking.

He said, "Okay. Where is Sister DeVault? Oh, there she is. Sister DeVault, is it alright if we baptize your baby girl?"

I couldn't see Momma over all the people but she must have nodded her head because the Pastor said, "Well, alright then. We're gonna baptize this child in a week or so."

Then he told me I could go back to my seat. I flat out ran back to the rear of the sanctuary and sat down in the pew in front of where the ushers sat. After my heartbeat slowed down and I stopped sweating, I turned around and looked at Daddy who was sitting just behind me with the ushers. He nodded his head and gave me a big smile. Daddy was the head usher at the time. Still is.

I was excited about getting baptized. The next morning at school, I told all my classmates about the coming event. Their attitude was less than enthusiastic. If I remember properly someone said, "So what?"

Those little heathens didn't seem to care about my big day but I remember my teacher was very happy for me. But she would be since she went to a sanctified church. She gave me a big hug and told me she was really proud of me.

The baptism was scheduled for two weeks away on a Sunday evening. All my family in Memphis came to the night service. Jean was still living and she brought her three children, Tina and her daughter as well as Wayne and Denise. I felt special that night.

As soon as we walked through the front door of the church, I could feel the dampness and smell the chlorine. That was because of the pool of water was right there in the sanctuary behind the pulpit.

Momma took me directly to the back of the church to the area just behind the choir stand. She helped me change into a white robe, white socks, and placed a white swimming cap on my head. Then she gave me the look that meant, "behave" and left me with one of the deaconesses so she could get her a good seat in the front of the sanctuary.

After all the candidates, (candidates are what they call the people about to be baptized) were dressed they told us to line up. Then they marched us out of the tiny dressing room. They took us down a short hall and around a corner to the bottom of the steps that led to the baptismal pool right behind the choir stand.

Up until that point, this was all fun to me. I really didn't realize the seriousness of what was about to happen. My mirth continued until I reached the top of the stairs and looked down at the pool. Y'all, I had never seen so much water in my whole life. Black folks didn't have pools where I'm from so the most water I'd ever seen was either in the tub or the Mississippi River. That baptismal water was deep! I knew they didn't expect me to get in all that water 'cause I didn't know how to swim. I was terrified. My seven year old heart went to pounding in my ears again as they nudged me forward.

It was my turn to get dunked but I was just standing there trying to figure out how to get the heck outta there. Finally, one of the church mothers literally pushed me down the stairs and into the warm water. Immediately, I lost my balance. I was so skinny I started to float away. They had to hold me down in the water because I kept rising up. The deacon standing in the pool caught me and pulled me over. Then the Pastor started his speech.

In a loud booming voice he said, "In obedience to the Great Head of the Church, I baptize you, my sister, upon the profession of your faith. In the name of the Father..."

Now, I'd heard this speech enough to know that he was getting ready to dunk me so I started to get really scared. I just knew I was going to drown.

"In the name of the Son..."

Uh oh. Here it comes. I knew the Holy Ghost name was coming next...I had to think fast. In a few seconds, I would be going under. I had to do something quick before they killed me by mistake.

"And in the name of the Holy Ghost."

Well that was it. It was now or never. I opened my mouth to yell, "Stop, I can't swim" but I never got the words out. As soon as I opened my mouth, they dunked me under that water, with my mouth wide open.

I was a sight. I took in so much water it felt like my

lungs were going to explode. I came up coughing and sputtering, thrashing around, and splashing water everywhere. See there, I had a feeling something like this was going to happen.

The deacon didn't even care about my misery. He just held me in a bear hug and walked me back over to the steps on the opposite side of the pool. Somehow they got me out of that pool. As I was walking down the steps, a different church mother was standing at the top of the steps looking at me with her nose turned up and shaking her head. She told me, "You're going to have to get re-baptized. You done coughed out the Spirit."

"I did WHAT?"

Do you have any idea how that sounds to a seven year old? I looked at her like she had two heads. It's a good thing I didn't have my breath back or I would have told her to go shave her moustache.

I didn't tell Momma what the church mother said to me. For a long time after that I thought I was going to hell for sure. But there wasn't anything I could do about that. There was no way I was ever going to get back into that water again.

ANGELS WATCHING OVER ME

Langston Hughes momma sho' did have it right when she said in that poem, "Life for me ain't been no crystal stair." I'm with her on that one. Because after I moved out of the family house in Memphis and settled in Los Angeles, I had all sorts of problems. Everything that could go wrong went there.

I've been broke, I've been sick, and I've been unemployed. Y'all name it and I've been it. More on that later. But, each trial brought a new revelation. Yes, I've learned a lot over the years as a result of going through a bunch of stuff. And, I'd like to share the conclusion I've come to, and here it is…all this pain and suffering and hurting has got to go!

I mean it! It just seems to me that if I do what I'm supposed to do and live like the Bible says, I should just walk on streets lined with rose petals. Those angels in the Bible, Gabriel and Michael, should be following me everywhere I go making sure I don't come up on any trouble during the course of my day. And, if someone dares to oppose me, they should rain down fire on their heads and obliterate them on the spot. Similar to the treatment Lot's wife got when she turned to a pillar of salt.

Okay, I'm exaggerating. I'm just saying that it seems like life should be easy and free from major stress if you're living right. Sadly, it's not like that at all. That gets on my nerves sometimes.

And just a doggone minute… Before you turn up your

nose and start looking down on me, I think you need to be honest with yourself. You know good and well, sometimes He lets things happen that gets on your nerves. You just don't want to say it out loud.

I can just hear you, "Humph…supposed to be a Christian and talking about she don't like how the Good Lord is running things. I'll tell you what her problem is. She thinks she knows more than God. That's the problem right there."

I know some of y'all are thinking something along those lines. I can feel it in my spirit. Well, I got a word for every one of you. Y'all can act self righteous if you want, like you've never had any doubts. But as for me, I'm in search of the truth. And the first step on that journey is to admit that I don't always agree with how my life is unfolding.

* * * * *

Let me say it this way…. Just because I don't always like how God does things sometimes, I have to give Him credit for sending angels to watch over me and encourage me when I've been down and out.

When I moved to Los Angeles, I lived with Mae and Henry for the first four months. During this time, Denise was living with Mark and his wife Margaret. We were both saving up to get our own place and the blessed day finally arrived when we found a beautiful townhouse in Inglewood, California. The place was a bit more than we could afford, but we were both hardworking girls and knew how to live on a budget.

Things went well for about two months when, wouldn't you know it, Denise lost her job. That meant we both had to live on my salary and that wasn't much. Y'all we wuz broke! We barely had enough food to eat. We would share a can of vegetables and a slice of cornbread for dinner each night and that was it. Meat was out of the question. It was a hard row to hoe, but we were determined to make it on our own so we didn't tell anyone how hard up we were. And then, guess what? Things got worse.

The management company decided to turn the townhouse we were renting into condos. We couldn't afford to buy so we had sixty days to get out. We managed to find a 1-bedroom apartment in the Mid-Wilshire district, which was a couple of miles from where I worked downtown and we moved without a day to spare.

I hated that tiny apartment. Hated it. I hated it and everything it stood for. The only good thing was, it was cheaper than our two-bedroom townhouse, and Denise was able to get a part-time job so financially, things improved. We weren't out of the woods, though.

I got the bedroom because, after all, I was the only one working. Denise slept on a daybed in the living room. Many nights I would cry myself to sleep because I was tired of being broke, I missed Momma and Daddy, and I hated not having a car and being able to move around. I hated life.

I was contemplating all of this when I was walking home from work one day. I wanted to take the bus home, but after three buses, filled to capacity passed me by, I decided to hike home, it was only about three miles.

I had made it to about two blocks from my street when a homeless man approached me. He was a black guy, filthy and smelly. His clothes were torn and covered with dirt. He was too for that matter. His afro hadn't been combed in ages and he had an overgrown beard. I turned my head because I didn't want to make eye contact with him. I was in no mood for any foolishness.

My ignoring him had no effect. Merrily he said, "Hello young lady. How are you today?"

I kept it short and sweet. "Fine."

He said, "Are you sure?"

There was something about his voice that caught my attention. I relaxed a bit and said, "Yes, I am sure. Thank you for asking." (That's how Southern Belles respond.)

He asked, "Do you think you could spare a bit of change so I can get something to eat?

I knew that was coming. I knew it. I can't tell you what happened to me, but the floodgate of my mouth opened up and I told that man every problem I had.

I said, "Naw. I ain't got no money. I'm barely making it myself. I don't even have enough to eat for myself. I need a car. I need to get my hair did. I don't have anythin' to wear to church. So, naw. I ain't got no money to be givin' you."

After I finished my grammatically challenged presentation, I looked at him with fire in my eyes waiting for him to curse me out or at least say, "A simple no was all you had to say."

I was ready for a fight and my posture said, "Now what do you have to say to that? Come on with it."

But the fight never came. I was surprised to see him smiling sweetly at me. His smile melted all of my anger.

He said, "I know you are having a hard time right now. You are being tried in the fire, but you will come out as pure gold."

The sound of his voice was so calm and peaceful that it melted my anger. Standing with him at the corner of Wilshire and Vermont, I felt ashamed to the depths of my soul. Shame for verbally attacking him in public. Ashamed that he took the high road and didn't sink to my level.

Quickly, I reached into my purse and pulled out a dollar. My last dollar, I might add. Bowing my head in shame, I handed it to him. He took the money, said thank you and turned and walked away. I stood there for a few seconds watching him go before I turned to make my way home.

It was about five seconds later that I had the urge to talk to him so I quickly turned back around to call out for him. No one was there. This man just vanished into thin air. I ran in the direction he went looking everywhere but he was gone. There were no buildings he could have gone into, no alleys he could have ducked into.

He vanished into thin air.

I realized that God had sent an angel to encourage me. It worked too. I felt like a million bucks and could have skipped home. I had a smile on my face for the rest of the night. Because, even though my situation hadn't changed, it made me feel better just knowing that God was aware of it. My whole outlook changed. You know what they say, "Just a little talk with Jesus makes it right!"

It wasn't until I got into bed that I thought, *Hey, that angel took my dollar!*

* * * * *

That was the first time God sent someone to me. The second time was a bit different.

I happen to be one of the few people in America who loves to work out. I love getting up early in the morning and going for walks or hikes, but usually I would have to wait until after work because of the morning traffic. I like to be outside communing with nature. No gym for me. Guess that's the Southern Belle in me.

When I lived in the mid-Wilshire district, and after I got a car, my favorite workout was to drive up to Griffith Park and walk on one of the trails. I used to do this all the time after work. I'd rush home, change into my sweats and head for the hills.

One day I made it to the park at about 6:00pm. It was the middle of summer so there was sunlight everywhere. Strange thing though, the park was eerily quiet. There were absolutely no cars in the normally crowded lot. I thought to myself, *That's odd, I wonder where everyone parked?* But

I didn't pay it no never mind.

Something else struck me as odd. There were no people around. I'm talking nobody. I was all alone. I don't think I've ever went to Griffith Park and didn't see one, single, solitary living being. Still, I thought it was odd, but I didn't pay it much mind.

I started walking when a strange feeling came over me. Like a jittery nervousness. In my head, I heard a still, soft voice say, "Go back."

I didn't pay it no never mind.

I kept walking. The jittery feeling was getting more intense but I kept moving because I'm rather fanatical about my workout and I really wanted to get it over and done with. I have a one-track mind and when I'm focused on doing something it's all I can think about until it's done.

In my head, the voice is a little louder. "Go back."

I didn't pay it no never mind.

I was still walking and finally reached the base of the trail. By now, the jitters were flutters and I was looking around and over my shoulder because the whole situation still didn't feel right. I began to wonder if I should probably be concerned that there was no one else on the trail. I made a mental note to be very careful and aware of my surroundings.

As I started up the trail, the still soft voice is no longer still or soft because the Lord knows I'm kinda slow.

In my head I hear one word, at a deafening octave, **"DANGER!!!"**

Oh, now I get it. I'm in danger.

Y'all, the Lord finally got my attention. I stopped in my tracks, turned tail, and ran for all I was worth. I was running so fast that I was unable to stop my momentum and passed my car. I jumped in from the passenger side and tore out of there on two wheels.

* * * * *

When I woke up the next day, I turned on the early morning news as was my normal routine. My mouth dropped wide open as I listened to the first report,

"The body of a young woman was found in Griffith Park by hikers early this morning. It appears the attack happened on the trail in the early evening on yesterday. The victim had been raped and beaten to death…"

Lord Almighty!

All I can say is, it's a good thing I was standing in front of the couch because my leg bone forgot it was connected to my knee bone and both eagerly went their separate ways. Y'all I flat out collapsed. It took me a moment to come to myself, but when I did all I could say was "Thank You, Jesus!"

It could have been me! My recollecting days would have been over. I felt awful for the poor young women who ran upon the devil in the park the previous day. But I was so thankful the good Lord was watching out for me when I didn't even know I was in danger.

God sho' is good, ain't He?

CHAPTER 30

PLAYING WITH THE GOD

Mae is my oldest living sister. If I'm not mistaken, she's eighteen years my senior, but I'm not sure. We are all at the "don't ask, don't tell" point in our lives as far as age is concerned. Still, it didn't bode well for me when, a few years back, Mae and I were sitting in church and a lady came to us and asked if we were twins. Mae thought it was funny, but I didn't crack a smile 'cause cataracts ain't funny.

To let Momma tell it, growing up, Mae got more whippin's than all of us kids put together. She had a hard head and knew how to use it. Her backside must be leather from getting tanned all the time. Mae wasn't scared of a whippin' the way I was. I ran from trouble. Mae embraced it. After years of witnessing Mae's antics, I sometimes wonder if the good Lord is up in heaven, shaking his head and thinking, *Who do I call on?*

Mae left Memphis in 1964 to live, first in Nashville, then Chicago and finally settling in Los Angeles with her husband Henry and son David. They moved around because Henry went to Tennessee State on a football scholarship and was drafted into the NFL by the Chicago Bears and was traded to the Los Angeles Rams. During this time of living away from the nest, Mae had time to continue to grow and mature into a fine wife and mother. She also had time to develop a few unsavory skills. Like cussin'.

I can remember it like it was yesterday, but it was in

the early 1980's because I was in high school. My
mother's brother, Uncle Andrew, had just died and Mae
came home to Memphis for the funeral. The funeral was a
somber occasion and we were all pretty shaken up about it.
After the service, Momma, Daddy, Mae, Denise,and I
crowded into Daddy's mint green Pontiac.

We were near the end of the processional of cars on the
way to the gravesite. Out of thirty cars, our car was
probably about number twenty five. Out of respect to
Momma, no one was talking. We were just riding along,
running the red lights and keeping up with the rest of the
cars. In spite of the occasion, it was a calm, pleasant ride
until the unthinkable happened. A man must have gotten
tired of waiting on our long processional to pass. He must
have thought, *If you can't beat 'em, join 'em* because he cut
in line and started riding along with us in order to run the
red lights.

Daddy was driving and saw what happened. He said,
"Would y'all look at this?"

Momma just shook her head.

Mae yelled, "Daddy, pull around him." All the while,
she was reaching over me like I wasn't there and cranking
down the window like she was going to pull that handle out
of the shaft. When I looked at her pursed lips, I knew that
what was about to happen wouldn't be nice, pretty or
Christ-like.

Daddy got out of the lane and sped up to catch the
man. I was thinking, *Daddy no!* and praying he could read
my thoughts. He couldn't. As soon as Daddy pulled up
next to that car, Mae proceeded to cuss that man out like he
was a demon straight from the pit of hell.

She called that man everything but a child of God. I
had never heard of such. I promise you, I thought I saw
steam coming out of her ears. I looked to the front seat.
Daddy had a shocked look on his face and Momma had
slumped down in her seat, probably praying that none of

our relatives could hear those words coming out of Mae's mouth.

She let loose on that man for a good two minutes and ended with, "Can't you see we're in mourning, you sorry @#%#$ *&!%>."

When she finished her monologue, she leaned back over to her seat and folded her arms, eyes looking straight ahead and an amazingly satisfied look on her face.

Nobody said anything for a few minutes until Denise broke the silence with, "Uh... Feel better?"

Mae said, "Yes."

After a few minutes her conscience must have started to get to her. She added. "Well, y'all know he was wrong."

She said it like she thought what she did was right.

* * * * *

Mae wasn't above playing with God either, bless her soul. It was in the mid 1980's and Momma had come to Los Angeles for a visit. We were having a good ol' time showing her the sights and taking her to nice restaurants. Sunday morning came and we all decided to take Momma to West Angeles Church of God in Christ where I was a member. Mae and Denise were still members of a Baptist Church that I had left to join West Angeles. Mark, Earl, and Wayne told us they would catch up with us for lunch after church. Heathens!

Anyway, we got up early and made it to the service in time to get a good seat. The Pastor, Bishop Charles Blake, was up preaching the word and working everybody up into a worshipful frenzy. I glanced over at Momma and I could see she was enjoying herself. Bishop Blake was almost finished with the message when I guess he got a word from the Lord. He said that the Lord wanted to deliver some people from smoking.

He said, with great authority, "I want everyone of you

who smokes to come up here to this altar so I can lay hands on you."

As an afterthought, he said, "And if you have any cigarettes, bring them with you and place them on the altar."

Mae was sitting there like she didn't smoke, but she does. Heathen! She was looking around, admiring the stained glass and acting like she didn't have a care in the world. I start to tell her about it, but then a definite need for life preservation as well as a desire to not get cussed out in church encouraged me to keep my eyes looking straight ahead. Denise did the same, but we both know Mae's acting up in church.

Again!

Momma ain't scared of Mae so out of the corner of my eyes, I saw her turn to Mae and give her a long, sorrowful look. A look that says, "Baby, you know you need to be delivered from smoking so why don't you get up and go up there and get some help. I love you." That's exactly what that puppy dog look said.

Mae sat there for a full minute before she sighed loudly, reached down and got her cigarettes from her purse and marched up to the front. There were about twenty people up there. Probably hundreds more should have been up there because the church seated about thirteen hundred folks so you know more than twenty people smoked!

It's like Bishop Blake was waiting for Mae because when she got up there, he started praying. He went to each person, laid hands on them and prayed for them. He got to Mae and placed his hand on her head and spoke a few words before moving on. Then he moved to the next person and started praying for them. When he finished praying for the next person he stopped, turned and looked at Mae, backed up and prayed for her again. That must have been the Holy Ghost telling him that Mae needed a double dose because while he was praying for her she was up there thinking, *I wish this man would hurry up, I need a cigarette.*

The whole thing took about five minutes and soon we were on our way to the townhouse Denise and I shared.

After dropping the three of us off to change for lunch, Mae said, "I'll be back in about thirty minutes." She then headed to her Beverly Hills condo where she and Henry lived.

Now, as soon as she got home, Mae pulled out her spare pack of cigarettes and lit it up for a smoke. You see, she had no intention of quittin gsmoking. She just went up for prayer to please Momma. Ain't that a mess? To let her tell it, she had tried to quit on several occasions and wasn't able to do it.

Well, guess what? God don't like ugly. As soon as Mae took the very first puff on that cigarette, she like to died. Sho' did. She got choked and was coughing violently. Her body was heaving and she couldn't breathe. She stumbled to the bed and was about to pass out when Henry came running in the room and caught her. It was a good thirty minutes before she could breathe properly.

Before she left the house to come and pick us up for lunch she threw the pack of cigarettes into the trash. But even after that coughing fit, she was only thinking, *This must have been a bad batch.*

The experience of not being able to breathe had scared her so bad that she had no desire to smoke for the rest of the day.

That was on Sunday. It was Wednesday when it dawned on Mae that she hadn't had a cigarette. To put it simply, she forgot about smoking. She had no desire for it. God took it. She had no withdrawals. She didn't miss it and she hasn't had a cigarette in over twenty years.

She called me and told me this. I was so happy for her. I remember the times when she had tried on her own and couldn't do it.

Ain't it something how God will bless you in spite of you?

* * * * *

It was revival time at West Angeles. I was so excited because I had heard of the big time preacher that was coming to my church. I had seen him on television and I knew he had a powerful ministry. I told Mae about it.

I had attended the first two nights of the revival before I called Mae and said, "Mae, you should come to my church for revival tomorrow night. The minister is very powerful. Everyone he lays hands on is slain in the spirit."

Mockingly, she said, "Slain in the spirit? Yeah right."

I asked her, "What do you mean by that?"

"That's okay for some people, but not for me."

"Why not?"

"I think some people are just weak. They see other people falling out and they fall out too."

"Mae, please don't say that. Look, why don't you just come and see for yourself.

"Can this guy preach?"

"Yes of course."

"Well, okay. I'll come. But I'm just coming to hear the word. I'm not interested in all that other stuff."

I agreed, "Fair enough."

Mae met me at church at 6:30pm and we hurried in to get a good seat. The service was high that night. The minister didn't disappoint. He reached the end of his message and started calling on people in the congregation to come down front for prayer. I got a little nervous because I didn't know how Mae would take this part of the service. I glanced over at her and saw her pull out her Bible and stared reading.

The minister called on four people. He prayed for them and as soon as he laid hands on them, they hit the floor. Slain in the spirit. I saw Mae look up each time the people went down. I saw her shake her head after each person went down. I marveled at her skepticism, but then remembered, that's how Mae is.

Anyway, he called a few more people up on the west side of the church and then he walked over to the side we were sitting on. I saw the minister point to someone in our section. My heart skipped a beat because it looked like he was pointing to me. And then, the horror! He was pointing at Mae.

I nudged her and said, "Uh, Mae, he's calling you."

Mentally, she was in another place. She said, "Who?"

"The preacher, he wants you to come up front."

She said, "I ain't goin' up there." Her dialect went right back to Memphis.

I went right with her. I told her, "You gotta go. Girl, he's callin' you!"

She finally looked at the minister and saw that he was pointing to her. Everyone in the church was looking around trying to see who was so slothful about getting to the altar. A battle was raging inside Mae. I could feel it. She wasn't above getting up and walking right out of the church saying, "Forget all of y'all. I ain't a member here anyhow."

But she didn't do that. Praise the Lord. Finally, she got up, slow as you please. I heard her mutter something under her breath. I tried to think happy thoughts.

She sauntered down to the altar and managed to make it before midnight. When she finally arrived, the minister walked over to her and started praying for her. I didn't bow my head for this prayer. I was looking straight at both of them.

It was a right good prayer too. But that's not the thing. I could tell by the tone of the prayer that the minister was about to wrap it up. Then it happened. Just when he was beginning to raise his hand and place it on Mae's forehead.

Mae hit the floor.

Now, wait a minute. Let me tell you again because I want you to get a good mental picture of what I just said. When the minister was BEGINNING to raise his hand to touch Mae's forehead, POOF! She hit the floor. He never even touched her. His hands were no where near her and down she went.

And she was out for a good while too. The minister said, "Let her lay there for awhile."

They did. Mercifully, the missionaries ran over and covered her with one of those large clothes so the people couldn't see all of her business.

When she finally came up, some of the men helped her to a seat. The minister had finished praying and it was time to go home.

Now, I'm a Christian. Try to be, anyway. But, I'm telling y'all the truth, it took every ounce of the Holy Spirit in me to keep from saying something like, "For somebody who don't believe in being slain in the Spirit, you sho' went down pretty fast. You could have at least waited until he touched you."

Nope, I'm a Christian. I don't do stuff like that. I decided to keep all my gloating on the inside where it belongs. I focused on the new, positive changes I would see in my sister as a result of the quiet time she spent with the Lord. I rejoiced because I just knew a new day was coming.

The last thing my sister said to me as we walked to our cars was, "I ain't never, ever going to your church again."

That girl is gonna be the death of me!

CHAPTER 31

REVEREND BEACON

Before I go any further, I think I need to clear the air. I've been telling you about my family and all the adventures and misadventures for a while now. I just finished telling you about Mae playing with the Lord. I was hoping y'all would get a chuckle out of some of the crazy things that girl has done.

Yes, she's a strong black woman. Yes, she's opinionated. Yes, she does not hold her tongue. Yes, she...well, you get my drift. She's all of that stuff. But now, I need to add something about Mae. She's the type of person who would take a bullet for you if you needed her to. She is a loyal and devoted friend and sister. She's smart. A problem solver. Not only that, she takes care of business. She doesn't spend much time sitting around ringing her hands about a situation. She gets results. That's why, when trouble comes, Mae is usually the first person to get the wake up call.

* * * * *

The phone call came in the early morning hours. In case you haven't noticed, calls that come at the ungodly middle of the night/early morning hours are never good news. Never. So, when your phone wakes you up from a dead sleep, just prepare to get the Kleenex or a good book. Chances are, you'll either be crying or so agitated that you won't be able to get back to sleep.

It was Mae's best friend, Doreen, calling. Doreen's sister, Monica, was suicidal. Mae knew that Monica's life was a rough road. She was a good girl, about 25 years old, who had made some bad choices, especially where men were concerned. She had been a victim of domestic violence and suffered from depression as a result. Monica said she no longer wanted to live and couldn't bear the thought of seeing another day. Doreen's family was on edge about how to handle this situation. As far as I know, black folk don't commit suicide that much.

After Doreen had delivered the burden into Mae capable hands, Mae spent the rest of the early morning hours trying to figure out what she could do to help. Knowing this problem was bigger than her, she decided it was a job for the Lord to handle. As soon as the clock struck 9:00am, Mae was on the phone calling the church to speak to her Pastor. The church secretary told Mae that the Pastor was out of town preaching, but gave her the number of one of his associates who was covering for him. Mae gave him a call.

The church secretary answered the phone, "Holy Trinity Baptist Church, can I help you?"

Mae said, "Yes, I need to speak to Pastor Davis?"

"May I ask who's calling?"

Sighing loudly Mae said, "My name is Mae."

"Hmmmmm, Mae. Are you a member of Holy Trinity?"

Sighing louder and with an attitude, Mae answered, "No, I am not."

In an effort to curtail any further questions, she added, "I am a member of Sacred Mountain Baptist Church. I have a problem and I need to speak with a pastor. Pastor Mitchell is out of town so they told me to call Pastor Davis. Can I speak with him now?"

"And what is your call pertaining to?"

"It's personal. Okay? It's a matter of life and death,

okay? Can I just speak to him?"

"Well, it's just that everybody calls wanting to speak to the pastor and he's a very busy man. Most of the time, they can speak to someone else on the staff."

To this, Mae said absolutely nothing. I admire her for that.

"Well, okay. I'll see if he's available. Hold please."

It was a good five minutes before Pastor Davis came to the phone. "This is Pastor Davis."

About time, Mae thought.

Her words came out in a rush, "Hello Pastor Davis. My name is Mae and I'm a member of Sacred Mountain. I called to speak to Pastor Mitchell, but he is out of town. I was given your number. This is a matter of life and death. I got a call this morning and a friend is on the verge of committing suicide. She..."

He interrupted her, "Just a minute. I'm sorry but I can't talk to you right now."

"Say what?"

"Since you're not a member of Holy Trinity I can't speak to you without speaking to your pastor first."

"Pastor Davis, I just told you Pastor Mitchell is out of town. He's off somewhere preaching. His secretary told me to call you. If he told me to call you, why do you have to speak to him first?"

"I have to make sure it's okay."

"That's well and swell, pastor. The only problem is, this is a matter of life and death. I don't really have time for you to call Pastor Mitchell for him to tell you what I just told you."

"Well, I'm sorry, but that's our procedure."

"The 'matter of life and death' means nothing to you, huh?"

"What part of the word 'procedures' don't you understand?"

"Pastor, thank you for nothing." Mae hung up.

Ain't that about nothing?

Mae was so mad she didn't know what to do with herself. When did procedures become more important than people? When did church become a long roll of red tape? What just happened here?

She didn't give herself much time to dwell on this foolishness. She went into her living room and got the phone book. Yes, the phone book…this was way before we even knew what a Google was. Mae flipped over to the church directory and found the number she knew she needed to call.

The receptionist answered the phone, "West Angeles Church of God in Christ. How may I direct your call?"

"Hello. I have a very bad problem. I have a friend on the verge of suicide and I need some help."

"Hold on. I'm transferring you to the counseling department."

Less than a minute passed. A soothing, calm, but concerned voice answered the phone. "Sister, this is Reverend Beacon. Tell me what's going on."

Mae went through the whole story and told him everything she knew about Monica's situation. While she was speaking, she could hear Revered Beacon encouraging her to continue. His tenor was the way you'd think a preacher would sound, deep, rich, and in command of the situation. He put her at ease.

When Mae finished her story, she said, "Do you think I can make an appointment to bring her in today?"

He said, "Yes, definitely. But we need to pray about this right now."

Mae said, "Pray on."

The good Reverend started praying, "Heavenly Father, Even though Monica is in a dark place we know that Jesus is a light and He can reach her even in the darkness of where she is right now. I'm praying that this prayer will touch her heart and turn her mind away from the thoughts that she is thinking. And by the power of the blood of Jesus we are touching and agreeing that Monica's mind is healed. It is done. IT IS DONE in the name of Jesus."

Y'all that's just a small portion of the prayer he prayed because he went on for about five minutes. Mae told me that his prayer was so powerful that she had to jump up from where she was sitting in her bedroom. She was pacing the floor and energy was flowing through her whole body. Mae said she knew it was done and that Monica would be alright. Mae's mind was at peace.

After Revered Beacon had finished praying they were both silent for a few minutes.

He was the first to speak. "Well sister, I believe God is going to work it out alright. Do you still want to make that appointment to bring Monica in?"

Mae answered, "Oh no sir. No sir. I don't think we need to do that anymore."

"Are you sure? She can still come in. We'd be happy to sit and talk to her."

"Well, it's up to her. But as for me, I believe it is done. By the way, what did you say your name was again?"

"It's Reverend Beacon."

"Beacon?"

"Yes. B-E-A-C-O-N. As in light."

Mae got her trusty black pen and wrote his name on the memo pad by the phone. "B-E-A-C-O-N. Got it. Well, I want to thank you, Reverend. You have been a blessing."

Mae tore off the sheet and placed it on the counter with the outgoing mail.

"No problem sister. Call back if you need to."

Mae got dressed and went to work with the assurance that all was well. She was so at peace that she forgot about Monica. She didn't think about her until well into the afternoon. She called Doreen to check on Monica.

Doreen said, "Well, you're not going to believe it, but I talked to Monica a few hours ago and she said she felt better than she's felt in years. She said the depression has lifted and she wants to live. She can't explain it. Monica keeps saying, 'I see the light. I see the light.'"

After Mae told Doreen about her call to the counseling department, they both had a good old time praising God.

I didn't find out about all of this until later that evening when Mae called me and asked me about Reverend Beacon.

Now, I had only been a member of West Angeles for a few years, but I did know one thing and I told Mae that. "Mae, we don't have Reverends in the Church of God in Christ. They're called Elders."

"Really. I could have sworn he said Reverend. Well, it doesn't matter. Do you know who he is?"

"No. I don't think I've ever heard of him, but I haven't been there that long. Let me ask my friend, Julie. She's been a member for over fifteen years. I'll bet she knows him."

I called Julie as soon as I hung up. She told me there wasn't a Reverend Beacon at West Angeles that she knew of. She also told me that the church doesn't use the title Reverend. I knew that.

I called Mae back and told her what Julie said.

Mae's reply was, "She don't know everybody in that whole church. Don't worry about it. I'll call the church tomorrow and get to the bottom of this.

Her curiosity was about to get the best of her. She could hardly wait for the next morning to come so she could get her answer.

When the receptionist picked up, Mae asked for the counseling department.

A friendly voice asked, "Counseling Department, can I help you?"

"Yes, I called yesterday and spoke with a Reverend Beacon. Is he there today?"

The receptionist hesitated before saying, "Did you say

Reverend Beacon?"

"Yes. Beacon. As in light."

"We don't have anyone on staff by that name."

Mae said, "There must be some sort of mistake. I called you guys yesterday, at about this time, and spoke to him. He told me his name was Reverend Beacon. He even spelled it for me. He told me it was Beacon – like the light. Then he prayed with me."

"I see."

"Wait a minute. Do your counselors use assumed names?"

"Oh no ma'am. We're Christians. We use our own names."

"But this doesn't make sense."

"Yes, I know. We didn't have a male counselor working here yesterday morning."

"Oh, I see."

"And another thing. We don't use the title Reverend. Our ministers are called Elders."

Mae was reluctant to let it go, but there's no use beating a dead horse. She said, "Well, I just wanted to tell him that the prayer had been answered and all is well."

"Well, praise the Lord! That's good to know. Thank you for the praise report sister. God bless you"

"Yeah. Uh-huh."

The line disconnected but Mae was sitting there with the phone still pressed to her ears. Her mind was traveling a mile a minute. She could still hear the sound of his strong, powerful, yet peaceful voice ringing in her ears. She could still feel the energy that flowed through the phone lines and had her doing the holy dance in her bedroom.

Mae was wondering if she could have been mistaken when she remembered something. She wrote his name on the memo pad next to the phone. She rushed to the living room and started going through the outgoing mail until she found the small slip of paper that she was looking for. As she looked at it, her hands started to tremble and she broke out into a sweat. She slowly eased herself down onto the barstool at the counter.

Her eyes were glued to the paper where the two words were written. True enough, it was just as she remembered. She'd written Reverend Beacon. The only difference was the words were now written in red ink.

Mae reached over and picked up the ink pen that was lying by the memo pad. The same pen she wrote with the previous day. She made a big circle and the black ink flowed onto the paper. She wrote Reverend Beacon in black ink. How did the words turn red? Mae knew neither she nor Henry owned a red ink pen.

Mae sat there for about fifteen minutes wondering who she had spoken to.

She still has that piece of paper to this day.

* * * * *

WHOA Nellie!

Don't go another further…

That means STOP!

I've been recollecting over the river and through the woods, haven't I? It seems like y'all know just about everything there is to know about me, my family, and the times we shared together. Well, not really, sorry to say. There is one more recollection I want to share.

It's what I was thinking about before I got that text telling me that M. Sue from Columbia, South Carolina had passed away. You remember the day my boss called in sick and I ate those delicious peanut butter cookies because they are my very favorite. And then, I found out I was a Southern Belle. And then I started recollecting on Great Grandpa Anderson and Big Mama Sarah and Papa George. And then….

Okay, okay, I'll stop stalling and get to it. But I gotta warn y'all. It's gonna get a bit rocky through here, but don't you worry yourself none. I suspect it'll be alright after awhile. So, here's the story that started it all. It's about *SAYING GOODBYE.*

PART EIGHT

SAYING GOODBYE

THE SWEET BY AND BY

She had made up her mind and nothing was going to change it. Mule headed is what we called her. That's how she was. Even if Momma threatened to whip her, she wouldn't change it. Once she saw the shiny teal blue swimsuit that our Aunt Cassie, Momma's baby sister, gave to our financially challenged family, she knew she had to learn how to swim so she'd have a reason to wear it. It was much too pretty to wear in the little plastic pool we used to fill up with the water hose in our backyard.

Mae wanting to swim was a shock to everyone, especially Momma and Daddy. They never, in their wildest dreams, thought any of their three daughters would have fallen in love with a piece of fabric and then practically demand to be taken clear across town for a swimming lesson. But this is Mae we're talking about. To tell the truth, they should have known better.

If anyone would have wanted to do something that no one else in the family had ever done before, it would have been Mae. Fifteen years old, nearly six feet tall, gate-mouthed, forceful, and determined Mae, in all her Mae-ness. Ain't scared of nothing or nobody Mae. And when she set her mind to do something, she'd upset the whole house until it was done. That's Mae for you.

Forget the fact that it was 1959 in Memphis, Tennessee. Forget the fact that the closest pool where black folk were allowed to swim was at T.O. Fuller State Park, way over on the other side of town, past Walker Homes.

Forget that Momma was pregnant, busy keeping house and cooking for her family of eight and that Daddy was working two jobs and tired. Forget that they both had better things to do with their time than carting six black children back and forth to the park. 'Cause, you know, if you took one child, you had to take them all.

Well, in spite of forgetting all those facts, it was a warm Saturday morning in June when Daddy pulled our Pontiac out of the driveway and headed toward the park for Mae's first lesson. Like I said, Jean, Mark, Tina, Earl, and Wayne went along for the ride. Back then, you didn't just drop your kids off in the park. No, if the kids went, at least one of the parents went also and Daddy was it because Momma was pregnant with my sister Denise. I wouldn't show up until much, much, much later 'cause I'm way younger than everyone else. And prettier, but that's another story.

The ride to the park took forever. Or so it seemed. Mae could hardly contain her excitement. She loved how she looked in the one-piece bathing suit. She held the white plastic swimming cap in her hand and she was still debating if she was going to wear it. Momma had given her strict instructions to put the cap on her head before she got into the pool so she wouldn't have to hot comb her hair again.

In fact, Momma's exact words were, "If you get your hair wet it's gonna be you and me."

Mae knew what that meant because even at eight months pregnant, Momma could still swing a mean switch.

Her heart was racing as she approached the pool, but when she got there, reality set in. *That sho' is a lot of water,* she thought, as she looked at the other people jumping in the water like it wasn't anything. She had no idea so many black folks knew how to swim.

Even though she was a bit afraid of the water, she was fascinated with the idea of a pool. Summoning up her courage, she put the swimming cap on her head and eased herself into the warm water. The sensation was totally foreign to her. She was delighted with the weightlessness that almost overtook her as she willed herself to go into the deep end. She was hugging the sides of the pool when she heard a friendly male voice behind her ask, "Are you okay?"

It took a while, but she finally managed to maneuver herself into a position where she could see who spoke to her. He looked to be about her age and height, well built with dark brown skin and very short hair. So short, in fact, that he appeared to be almost bald. He had a good-looking face, handsome actually. His red swimming trucks had the word "Lifeguard" written on them. He made her a little nervous. When nervous, Mae says stupid stuff.

"Are you a lifeguard?" she asked. Smooth.

He didn't even look at her like she was stupid. He answered, "Yeah. Are you okay?"

"Yeah."

"Do you know how to swim?"

I'm guessing the death grip she had on the side of the pool was his first clue.

Mae answered, "No."

"Are you afraid of the water?"

"No. Well, yeah. A little. I'm gonna stay near the edge so I can hold on."

"There's nothing to be afraid of. Come on. Let me float you around. We can go to the deep end if you like."

He didn't have to ask her twice. He swam over to her and before long she was floating around the pool with him.

During the course of their time in the pool, she learned that his name was Jonathan, he was sixteen years old and an only child. He went to Mitchell Road High School, one of the eight high schools for blacks in Memphis at the time. She told him that she went to Carver High School and was the third oldest of six children with another on the way.

Under the ever watchful eyes of Daddy, who was sitting under a tree chatting with some of the other fathers, Mae and Jonathan hit it off just fine. She hung around him for the remainder of his shift. After a couple of hours, Daddy gave the signal that it was time to leave and went off to collect his five other children who were scattered all over the park. Jonathan asked her for her phone number.

She eagerly told him, "Whitehall 2-7715."

He called that same evening.

Now, before I go on let me tell y'all something. My parents were very strict, but they didn't have a problem with Mae talking to Jonathan on the phone. Our phone was in the main hallway of our tiny South Memphis home. And believe me, there wasn't any such thing as a private phone call with eight people living in a two bedroom house.

Privacy wasn't the only issue. You could wind up hurt when talking on the phone if you didn't watch out for the attic stairs which folded down into the tiny hallway. The attic is where my brothers Mark, Earl, and Wayne slept. And let me tell you, if they had to go to the bathroom or had a hankering for something in the kitchen they would fold those stairs right out onto your head if you weren't paying attention.

Well, it wasn't long before Jonathan was calling two and three times a week. There was nothing romantic about the calls, just two friends chatting, getting to know each other and catching up on what was going on in their parts of town. Mae even snuck and called him a couple of times, but my parents frowned on that sort of thing. It wasn't ladylike. So, usually Jonathan was the one who did the dialing.

After weeks of talking almost daily, Mae realized that she hadn't heard from him in four days. School was back in session by that time and she was so busy getting situated into high school that she hadn't realized that he hadn't called. With Momma's permission, she decided to call him.

His mother answered the phone.

"Hello Mrs. Sullivan, how are you doing?"

"Oh, I'm doing fine." But she didn't sound fine. Mae noticed that right off.

"I was just calling to talk to Jonathan. I haven't heard from him this week."

"He's in the hospital."

"Oh."

That's all Mae said. That's all she could think to say. She didn't try to find out why he was in the hospital or how he was doing. She just said, "Oh." Then she managed to say, "Okay then, I'll call back later." She quickly hung up the phone.

She was stunned speechless. Mae had never heard of a young person being in the hospital before. In fact, she had never been in a hospital before. With the exception of Wayne and three month old Denise, Momma had all her babies at home, with the help of a midwife. Hospitals were a foreign concept to her. She had never known a teenager sick enough to go to one.

Mae waited until after school three days later, on a Friday, to call Jonathan again. His mother answered the phone. Mae could tell by the sound of her voice that bad news was coming.

"Hello Mrs. Sullivan. It's Mae DeVault. Is Jonathan okay?"

"No baby, he isn't."

"Will he be getting out of the hospital soon?"

"No. He won't. He's very sick."

"Oh, I'm sorry to hear that. Can I visit him?"

"Yes baby. That will be fine. I think he'll like that. He's in room 421."

Mrs. Sullivan didn't have to tell Mae what hospital Jonathan was in or try to give her directions on how to get there. Mae knew that Jonathan was in John Gaston Hospital, near downtown Memphis. John Gaston was the only hospital where blacks were allowed to go for medical help. After my family moved to Memphis, Momma gave them all her business.

After Mae hung up the phone, she went to the living room where Momma and Daddy were sitting. Just so y'all know, the living room was the only room in the house where people could sit comfortably. We didn't have a den or family room back then. Anyway, my parents were very quiet so they must have been listening.

Mae told them, "Something is wrong with Jonathan. His Momma said he's very sick. I told her I was going to visit him. Can I go tomorrow? I'll catch the bus. I know where the hospital is."

Daddy told her, "I'll take you."

They went the next day.

When they got to the fourth floor, the tiny waiting room was filled with folks who looked like Jonathan. She knew it was his people. They didn't say anything. They just looked at her and especially Daddy. Daddy always gets a lot of attention, especially from women because he is a very handsome man, and I'm not just saying that.

As they approached the waiting area, Jonathan's parents got up and walked over to Mae and Daddy. After introductions were made, the four of them walked to Jonathan's room. Mae didn't know what she was expecting to see, but relief washed over her when she saw Jonathan. He didn't look sick at all. He looked the same as when she had seen him at the pool that hot day in early June. After Mae introduced Jonathan to Daddy, the adults went outside and left them alone.

Mae and Jonathan picked up where they left off. They were laughing and talking as if he weren't sitting there in a tiny hospital bed wearing a faded, dingy blue and white hospital gown and surrounded by funny looking equipment making strange beeping sounds. Like nurses weren't barging in and out of the room looking at the machines and making notes on the chart at the end of his bed. Like there wasn't that stinky hospital smell.

Mae stayed there talking to Jonathan about this and that for thirty minutes, give or take, before she gave him a hug and went back to the waiting room. She felt much better since she'd seen for herself that he was all right. After they got to the car, Mae told Daddy that Jonathan was just fine and would probably be going home soon. Daddy just nodded his head and didn't say anything. In fact, he didn't say much of nothing all the way home. Mae didn't think much of it.

Daddy's a quiet man.

* * * * *

Mae was in a good mood when she called Jonathan's house three days later. She wanted to give him time to get home and get settled in. His mother answered the phone.

"Hello Mrs. Sullivan. How's Jonathan?"

"Oh baby. He died."

It took Mae a whole minute to form her next question. It wasn't a good one.

"He what?"

"Yeah baby, he didn't make it."

Like I told y'all. My sister is a very intelligent person, but when she is shocked, she says the first thing that comes to her mind. "Is there going to be a funeral?"

"Yes, there's going to be a funeral. It's on Friday at 11:00."

"I'll be there."

"Thank you baby. Mae, you have been a good friend to my son."

Mae could tell that Mrs. Sullivan was about to cry so she quickly got the name of the church where the services would be held and hung up. She didn't ask what happened or what he died of. I guess we'll never know.

Numbly, she walked into the living room where Momma and Daddy were sitting. Again, they were quiet and she knew they had been listening but she had to say the words so that they could become real to her.

"He's dead."

That's all she said. Then she turned around and walked through the kitchen and out to the back yard.

News travels fast in a small house. Everyone thought it best to give Mae some time to herself so nobody bothered her. She sat there on the green and white nylon chaise lounge under the huge cherry tree thinking about Jonathan. She didn't cry. She couldn't. She's not like that. She missed dinner.

After two hours, Momma came to the back door and said, "Mae, come and eat your dinner. I kept it warm for you."

"I just want to sit our here for awhile Momma."

Now, Momma means well, she really does. But, she's a strong, no nonsense Christian woman who lives by the Bible. She is not given to crying and emotional displays. That's how she is.

Momma said, "Child you come on in here and eat. Ain't no reason to be sad. You know what the Bible says…"

She was just getting ready to launch into a sermonette about being absent from the body and being present with the Lord. I promise you she was. Thank the Lord, Daddy intervened.

"Beulah Mae, leave her alone. Let her sit out there if she wants to."

Momma didn't say another word. She sighed and eased back into the kitchen.

Mae stayed outside for another hour before she came inside and told Daddy she wanted to go to the funeral.

"When is it?" he asked.

"Friday at 11:00."

"I'll take you."

She floated through the week, dreading Friday. She'd been to a funeral before, but this was different. This was for a young person. This was for a friend. She didn't know what to expect, but she did feel better because Daddy was going with her. Daddy's presence would be a good distraction.

She loved going places with Daddy because she liked watching people's reaction to him. He wore his black suit, slick from too many ironings. He even slicked down his curly hair. The way he carried himself was impressive. She was always proud to be with him.

When they arrived at the church, the family was just starting to walk in. Mrs. Sullivan asked Mae and Daddy to walk in with the family and they did. Many people were looking at Daddy, probably trying to figure out if he was black or white. He kept his arms around Mae and his eyes straight ahead. He was used to the attention but he didn't have the big head about it.

The funeral was a surreal process. Jonathan's people were the dignified type so they weren't falling out and trying to jump into the casket. It was a nice service. At least, the part that she actually heard was nice. Mae's thoughts were across the board. She was remembering phone calls, jokes…floating in the pool… room 421… beeping… baldhead… charts…Baby, he died…You were a good friend to my son.

"…in the name of Jesus amen."

The voice of the minister pulled her back to the present. She didn't even remember standing up. *Oh, it's over,* she thought.

Daddy leaned over to Mae and said, "I reckon we can leave after we march around."

"Huh…oh, okay Daddy."

Oh Lord. Mae had no intentions of marching around. She didn't want to see him dead. She wanted to break and run out the back of the church, but when the usher came to their row and held out her hand directing them to the front of the church, where the casket was, she just fell in line after Daddy. When they made it to the casket, she looked at Jonathan out of the corner of her eyes and rushed out of the church, practically running up Daddy's back.

Mae was silent for most of the drive home. The more she thought about Jonathan the more confused she became. It took a while before she was able to put her confusion into words.

Finally, in a voice filled with frustration, confusion and anger she said, "Daddy, I don't understand why he had to die. He was a good person. He never hurt anybody. He was a lifeguard. It was his dream to be a preacher. He wanted to save lives and save souls. He was Mr. and Mrs. Sullivan's only child. Now they have no one. Why Daddy? Why did God allow this to happen?"

It was an impossible question.

Daddy thought before he answered. "Child, I really don't know. Sometimes we just don't know why God does the things he do. It's His way and I can't answer for Him. But I do know this, God knows what He's doin' even when we don't. He's been God a long time. Our job is to just keep on lovin' Him even when we don't understand Him. I reckon it's just one of those questions you'll have to ask the good Lord in the sweet by and by."

It was an honest answer.

* * * * *

Years later, when Mae told me this story she said the answer Daddy gave her actually made her feel a bit better. She appreciated the fact that Daddy was honest with her. She said it helped her to know that even if she didn't understand why God does things the way He does, that there was a purpose to her grief.

I'm glad my sister was able to find a place of peace.

Good for her. But that was in 1959. As for me, in October of 1997, that sweet by and by stuff didn't do me a lick of good. 'Cause when I needed God, I couldn't find him anywhere.

But I'm getting ahead of myself…. Guess I should go back and start at the beginning so y'all will know what the heck I'm talking about.

CHAPTER 33

A STORM'S COMIN'

My brother died.

I tried to prepare y'all for this shocking revelation by telling that story about Mae and her lifeguard friend, Jonathan. Hope it worked. My master plan was to get you in the mindset of thinking about death so it would help to soften the blow of me telling you flat out about my brother being dead.

I hate to be all blunt about it, but that's how death is. It feels like the smell of a dead cow. It hits you in the guts and then wraps itself all around your insides until it winds up gnawing on your liver. Then, it just hunkers down and sits there day after day, month after month, and year after year until you can find a way to pass it out of your system…like gas.

At least that's how my brother's death felt to me. Not like gas, but like something was trying to eat me up from the inside out. Like something was trying to squeeze the life outta me from the inside out.

Almost did too.

I'm telling you, I just about lost my natural mind when that call came saying, "He's gone." That's exactly what his step-daughter said when she called at that ungodly hour. "He's gone." And just like that, my brother was no more. I didn't think I would ever recover. I was jittery and nervous, I couldn't eat or sleep and I didn't care squat about how I looked.

I stopped wearing makeup and combing my hair. Now,

y'all know when a sister with hair from the motherland stops taking care of her "do" the pain is real bad. I was nothing pretty, but I didn't care. I was embracing the Buckwheat look and totally fine with it.

But, wait. I'm getting ahead of myself again. Trust me, I'm looking for a support group.

When did death get so sneaky anyway?

Back in the old days, 1985 to be exact, when my beloved sister Jean died, death gave us some notice. Death started working on poor old Jean a good twenty years before it actually took her to the bosom of Jesus. Jean first got sugar when she was in her early 20's. Oh, 'scuse me...diabetes is what folk call it nowadays, but back in Memphis, Tennessee in the 1960's and 70's, we didn't know nothing about no diabetes. All I ever heard was, "Jean got sugar."

To be honest, I'm kinda glad they changed the name to diabetes because calling it sugar confused me to no end. I mean, I was a child when Jean was a grown woman so I didn't have a real good understanding of what was wrong with my sister. All I knew was, Jean used to eat boxes and boxes of starch. The same starch my momma used when she ironed our clothes.

Jean would take that red and white box of starch, get her a spoon, prop her feet up and go to town. So, me being a young child, I always wondered why they didn't say, "Jean got starch." Granted, she ate her fair share of sweets, but that starch was her first love.

Uh, 'scuse me again...I think I've kinda drifted from my point.

Anyway, in March of 1985, Jean departed from this world, practically in front of my eyes because I was the last one in the family to see her alive before the doctor yelled out, "Harvey Team to ICU STAT!" and rudely pushed me outta her room. I ran down the hall to wait with the family because I kinda knew Jean wasn't long for this world.

At first there was total chaos with doctors and nurses running and yelling like the world was coming to an end. I'd say it was about a good five minutes of them trying every which way to squeeze a little bit more life outta Jean, but she wasn't having it. It wasn't long before that room got as quiet as, uh…as quiet as…something really, really quiet. Then one by one they left the room with their heads hung down and the head doctor came and told us that Jean was gone.

She left without saying goodbye.

So you see, the family had a good twenty something years of seeing Jean struggle with the sugar, uh…diabetes, to sort of prepare us for the possibility that she might not be getting an AARP card. We comforted ourselves with cliché stuff like, "She's in a better place" or "She's not suffering anymore." Thinking like that helped because it was totally true. Jean's life was a daily dose of pain, medicine, hospitals and needles, so knowing she was at rest took the sting out of her death. Or maybe I should say, it made it easier to swallow 'cause it still stung like the dickens. But with my brother, we weren't saying none of that "better place" stuff because we got nothing.

No notice, no prolonged sickness, no warning.

Just death.

Sneaky death.

His dying totally upset the balance of my life because when I first got the news to come to the hospital, I started praying like there was no tomorrow. That's what I'd been trained to do. Y'all, I prayed longer and harder for that boy than I had ever prayed for anything and anybody in my whole life. Even harder than I pray for God to send me a husband…and that's some mighty hard praying.

Nobody could tell me that my brother wasn't gonna recover from his mystery illness because I had faith. And not some little mustard seed faith either. I'm talking big kosher salt size faith, if we're talking condiments. I also had the prayer chain going. Not only that, I was walking by faith and not by sight because even though he was getting sicker and sicker, my faith was not moved. I just thought it would give him a better testimony when he recovered. So, I was totally in "my brother will live and not die" mode.

Praise the Lord!

In Jesus name.

Amen.

But, guess what.

Y'all, my brother died.

Died like I hadn't said a cotton pickin' word.

Suffice it to say, I didn't like how the Lord handled it. Not one bit, I didn't. And that's how it all started. This little tussle between me and the Lord. As you can probably guess, things pretty well went downhill from there.

From the day my brother died until the day of his funeral was a good three weeks. Lord have mercy! Y'all know they not supposed to keep black folks out that long. I mean, we do better than white folk, but goodness gracious!

Let me just say that during this time, I experienced a great falling away.

CHAPTER 34

THE BEGINNING OF SORROWS

I usually answer the phone when it rings in my home, but not this time. Not when it rang at 3:00 AM. I didn't move a muscle. It could have rung all night for all I cared. Besides, I knew it was either my sister-in-law Laura or my step-niece Juliette. I knew when I left the hospital that night that the phone would ring at some ungodly hour and it would be one of them. Not only that, I knew exactly what they were going to say.

Denise called me from downstairs where she was sleeping on the couch. She didn't wait for me to answer. "That was Juliette. He's trying to pull the ventilator out of his mouth. She thinks we should come to the hospital right away."

"Y'all go ahead. I'm not going."

I had already made up my mind about that.

"OK" she replied after a brief pause. She didn't ask again. I really appreciated that. I hate when people try to manipulate you into doing what they feel is right. I didn't care what anyone thought. At that point, it was every woman for herself. I was going to do what was right for me.

I could hear Tina stirring in the bedroom across the hall. She had flown in from Memphis to Los Angeles two days earlier to see how our brother was doing. She was about to find out.

Denise had already called Mae. Mae lived about five minutes away so they hurried to get ready. I hadn't seen them move that fast since the time we found out the all you can eat Sunday brunch at Sally's Soul Food was over at 2:00 instead of 3:00. Panic always puts a little pep in your step.

I heard all the activity going on downstairs and across the hall, but I didn't come out of my bedroom. I just lay there, feeling helpless. Knowing I was unable to change what was about to happen to my family. I was nestled under a blanket and the worn quilt Momma gave me that Big Mama Sarah had made with her own hands. The covers were pulled up to my chin but I was still cold. I thought, "This is what it feels like to be in a coffin." Just thinking about a coffin spooked me a little.

A few moments later, the phone rang again. The way it rang, I knew it was bad news.

Denise called my name again. I didn't answer, hating the fact that I ever told her my name. Hoping she would forget about me. But y'all know she didn't.

She called me again.

"What?" I said, not even trying to keep the irritation out of my voice.

"He's gone."

Do you know that feeling you get when you narrowly avoid an accident? Or when you see the person you've got a secret crush on with someone else. You know that hollowed out, numb feeling that starts at your neck and goes all through your body like venom.

I got that.

You know, as hard as you try to prepare yourself, no matter how you brace yourself and no matter how sick a person is, you can never, ever be prepared to hear that someone you love is dead. That kind of pain you can't prepare for. It hits you too deep.

I don't rightly remember the next few moments.
I hurt.
I felt like I wanted to die right along with him but I

didn't have it in me to cry. I'd had enough of that. I'd been crying for the eight days he was in the hospital. Now, I just laid there, looking at the white ceiling and the white walls, wondering why I never bothered to paint my room. I sat up and looked around the crowded space. *Why would one person need so much furniture?* Every inch of space in my cramped little room was taken. Why did I choose cherry wood furniture? It made my room look dark and depressing. I decided I would give all my furniture to the poor and start over with a new decor. Maybe a lighter color, like yellow.

Now that that was settled, I realized that I couldn't think of anything else to think of so I stood up. I didn't move at first. I just stood there next to my bed. Trying to think and not to think. Trying to open one part of my brain and close another.

I made the bed. That killed a few minutes. *What to do? What to do?* I asked myself, trying to occupy my mind. Well, I couldn't think of anything and I felt stupid just standing there like a moron so I decided to go downstairs because I thought it would be rude to not do something with my sisters.

When I walked into the living room I saw them. Denise and Tina, two of my three living sisters. By then, Jean had been with the Lord for twelve years. They were sitting on opposite ends of the sectional sofa waiting for Mae to arrive. *I hate this room,* I thought. The colors were too bright. Denise and I chose mint green and peach furniture because the carpet was sea foam green. A friend told me the room looked like a doctor's office.

We aren't friends anymore.

When I could bear it, I took a few moments to take an emotional inventory of my sisters as they sat quietly in that room. I saw that it wasn't just me. The shock of the announcement prevented them from crying too. Then again, that's how we are. I imagine some folks start crying right off the bat. Not us. Not the DeVault girls. That's not how we do things. Don't get me wrong. We're gonna cry, just not right now. We save our crying for when we are alone.

When nobody can see us.

Just like Momma.

They were in a daze, both staring straight ahead. Tina was the only one who had the ability to speak, but she wasn't talking to either of us. She kept shaking her head and saying to herself, "Lord have mercy."

That's what black folks say when they can't think of anything else to say. Tina meant it this time. To tell the truth, that just about said it all. I didn't trust myself to say amen so I started cleaning the living room.

I allowed my mind to drift back over the last few days. One minute the doctor would say that he was improving. The next minute he was at death's door. Why, only two days ago we were all laughing and praising God when he made it through a critical period. The doctor had told us that if he made it through the next twenty-four hours his chances of recovery were good. Well, not only did he survive for twenty four hours, but another twenty four hours after that. We thought he was home free. We thought everything was going to be alright.

As we drove home from the hospital that night, well after visiting hours were over, we were all singing, "What a mighty God we serve" in the car. Y'all, we were havin' church in that Corolla. Finally, the doctors had given us a good report. We had hope. I honestly believed this nightmare would soon be over. Things were finally looking up after five days of touch and go hell.

But then, without warning, he took a turn for the worse. It came from nowhere. First, they said his temperature wouldn't go down. Then they said his blood pressure was too high. Next they said he wasn't responding to this. Then he wasn't doing that. It was all a bunch of medical jargon to me. I ain't stupid, but I couldn't really understand any of it. I told y'all how I tried to keep the faith, but right near the end a cold, clammy feeling came all over me. That was when I knew he wasn't going to pull through.

I just knew it.

That was when I first started to feel betrayed by God.But before that, I really thought he would be okay. He was scared of dying, it was his worst fear of all. That's how he was.

He ain't going nowhere, I thought, *he's gonna fight this thing.*

In fact, when the constipated, grouchy old surgeon told us on Sunday evening that things didn't look good, I stood in front of him shaking my head. He seemed to resent my rejection of his prognosis.

He snapped at me and said, "You go ahead with your faith, I'm giving you the facts."

I knew he was just doing his job, but every fiber of my being told me he was wrong. That this was just a faith test. I would not let this doctor penetrate my armor of faith. Perhaps he didn't know Jesus. Maybe he didn't understand faith. But I did. You know what they say, "prayer changes things." That's what they say all the time and I believed it. My brother was gonna live. Nobody could tell me anything different.

I remember the first time I saw him after he was in ICU. The room was filled with machines that were beeping and humming so loudly I could hardly concentrate. There was so much equipment in the room there was hardly any place to sit. I couldn't believe my eyes. It was hard for me to look at him laying there with all those tubes sticking in him. He looked awful. He wouldn't have cared about how he looked though. He was in a coma. His whole body was swollen, maybe to twice its normal size. He hardly fit in the bed.

Worse than that, his body was jerking. It looked like something was shocking him and he responded with tremors so hard the whole bed shook. I think it was the ventilator because the jerking seemed to be connected to his breathing. He looked so different that for a moment I was confused.

Is this my brother? I thought. I wondered if I had the wrong room. Wished I did. I didn't.

At first, we were told he had a stroke so I focused my praying on stroke-like stuff. But then, while I was praying and talking to him, trying to bring him out of his coma, my hand went to his stomach, practically on its own. I didn't think anything of it at the time. I just continued my prayer vigil until it was time for the next person to come and spend some time with him.

A few hours later, a nicer, younger doctor was examining him. He said that when he touched his stomach, he jumped. They decided to run an MRI and found that the problem was a twisted intestine. Now, who ever heard of such a thing?

Well, since that was the area my hand went to, I thought I had been led by God to pray for his condition in advance of knowing that was where the problem was. So, you see, to me, I had positive, 100% proof that he would be healed. At least, that's the connection I made.

I became more certain that this was God trying to get my brother's attention because that's how God does things sometimes. That's how He is. The way I figured it, God was going to bring him back from the very brink of death and give him a wonderful testimony. Then he would be so grateful he would start preaching or something like that.

So, that is how I was thinking about the situation. God was going to fix the problem and I told everyone that he would be well. For some reason, nobody seemed to believe me but I didn't care. I thought to myself, *they aren't as spiritual as I am.* Even as his condition began to rapidly deteriorate, I still believed. I believed until almost the very end.

Well, my belief couldn't save him. I waited and waited for God to heal my brother but He never did. In 1997, on a chilly Wednesday morning in October at 3:16 AM, my brother died. I knew it was coming, but when it actually happened, y'all could'a knocked me over with a feather.

AGAIN

Now, there I was. Sitting there in the middle of my living room feeling like an idiot and asking God the same questions Mae asked my daddy thirty eight years prior.

Why?

Why did this happen?

I wanted to shout it out….*WHY????*

One thing I can tell you right now, that sweet by and by stuff wasn't going to cut it this time.

God let me down. That's all I knew. My faith didn't work and I didn't understand why. I did exactly what the Bible says to do, but with all of my praying, I had to face the grim fact that my brother was just as dead. Just as dead as anyone lying out in the morgue.

I could feel the anger building up in me. I tried to be angry with my brother, but that's just plain stupid, with him dead and all. When I realized who my anger was really directed at, I quickly shifted to denial. I couldn't admit that, for the first time in my life, I was angry with God.

Y'all have to understand. I was raised in a strict Southern Baptist home. It had been drilled into my head that you don't question God. That you had to accept things that come your way whether you liked it or not. In light of that, I tried to comfort myself by thinking stuff like, *God's will be done* and *God knows what's best* but in my heart I wanted to scream. *How could You let my brother die? Why do You tell us to stand on the Scriptures if they don't work? Don't You care?*

There were so many emotions raging inside of me, but I never said a word. I just kept cleaning the living room.

For the life of me I couldn't understand why my sisters still wanted to go to the hospital. They knew he was dead. There wasn't anything they could do about it. They said they wanted to see him one last time. To me, that was crazy. What good would that do? It seemed important to them but it wasn't to me. I didn't want to see him, with his dead self.

I didn't go see Jean when she died either. I didn't even go to the wake. I got this thing about dead people. I don't want to be anywhere around them. They look like mannequins and they smell. In fact, the smell makes me sick. I sometimes wonder if growing up down the street from a funeral parlor made me like this.

I can remember the first dead person I saw. She was my friend, Andrea, and she was about ten years old, just like me, at the time. When I first heard that Andrea and her aunt were killed in a car accident while driving from Mississippi to Memphis, I refused to believe it. I remembered the fun we used to have on the playground at recess or how we would laugh and share secrets at the lunch table. We were young, with our whole lives ahead of us. But, she was dead alright and there I was, walking up the street to the funeral parlor on the corner. Parlors are what we called them back then but it was really a converted house.

Anyway, Momma was working in the kitchen at my elementary school and Daddy didn't get home until it was almost dark outside and I sho' wasn't going to no funeral parlor when it was dark outside. Since I walked past the place on my way home from school everyday, I just trotted up there alone, telling myself with each step that I wasn't scared. And, truth be told, I wasn't scared. I was terrified.

My boney knees were knocking as I walked up the front stairs to the entrance. It took nearly all of my strength to open the heavy wood door. As I tipped inside, I remember listening to the door slowly, slowly, slowly creak shut behind me. I looked around, but no one was at the reception desk so I stood there in the lobby looking around at the dark furniture and burgundy carpet and smelling that dead smell.

Trying to calm myself, I thought, *This place ain't that bad. It looks like someone's living room.*

I had started to relax a bit, but then, all of a sudden, that creakin' front door slammed shut. I had forgotten all about it, that's how long it took that dang thing to close. The sound was deafening. It scared the life outta me. I'm telling the truth, y'all, I must have seen every dead body they had in that place on that day because I took off running straight down the hall of that place. Past parlor one, past parlor two, over chairs and over people until one of the workers finally grabbed me. I could tell by his eyes that he wanted to laugh but I didn't see a thing funny so I decided to play it off. You know, like I planned to run down the hallway of a funeral parlor. Like, that's what I do in my down time.

Anyway, I looked that brother dead in the eyes (no pun intended) and said, "I'm looking for Andrea Jones, and I'm in a hurry, where is she?" Now, if you ask me, that was a pretty good comeback for a ten year old. I guess I didn't fool him because he laughed right in my face. Stupid sapsucker.

After he composed himself, he took me to the room where my friend was lying in state. I was so glad I hadn't passed it. He let me have a few minutes alone with her. I tiptoed over to the casket and peeped in. She didn't look like herself, mainly because she had on make-up, a curly afro wig and her skin was about two shades darker than normal. I heard that she had been ejected from the car so I knew she would look bad, but I wasn't prepared for her to look so different.

I remember thinking, *Her momma would never let her wear makeup.*

That was all I could think of to say. I didn't cry. I didn't say anything. I just looked at her, feeling confused. I stayed there about a minute and then I left. That door slamming incident had ruined the moment. When I walked past the front desk there were a few people seated doing some paper work. They pretended to ignore me so that I could leave with some dignity, but I knew they wanted to laugh. You know, to this day, I believe they rigged that door to slam shut like that.

* * * * *

Anyway, I like to remember people the way they were when they were alive. I didn't want to see my brother as a waxen, frozen corpse. No one pushed me to go to the hospital or tried to make me feel guilty. I could be pretty mule headed about some things so they knew better. When Mae finally arrived she rang the buzzer to our townhouse and my sisters quietly walked out.

When Denise got to the door, she told me to call my parents, who were living in Memphis, and tell them he was dead. We didn't discuss this, she just told me to do it. I said okay because I wanted them to get out of the house. At the time I didn't have a problem with making the call. I'll just call them and tell them he's gone, no problem. That's what I was thinking.

When the door closed behind them I breathed a sigh of relief. *Alone at last,* I thought. As the moments passed my sanity returned to me. *Hold up...What did I just get myself into*? Exactly how do you tell a parent that their son was dead? What can take away the sting of the harshness of the word "dead?"

I began to rehearse how I would break the news. Since Momma always answers the phone. I thought I would say,

Mother, the Bible says that there is a time to live and a time to die. This was his time to die. I'm sorry, he's gone.

Nah, that didn't work for me, it was too simple. My brother deserved better. OK, I'll use Momma's words. I'll say, *Momma, the Bible says that to be absent from the body is to be present with the Lord. Your son is with Jesus, Praise the Lord.* Using the Bible and Jesus. Two of Momma's favorite things. Now that approach could work.

At the time that I agreed to this arrangement, I didn't think it would be too big of a problem. However, as the minutes ticked by I began to think that there is probably nothing worse than losing a child, especially a son like him. He was the one who would always call home to check on them. He would send money to my parents when he had a little extra. He would go home for a visit and do odd jobs around the house, like painting or trimming the trees. That's how he was. He was a good son and a good man. Now I had the job of calling my parents to tell them their boy was dead. I wondered if it was too late to catch my sisters.

While I was waiting, I called Tina's daughter, Renee. We concocted a plan on how I would tell them. She would go to their house at exactly 8:00am, pretending to check on them. I would call at exactly the same time. That way she would be there to comfort them when I broke the news. I was so glad she would be there for them. With her studying for her doctorate in Christian Psychology, I knew she would be able to offer them some words of wisdom and support to ease the blow.

At the appointed time, I picked up the phone and called home. Momma answered the phone on the first ring so I knew she was sitting in the den, my old bedroom, in her La-Z-Boy recliner with the arms and the headrest covered with plastic. She sounded anxious, like she knew something was wrong. Thankfully, my niece was already there, one of the rare occasions she was on time.

I tried to sound chipper. "How ya doing Momma?"

Now, Beulah Mae is a no nonsense woman. She is the epitome of the strong, black woman. Direct, to the point and not taking any foolishness. I love my Momma. She took care of all of us when we were sick and whipped us when we misbehaved. Still, it is extremely rare to see her show emotion. It's not her thing, but that's alright. That's how she is.

"How's he doing?" she asked, ignoring my pleasantries.

All of my rehearsing went straight out the window. Y'all, I couldn't remember my speech to save my life. My first impulse was to ignore her question and say something like "Who?" or "I asked you how you are doing first" but I knew better than to make her wait.

The only thing I could tell her was the truth, "I'm so sorry Momma."

"He didn't make it?" She sounded small and confused.

"No Momma. I'm sorry. He's gone."

I could hear the soft whimpers and I was glad I wasn't there to witness the tears flowing down her ebony cheeks.

"*What*?" I thought to myself. *I don't believe this. She's gonna cry now. She didn't cry out loud for Jean. After all these years, Momma's crying out in the open. This is just great.*

Now I was confused. I wasn't prepared for this. I listened to my Momma cry for about a minute, totally unable to think of anything I could say to make it better. I wanted her to stop. The sound was foreign. It was killing me. Finally, I couldn't take it anymore and I cried along with her. This was a major breakthrough in my family. Two people crying at once like that. And one of them being Momma.

She said, "I was praying he would pull through."

"I know Momma. I was too."

It was at this time that I heard an ultra sonic scream in

the background. I thought Jesus had just cracked the skies and the world was coming to an end. Turns out it was my niece, the future doctor/counselor. That girl let out a yelp loud enough for me to hear in LA without a telephone.

I asked Momma, "What happened?"

Momma said Renee jumped up and ran to the bathroom where she retrieved a whole roll of tissue. She returned to the room still moaning and groaning, tore off a big swag of tissue for herself and handed the rest of the roll to my mother.

"Oh, Lord help us. That old devil. This ain't nothing but the devil" I could hear Renee screaming in the background.

So much for Christian Psychology.

The good thing was Renee's display dried Momma's tears. The bad news was all the commotion brought Daddy in from his garden in the backyard. I heard him ask for the phone so I said "No Momma. Don't' give him the phone. I gotta go. You tell him."

She was too upset to hear me. Or maybe she didn't want him to hear it from her. She handed Daddy the phone.

Jesus, I whispered to myself and braced for the worst.

I especially didn't want to talk to him because he's the emotional one. Daddy is really sensitive when it comes to his children. He acted like he wanted to die when my oldest sister Jean died. He's the one who prayed and asked God to not let him see any of his kids die because he wanted to go first.

This was the second time God said, "No."

Daddy cried over Jean more than all of us put together. To this day I still don't think he has fully recovered and maybe he never will. Now, when I told him about his son he cried again.

This had quickly become the worst phone call of my life. I wanted it over. Thankfully, by the grace of God, I was able to change the subject after a while and we started to make plans to get them to L.A.

The next thing I knew I was off the phone. I sat on the floor of my doctor's office looking living room, staring at nothing. It was quiet.

So quiet.

And still.

This was the time I had been dreading. This was the time when I would have to deal with the hundreds of emotions and questions that were pulsating through my mind. I still didn't feel bold enough to ask God why He thought it was necessary for my brother to die when I asked Him not to do that. So, I pushed the thought aside. I couldn't bear to think that the Bible's promises weren't true, but in the back of my mind, coupled with the devastating reality that my brother was dead was the wrenching thought that prayer doesn't mean anything.

I tried to reconcile the negative emotions that I was beginning to have toward God through denial. It worked for a while. "No," I thought, "these thoughts are wrong and I won't entertain them."

So, I got up, went to my bathroom, washed the tears from my eyes, brushed my teeth, took a shower and then I did what anyone who has been raised to believe that you don't question God would do. I got up and began to vacuum the carpet.

Again.

ANGRY

My grief covered me at 7:30am. I tried to hold it back as long as I could, but that's when it became real. It covered me like white on rice. It hit me hard and I didn't hit it back. I just went with it because there was nothing else to clean. I couldn't hold back the separation and loneliness I felt. It was like something from the underworld grabbed my foot and was pulling me down to the depths of hell. If I knew what drowning was like I would say it was like that. With each passing minute my brother was deader and deader. Nothing would ever change that.

I couldn't ignore the darkness that was hanging over my head like a bad weave. I didn't try. I wanted to scream but I didn't. I wanted to run. Didn't do that either. All I could do was cry. I sat there on that sea foam green carpet and before long I was all rolled up in a ball and crying like it was an Olympic sport. The fetal position is really made for crying like I was doing it. That jerking kind of crying you do when the pain is really bad and deep. I cried like that for a good thirty minutes.

There was nothing else to clean.

I could hear my neighbors stirring in the townhouse next door. I could hear cars moving up and down the street. Just right outside my window, children were walking to school, laughing and having a good time. Flags were flying full staff. Life was going on as usual. That made me mad. I wanted to open my window and tell

everyone that the world had changed while they were
sleeping. I wanted them to know that someone special had
died. Someone who really mattered. I wanted everyone to
go back home and mourn with me. I wanted everyone to
shut up and show some respect for the dead. But I couldn't
do anything like that. I just sat on the floor of my bedroom,
rolled up in a little ball, rocking back and forth like a crazy
person.

* * * * *

It's a shame he died on such a beautiful day.

It was the kind of day that makes you glad you live in
Los Angeles. Even though it was early October, it warmed
up to about eighty degrees by noon. It was sunny and the
skies were so clear I could see all the way to the Hollywood
sign from my bedroom window. I must have stared at that
sign for hours that morning thinking about how much my
brother loved a good movie.

I was still in my room staring at that sign when I heard
the key turn the lock downstairs. By the time my sisters
returned from the hospital, the apartment was spotless. The
dishes were sparkling and the furniture was glowing. You
could see yourself in the carpet. I had recovered from my
fit thirty minutes earlier so I made my way downstairs like
everything was okay. I knew they would want to give me
all the details, but I really didn't want to know. If I had, I
would have gone with them.

Nobody thought of that.

"He didn't look like himself," Tina started, before I
could get down the stairs good.

I heard dying can do that to you. That's what I thought
to myself.

Tina said to me, "Girl, he was so swollen. He looked
like he was going to explode." She continued, "The
doctors said his intestines just shut down and all his body

fluids backed up inside his body. His body poisoned itself."

Why is this woman still talking? That's what I thought to myself.

She finally said what she really wanted to say. "I hope he didn't suffer."

I spoke my first words. "He was in a coma. I'm sure he didn't feel anything," I said this also trying to convince myself, but I don't know much about that kind of stuff.

Thankfully, Denise changed the subject. "I guess you were wondering what took us so long."

As a matter of fact I was wondering just that. I mean, how long does it take to look at a dead body and come home? They were gone for over four hours. Still, I didn't say anything because I knew she would keep talking on her own. She told me that my two brothers also showed up at the hospital. I guess Juliette must have called everybody. Anyway, after they finished looking at him, they went to a coffee shop near the hospital.

For the life of me, I didn't know how they could eat at a time such as this. But they did. Potatoes, pancakes, and sausage. That kinda stuff. Greasy, fatty stuff. They said the food was good. I didn't say anything.

Denise saw my reaction and quickly added, "We just wanted to console each other. Everyone was there, except you."

I was feeling generous so I let her have that one.

* * * * *

I floated through the day of his death. Everything happened so fast. The four of us sat around talking for a few hours. At around noon, Tina, Denise, and I piled into Mae's car and went to Lane Bryant so Tina could shop. She didn't think to bring a black dress. I guess she didn't think she would need one.

Later, we ate lunch at our favorite Chinese restaurant in West LA. Denise said something funny and for a moment we were laughing like nothing was wrong. It felt good. But, after awhile, reality kicked back in. It grew quiet.

We remembered.

I kept thinking that eight lousy days ago everything was fine. My brother was alive and life was good. That is, good compared to now. Then, one day he started complaining of a stomachache. The next day he went into a coma at the admitting desk in the emergency room. A few days later, he was dead. The coma should have been my first clue.

I have a confession to make. Remember how I told you about my undying faith? You know how I prayed and asked God to spare his life. Well, to be honest, right at the very end, on that last day when things began to go downhill, I changed my prayer. When I saw that there was no hope, I begged God to just let him regain consciousness for one minute. I was begging for just one lousy minute so I could have one more conversation with him. I would have done anything to have him open his big brown eyes and look at me for one lousy, stinking minute. I just wanted to tell him goodbye.

We hadn't spoken for at least a month before he died. Nothing was wrong. It's just that he was one of the hardest working men I ever met. He was always so tired. I was always so busy. Still, looking back, I could have made the time to pick up the stupid phone and make one stupid call. One stupid phone call.

I think most people harbor feelings of guilt when someone dies. It always seems that more could have been done. Like you could have spent more time with them or listened more. My mind drifted back to when Jean died. I went through the same guilt thing with her death because I was angry with her when she up and died.

Jean was diabetic and needed dialysis because the disease tore up her kidneys. Just like my brother, Jean died while she was in a coma. Come to think of it, I guess my family don't do well in comas. Anyway, hers came during a dialysis treatment and she never regained consciousness. I can still see myself now, hunched over her deathbed begging her comatose body to forgive me. Saying "I'm sorry" to an empty shell. She was gone. What a mean thing for her to do! She up and dies and I'm the one who's forced to live with all the guilt. She died over twelve years ago, but I remember it like it was yesterday. It was on a Monday morning.

I hurt over Jean but, to be honest because she was in pain day in and day out I just couldn't bear to see her suffer anymore. That helped me to accept her death a lot better. I asked God to take her and if you had seen her on that last day you would have done the same thing. So, Jean going to be with Jesus, I could deal with.

Wayne's death...

Totally different.

CHAPTER 36

THE SIGN OF THE APOCLYPSE

Time passed slowly while we waited for them to release Wayne's body to the funeral home. In the meantime, my family all chipped in to pay for Momma and Daddy's airfare and within two days they were on their way. At first Momma acted like she didn't want to come, but we weren't trying to hear that. If there was ever a time when we needed "The Rock," it was now.

My sisters and I arrived at the gate a few minutes before the flight was due to land. This was way back in the day when you could walk right up to the gate and watch people get off the plane. For some reason, I had a bad feeling about them flying. They were both in their late 70's and Daddy had developed a heart condition and Momma got sugar...uh, diabetes. Call me paranoid, but I had been having nightmares about the plane hitting some turbulence and Daddy having a heart attack and dying right there on the flight. Thankfully, the plane pulled in and nobody looked alarmed at the gate so I figured they were still alive and breathed a sigh of relief. They made it.

Matthew and Beulah Mae were the last ones to get off the plane. I mean, after what seemed like hours, I finally saw them slowly walking down that long corridor. I took a moment to study them. They looked old. A lot older than when I last saw them about six months prior. I'm guessing this whole business with Wayne put a couple more years on them.

Daddy's still a nice looking man with a head full of

wavy salt and pepper hair (way more salt than pepper) that he wore in his signature slicked down style. Years of working outside in the Memphis sun as a supervisor at a trucking company had darkened him up to a nice caramel color. Momma still carries herself with pride, walking with her head held high like, she owned that United terminal. She's a little taller than Daddy and wears her size 18 well. I walked to them and gave them both a hug while taking Momma's bag. She smiled and kept on walking.

"What took y'all so long to get off the plane?" I asked.

Daddy answered, "We're old."

"Oh, right." Guess he told me.

We began the long walk to baggage claim and immediately, Daddy starts asking questions. The cat's got Momma's tongue so she doesn't a say word.

"Have they released the body?"

"How's Laura?"

"Have we found a place for the service? In a nice church, I hope."

His questions all come out rapid fire, like bullets. Then, just as quickly, he looks like he wants to cry. I walk over to him and put my arm around his shoulder. He reaches into his pocket for his handkerchief and dabs his eyes. Nobody says anything, he would have wanted it that way. We finish the walk to the baggage claim area in silence. I'm very glad they are here. Their arrival was a momentary, welcomed distraction from reality.

* * * * *

Wayne's wife, Laura wasn't emotionally able to take care of making any of the arrangements. As usual, Commandant Mae took charge of everything. Nobody asked her to, she just did so because that's how she is. I think she wanted to keep her mind occupied with the details of what needed to be done so she didn't have time to think about anything else. Fine by me and everyone else.

I helped out as much as I could. But basically, Mae had everything under control. Four days before the funeral, Mae said she was going to the mortuary to sign the papers for the service and something was telling me I should go with her.

I said, "I'll go along for the ride."

My family looked at me, but they know I'm kinda different so no one said anything.

Now, I hate funeral parlors, y'all know that. Walking into the parlor this time, I held the door until it closed all the way. You know, they really try to fix these places up so they look nice and homey, but they aren't fooling nobody. One whiff of that dead smell lets you know where you are and that there are bodies right down the hall.

Things were going fine at first. The funeral director escorted us up the stairs to his office on the second floor of the converted house on Crenshaw Blvd. I was sitting there taking in the burgundy décor and matching thick carpet. Occasionally, I would nod my head when he asked a question, but there wasn't a need for me to say anything because Mae was doing most of the talking. They were discussing stuff like how many limos and traffic officers we would need, what time they would pick every one up and what time the service would start.

The subject of the casket came up and Mae didn't miss a beat. We weren't working with a whole lot of money so we had to plan his funeral on their super savers program. The funeral director pulled out a brochure and we picked the silver-blue casket because the other one looked as cheap as it really was. He told us we were in luck because they had the model we chose in the showroom and we could see it if we wanted to. Mae quickly answered okay for both of us but, to tell the truth, I could have done without it.

He led us downstairs and outside to the back of the place to what appeared to be a garage. That's what he called the showroom, which was stretching it. It was a garage.

I told y'all we were on a budget.

Anyway, that's where he took us to look at the casket we would be getting. And that, my friends, is where it happened.

The sign of the apocalypse....

As soon as that funeral man lifted the garage door and we stepped in Mae lost it. When she got a look at those wall-to-wall caskets, she broke down. I mean all the way down, too. She started crying and shaking like I did when I was knotted up on my living room floor. I thought she was having a nervous breakdown. I think seeing the casket made her realize that Wayne was really gone. I think all the emotions she had been holding inside her for her whole entire life burst out right then and there. Right then and there in the garage they called a showroom in the funeral parlor that was really a house.

I was stunned. I couldn't take my eyes off of her. Looking back, I wish I would have done something helpful like pat her on the back and say, "There, there..." But my feet were nailed to the concrete and my mouth was wide open. It was like when you look at a bad accident...morbid curiosity is what I think people call it. I had a bad case of that 'cause I had never, ever, in my whole entire life seen/heard/or imagined Mae crying. I didn't think her eyes worked like that.

I ain't lying. The whole "strong tower" thing describes her completely. Mae is like momma in that respect. When my curiosity had been satiated, it kicked in to my brain that this was a sad moment so I started crying too. I'm always good for a tear or two. Finally, I went over to try to console her, but she didn't want any part of that. As soon as she realized what I was trying to do she high-tailed it out of there. She started walking so fast that I couldn't catch her. I don't think she wanted me to touch her.

The director stood there totally unfazed by the scene playing out before him. He obviously didn't grasp the magnitude of the situation. I guess he was used to this type of behavior. On my way out, I told him in passing that we would call him a little later. On the drive home I didn't say a thing to Mae and she didn't say a thing to me. In fact, 'til this day, we have never discussed the matter, which is fine by me.

* * * * *

To be honest, I didn't totally accept the fact that he was dead until the day of his funeral. In fact, two days before his funeral the whole family was sitting in our townhouse when Mae arrived. She seemed really happy so I jumped up and asked, "What happened, was it a mistake. Is Wayne really alive?"

Oops. Where did that come from? I regretted my words as soon as they left my mouth but Wayne being alive was the only thing I could think of that would make me happy. So I logically jumped to the conclusion that God had raised him from the dead even though there was no precedence of Him doing that kinda thing after more than three days.

After the words left my mouth, I wished I could have taken them back. The room grew quiet. They all stopped and looked at me like I was crazy.

Mae looked at me with one eyebrow raised and said, "Uhhhhhhh, no. He's still dead, but I was able to work out a deal with the funeral home so that we won't have to spend as much as we thought."

"Oh."

That's all I could say. Then I slunk back over to my corner of the room and waited for the attention to shift to someone else. They were still looking at me. I know they were thinking I was going to need therapy when this ordeal was over.

The day before the funeral, we tried everything we could think of to keep Daddy from going to the wake, but he had to be there. Mae was brave enough to go the mortuary to get an early look so she could warn us, if necessary. After she saw him, she called us and said, "Don't let Momma and Daddy come out here. He looks really bad."

Momma said, "Thank you, I will be staying at home."

Denise stayed with her.

Daddy, on the other hand said he had to see his son one more time. We tried to talk him out of it because of his weak heart but our talking didn't do any good. He was determined to go. Since we had decided on a closed casket funeral, Daddy knew this would be his last time seeing his son. Tina and I went with him. I drove them there. By the time we got there Mark and Earl were standing outside on the front porch waiting for us. Mark smiled as we approached. Earl's face looked like a piece of stone.

Mark stood to Daddy's left and Earl was on the right. Daddy hobbled into the mortuary and went into the salon to look at what was left of his son. About ten minutes later, he came out crying like a baby, just like he did with Jean. Looking at him, I remember thinking, *My Lord, how did we get here again?*

To distract myself from the sight of Daddy breaking down like that, I willed my mind to go someplace, anyplace but this funeral home on Crenshaw Boulevard. I couldn't help but think that if God had just answered my prayers and let my brother live, I wouldn't have to witness all this pain and agony.

But He didn't.

That thought made me tired.

CHAPTER 37

DAVID'S EULOGY

We woke up early and, in a room full of people, ate a lonely breakfast. I remember that my friend and her minister husband came over to drop off some orange glazed Cornish hens and prayers. I was numb with pain at that point but I thanked them as best I could.

Everyone started getting dressed and before we knew it, it was time to head to West Angeles Church for the funeral. At that point, I didn't even know my name. All I wanted to do was to get it over with.

Earl, Mark and their families met Mae, Tina, Denise and the parents at the church. We decided to drive our own cars to West Angeles and wait for Laura, Wayne Jr., the stepchildren and the rest of Wayne's extended family to arrive in the limo. We didn't have to wait long, less than ten minutes. Laura was taking it hard. I could hear her crying as the limo pulled up...and all the windows were still up. Good Lord, this was going to be a long, bad day!

Since Wayne Jr. was eleven at the time, I would say Laura and my brother had been married about thirteen years give or take. In light of that, I guess it was asking too much of her to try to hold in together and make it through the short service we planned. I wish she could have for Momma and Daddy's sake, but I could see that wasn't going to happen. Sighing to myself, I could see it was gonna be one of "those" kinda funerals.

Momma and Daddy joined Laura and Wayne Jr. at the beginning of the line and the rest of us fell in after them as we started the processional up the center aisle. My main goal in life, at that moment, was to make it to my seat without crying. I kept my head in front of me, but was able to see a few of my friends and coworkers out of the corner of my eyes. They were nice to take off work and come and grieve with me. I was grateful.

I looked into the pulpit and saw my pastor, Bishop Blake sitting there. I was shocked and elated that he had time in his busy schedule to be at Wayne's funeral. I mean, Wayne joined the church years ago but because of his work schedule and where he lived, he only came one or two times after that.

But even with the support of my friends and the presence of my pastor, Wayne's funeral was cold.

Or maybe it was just me.

I looked around the family section and saw my brothers. Mark was crying openly. My eyes were then drawn to Earl. He looked incredibly handsome in his black suit and red tie, but his face looked like death. Earl and Wayne were especially close and I know he must have been feeling bad, but his expression was like a blank sheet of paper. Nothing there.

I sat there stone faced like that death angel myself, barely listening to the people who got up and spoke about what a good man my brother was. I knew all that. He was a loving man. A devoted man. A hardworking man. I knew all of that too so I didn't feel obligated to listen.

I know I told y'all that Wayne and I fought like warriors when we were coming up, but that was a long, long time ago. That's what brothers and sisters do when you're young and stupid. Over the years, Wayne and I became friends. We would talk on the phone for hours. Sometimes we would both call in sick and meet for lunch. He was the brother I could really depend on when I needed help. I can't count the number of times he moved "Gibraltar."

See, even though I'm totally a brilliant and conscientious employee and a flat out joy to be around, I seem to have difficulty retaining a job. I'm a layoff magnet. I'm telling you, if there's a downturn at a company and somebody has to be let go, it will be me. I must have a big sign over my head that says, "Pick me! Pick me!" because I've been laid off seven times. My employers tell me, as they are showing me the door that it's nothing I did…just downsizing. I gotta tell y'all, that kinda stuff can really mess with your self-esteem.

But, God has been faithful and I've always been able to get a new job pretty quickly. And when I get a new job, I usually strong arm my roommate, Denise to move close to the job because I'm not into long commuting in the LA traffic and she works at night when there is no traffic. Well, with each move I would call Wayne and he would huff and puff about it, but he would arrive bright and early to help Denise and me.

With each move, the last item to get carried to the truck was a piece of furniture we lovingly called "Gibraltar." Gibraltar is a thigh high cube of white marble with blue streaks in it. Denise and I got it for a steal on sale at JC Penney. I think I know why it was on sale because that thing was a hernia waiting to happen. That stone had to weigh about three hundred pounds and it would take all three of us to even budge it.

The last move to the condo in Westchester was the worst of all because there were two flights of stairs and no elevator. We wrestled with that cube like it was Hulk Hogan. We'd lift it a little bit and someone would start giggling (me) and then it would start to slip and Wayne would yell at me. It would take longer to move that cube than it did the whole apartment full of furniture.

I can remember the last thing Wayne said to me and Denise when we finally got "Gibraltar" into the living room.

Sitting there, sweating and puffing like he just ran a marathon he said, "I got something to say and I want both of you to hear me good. Y'all my sisters and I love you, but I done moved that blasted rock all over Southern California and I have had enough. I'm too old and this is the last time."

Looking at me, he added, "The next time you get laid off, y'all on your own. Man…trying to kill a brother."

I sat there laughing to myself at that memory and experienced the first warm feeling since I got to the funeral. But then, I remembered that it really was the last time he would have to move "Gibraltar." Wayne got his wish. He didn't have to worry about that stupid marble anymore. Tears threatened to spill down my cheeks but I was saved when I looked up and saw Mae's son David walking up to the pulpit. I had totally forgotten that we asked him to speak for the family.

David, an attorney, is a commanding presence at six feet four; he got that from Mae's husband, Big Henry. He's brown skinned with a handsome, chiseled face with a bit of studiousness mixed in. He's the kind of person you look at and know he's somebody.

I had no idea what David was going to say, but I sat up a little straighter in my seat in anticipation and I noticed that others did the same thing. I had a feeling it was going to be important.

* * * * *

He began, "As I was thinking about what I wanted to say, I think the first thing that came to mind was an analogy. I knew a friend who had a visitor from a foreign country to come and stay with the family. This person was an exchange student. The family got to like this person so much because he was actually fun to be around, a very amiable person.

A person that was very caring, open, generous and

giving, like Wayne.

It got to the point that my friend was actually complaining to me because his family began to like the exchange student more than they liked their own children. That's how much of a joy it was to be around this person.

Ultimately, the father of the exchange student called and said, you have to come home now, you're needed here. And they were sad, the adopted family, naturally because they looked upon this person as a gift. They didn't want him to go home because they knew they were going to miss him because he was such an integral part of the family, because he brought so much joy to the people because they depended on him to be a light in all of their lives. But the time came that his father said that he had to come home.

So they greeted him at the airport when he came and when he left, they went to the airport. They were a little heavy hearted but they knew ultimately that it was best that he go back to his father because it was his father's will that he go home and that it was time for him to go home.

And that's exactly the situation we have here. Like that exchange student, Wayne was a gift from God. Everybody in this room is a gift from God. We come into this world, we don't know how long we're going to be here. What we have to do is soak up one another, love one another as much as we possibly can.

There is an old saying in Hebrew scripture that says, "It takes three people to make a child. The biological mother and father and God." God the Spiritual Father. Wayne's Spiritual Father, God, called him home. That's what happened here.

Now, I know everyone may be feeling sad, but you have to look at this, not from a human perspective, but from a divine perspective. You feel sad for you, but don't feel sad for Wayne. Wayne is in a much better place now.

When we all leave here we have to get in cars, we have to go on with our lives. We have to worry about making the rent. We have to worry about getting sick. We have to worry about physical pain and family. Wayne is free from that. He will never have to endure these things. You all look forward to the point that you can come face to face with your Maker and live in tranquility in a pure light. Wayne is already there, and when you get there, hope that he will greet you at that time because he's enjoying it right now.

Wayne has been called home. That's all that's happened. So while you may miss him, don't feel sorry for him. Realize that he is happy and in a much better place. I want to say one other point. This reminded me of a Psalm. Psalm 23. I'll just go over the first line. "The Lord is my Shepherd." I don't think you have to go any further than that. Because the basic tenants of the relationship between a shepherd and his flock is that the shepherd stands at the front and guides. Nothing happens to that flock that the shepherd does not want.

The question being asked in this event, which is a sad event for some, but again, as I said, try to see it through divine lenses, and let the scripture help you do that. But, the question is do you have trust in God? Do you have faith in God? Do you believe in God? Do you think that everything that God does is for His glory and for your good?

If you believe that, if you know that God is the shepherd, if you know that He does not let anything happen to His flock that is not good, and if you know that God is good all the time, I should see some smiles. Because I want you to get a picture of the happiest time that you spent with Wayne, the biggest smile on his face that you can possibly imagine. The personal moment that you had with him where he was the happiest he could be as a human being in the flesh. Now, magnify that times 50. Magnify it times 1000. Magnify it times 1 million. Magnify it to INFINITY. And you still can't comprehend the happiness that he has now. And if he's that happy, then why don't you partake in his happiness? Honor his memory with joy because that's what he's feeling right now. Not with sadness.

I just want to close by saying that the basic point about having faith is that it is not a result oriented process. You don't say that I believe in God and trust in God if things work out the way I want them too. You see, the sheep follow the shepherd not knowing what particular pasture or where the destiny will be because they have faith in that shepherd. You have faith. Particularly in a moment like this.

And if you realize that it's not in a result, but in the process of living in God, having faith in God all the time, then you come to the conclusion that God is good all the time. All the time. And on that note I want everyone to have a happy thought when they think about Wayne because this is an occasion of joy.

Wayne is where he should be because his Father has called him home. "Thank you."

And with that, David walked back to his seat and sat down.

CHAPTER 39

IT HAD TO HAPPEN

His words were like a blanket that covered me.

My confusion and doubts melted away like butter on hot cornbread.

The more David spoke, the more my heart burned. Not that his words directly answered the question I had asked God earlier, "Why did my brother die?" It ain't for him to answer. I guess the words that Daddy spoke to Mae over thirty years ago finally rang true to me. If I ever find out the answer to that question it will be in the sweet by and by.

I had been grasping at straws and doing everything in my power to have things make sense. My seemingly unanswered prayer didn't make sense because my thinking of God didn't include allowing pain to be a part of His plan for my life. Suffering was not on my agenda. But, doggone it, now I know that's not really how this Christian walk plays out. The truth is this: at some point, I'm gonna have to bear some kinda cross. Somewhere, somehow. That goes for y'all too. There ain't no getting around it.

Wanna know what it felt like? Felt like scales were falling from my eyes. Like I now saw something very basic and simple that had been right in front of me all along. Wayne had his time...short as it was. He was on loan from God. And when that loan had reached maturity, the good Lord called my brother home and Wayne was outta here quick and in a hurry. Way sooner than what I'd hoped for, but I guess that ain't for me to say. That's God's business.

It kinda put me in the mind of the times when I was growing up and would ask Momma for something and she would respond with a disappointing "No."

If I were feeling brave, I would ask her "why not?"

She would almost always respond with the dreaded, "Because I said so."

Not wanting to feel her hand on my backside, I would go away and pout about not getting what I wanted. I used to think she was just saying no to be mean, or to keep me from having something I really wanted, but now I see that wasn't it at all.

Sometimes Momma's "No" was to help mature me, to keep me from becoming spoiled and to train me not to expect to get everything I asked for. Because life don't work like that. Sometimes my request was out of order with other plans that she had for me. Sometimes Momma's "No" meant that she knew what I was asking for wasn't good for me. Sometimes her "No" was because she knew what I was asking for could cause me problems down the road.

Oh, I got a perfect recollection to prove my point.

A few years earlier, I was diagnosed with having fibroid tumors and was told that I had to have surgery. Now y'all, I really, really didn't want to have surgery. What I wanted was for God to heal me. So, I started praying something fierce and in my mind I totally believed I would be healed. I prayed everyday for about three weeks, right up to the day before the surgery.

The night before the surgery, I went to a revival at my church. Matter of fact, it was the same minister that had Mae slain in the spirit a few years prior so I knew he had the power. At the end of the service, he had an altar call for those of us who wanted to be healed and I led the bunch hot footin' it to the altar. While he was praying, I felt a warmth ooze over my entire body and knew it was the presence of

God. Y'all, that hot flash was all the sign I needed to let me know I had been healed. Even Moses couldn't tell me no different. I came home after church and called everybody and told them I had been healed.

Mae was quick to say, "Uhhh, that's good, but you're still going to the hospital in the morning right?"

She didn't believe me but that wasn't surprising. Oh, she of little faith! I just shook my head but answered, "Of course I'm still going. I have to tell the doctor what happened. It would be rude not to show up since everything is scheduled."

I woke up at early the next morning, got dressed and Denise and Mae took me to the hospital. I obediently put on the gown and got on the table as instructed even though I knew it was all a big, fat waste of time. The staff was puttering around me, doing all their pre-op stuff while I sat there with a smug look on my face.

When the doctor came in to talk to me about ten minutes before the surgery was scheduled to start, I told him, "Doctor, I hate to tell you this, but I'm not going to need this surgery."

He slowly turned and looked at me. "Why do you say that?"

No shame in my game. I boldly replied, "Because I went to a revival last night and the minister prayed for everyone who wanted healing and I felt the presence of God all over me. I believe God has healed me and the tumors are gone."

He didn't miss a beat. "I see. Well, do you mind if we do a quick pelvic exam…uh, just to make sure."

I knew he didn't believe me either, but I didn't care. I would have the last laugh.

"Sure. No problem," was my confident reply.

I leaned back and waited for him to finish his exam. It didn't take him long. About three minutes later, I almost fell out of those stirrups when he said, "Yep. Tumors still there. Roll her in."

He didn't even look at me.

I'm telling y'all, they rolled me into that operating room with my mouth wide open. I couldn't believe it! I was so sure God had answered my prayer. I just knew I had been healed.

The last thing I said before they knocked me out was, "But…but…"

A few hours later, when I woke up, I was HOT as fish grease!

How could God do me like that? Why give me the warm, fuzzy sign? What was that all about? If it wasn't a sign of my healing, what was it? Needless to say, I sat there on my hospital bed with my arms folded across my chest in righteous indignation. I wasn't on speaking terms with God for the remainder of that day. I didn't have much to say the day after that either.

Two days after my surgery, the doctor was making his rounds and came into my room, sat on my bed and asked me, "So, how are you doing today, Missy?"

I was still embarrassed about my erroneous declaration of healing. I could hardly look him in the eyes. I knew what he was thinking, with his Jewish self… *Holy Roller*.

I mumbled, "Oh fine. Can I go home?"

He answered, "Nope. Not today. Maybe tomorrow, but we'll see. Let me check the staples."

As he began the examination, he started talking, "You know, it's a good thing you had this surgery because I found another problem. You must have endometriosis and the start of a nasty infection. I'm surprised you didn't have a fever. It had been there for awhile. The infection was in a place where it never would have been detected with an x-ray. Since you weren't having any symptoms, it would have continued to grow. Left untreated, this could have led to an even worse infection, sterilization, who knows, even cancer. It was only by going in for the surgery that I was able to see it and treat it."

He finished the exam. Standing up and smiling he said, "Everything looks fine, young lady. You should be able to go home tomorrow."

I sat there in bewildered silence for about ten minutes. God did it again.

He was taking care of me when I didn't even know there was a problem.

You know, I'm always losing these little power struggles with God. You'd think I'd learn my lesson. It's the classic struggle ain't it? Me trying to conform God to my will and God trying to conform man to His will. I was praying for healing and to be released from the surgery, but God said "No, my daughter. This surgery has to happen!"

Same thing with Wayne. Him living even one more day wasn't in the plans God made for him either. I have come to accept that fact. The challenge is to remain steadfast when my prayers are answered with a resounding "No."

And in those times when I ask why and He doesn't respond, I take it as a "Because I said so" kinda thing and trust His plan. Y'all, sometimes that's a bitter pill to swallow, ain't it? Sometimes it takes the faith of Abraham, Isaac, AND Jacob to get me to the place where I accept that God's "No" always has a meaning that is rooted in love.

So, I'm sitting there in the funeral and I began to see the past few weeks of my life in a new light. I wanted a miracle, but miracles don't happen that often, and for good reason. If God responded with miracles every time I asked where would it end? How would I grow and mature as a Christian if God had to move heaven and earth and defy the laws of nature every time my back was against the wall? Where would it end? Isn't a large part of faith still believing even when the answer is no?

Don't get me wrong. Miracles do happen. But miracles happen just enough to let us know that God is still able. God doesn't necessarily speak every day, week, or month, but just enough to let us know without a doubt that He hears us when we call Him. That is why I couldn't walk away from Him. Lord knows I tried. But I'd had just enough experience with Him to know He was still there. And He trusted me, just enough to know that I would work through my doubts and anger and our relationship would grow stronger.

Now I understand. God is cooking up a blessing that includes every tear, every blessing, every heartache, every smile, and every doubt I've ever experienced as the main ingredients.

Now I understand. There is a balance to the scriptures. For every "ask and it shall be given" there is a "in this life ye shall have tribulations." For every, "with His stripes we are healed" there is an "all that will live godly in Christ Jesus shall suffer persecution." Almost every story in the Bible has pain before glory. The Bible is a whole book and partial understanding and usage of all the "happy" scriptures will stunt our growth.

Now I understand. What I have lost, I had to lose. What didn't work out wasn't supposed to work out. Everyone who left me was supposed to go. When I'm crying, I'm supposed to cry. Each and every step I make is ordered by God.

Now I understand. When I'm going through something that makes me think that God is not on my side, that's the very problem God has sent to let me know that He is.

Now I understand. With all the good stuff that I will experience in life…a fair amount of awful stuff will be there too.

Now I understand. When people die it hurts, but it's supposed to hurt. Hurting is a necessary by product of living, loving and loosing. Hurting is necessary. Hurting reminds me that I am human. The ability to stay on the team in spite of my pain shows that I am growing.

What happened had to happen. It still hurts, but it had to happen.

And in the end, God is saying, "I need you to trust me on this."

And I do….

* * * * *

Bishop Blake was finishing up the eulogy when I came to myself. I didn't hear most of it, but it's alright cause I reckon I got just what I needed from the good Lord Himself.

And I close my eyes, lift my head and look up and in my mind's eye, I can see them all. Wayne, Jean, Big Mama Sarah, Papa George, Aunt Adele, Uncle Robert Lee, and the rest of my uncles, Cousin Louise and everyone who has crossed over to the other side looking down at me.

Smiling!

Happy!

Free!

Not them… Me!!

TRIFLIN'

Growing up, Wayne and I used to fuss and fight like cats and dogs. I told y'all about that. But, you know, looking back, I can now see that we were a lot alike. We both had our struggles trying to understand God and how He answers prayers.

I recollect the time…

* * * * *

Not long after I moved to Los Angeles, we all decided to go to Las Vegas for the weekend. Tina had come to town for a visit so it was me, Mark, Mae, Earl, Wayne, and Denise making the trip. We rented a mini-van, hit the road early on Friday morning, and drove five hours to the hotel where we were staying on the strip.

Now Wayne was excited about the trip, way more than everyone else. That boy had cashed his check and I could practically see his pants smoking 'cause that money was burning a decent sized hole in his pocket. He kept saying how he had a good feeling about this trip and how he was gonna hit it big and how he was gonna come back to Los Angeles a millionaire. We just let him talk because that's how he was. He had such a vagabond spirit. He was always trying to find some kind of get rich quick scheme because working a nine to five wasn't his thing. (Remember all those W-9's he spread out like a fan?)

As a matter of fact, I'm surprised his bosses at the bus company he worked for even allowed him to take off work because that boy was always calling in for some reason or the other. Calling in wasn't nothing but a word to him. His attendance was horrible.

Like the time when he decided he wanted to go home to Memphis to see Momma and Daddy...for no reason at all except he wanted to. Wayne picked up that phone called in and in his most sorrowful voice told the dispatcher that he needed to take the week off because his grandmother had died and he needed to get to Mississippi for the funeral.

The dispatcher told him to hold on for a minute then came back and asked him, "Boy, how many grandmothers do you have? That's the fifth time she's died."

I don't remember how Wayne got out of that one. Probably made up another lie. When he told me that story, he ended it muttering under his breath, "Blasted computers..."

I told him, "That's what you get, you lyin' demon."

His retort was, "Big Momma Sarah been dead and gone. It's only bad if I said that and she had still been living."

I let it go.

So, back to our trip, we finally made it to our hotel room. Mae and Mark went to check in while the rest of us stayed hidden in the car. After they got the key, we each went up in shifts because we only had one room for the five of us.

Hey, don't shake your heads at me like you've never done that!" In our defense, this was back in the 80's, way before we got sophisticated.

After we were all settled in, we hit the casino at Circus! Circus! Now, none of us are real gamblers. Matter of fact, I don't gamble at all. Everyone else was playing the slots and I was watching. I hung out with Wayne since he was bubbling over with enthusiasm. I wanted to be there when he "hit it big." He found himself a machine and started feeding it.

Each time he would pull the handle, he would say over

and over again, "Please Jesus…"

Sometimes he'd switch up and say, "Lord remember me!"

With every pull, he'd be calling on the Lord. I thought it was ridiculous but I minded my tongue. I sat with him until I got bored and went to watch one of the circus acts.

Hours later, we met up at the buffet. Over dinner, I found out that everyone had won a little bit of something. Mark won the most, but still it was less than a hundred dollars. Wayne was mighty quiet. He had definitely lost some of his effervescence.

I'm a brave soul so I asked him how he did.

He was staring at his dinner, just picking at it really. Finally he answered, "Aw right."

Everybody was snickering under their breath. He looked up, but they all avoided eye contact with Wayne. They knew something I didn't. I didn't think it was wise to continue that line of questioning.

I let it go.

Well, Saturday morning brought a return to Wayne's declaration of future millionaire-dom. He was the first one up and after a hearty buffet breakfast and a bit of shopping, we hit the casinos again. And you know what? By the end of the day, the results were the same. No one won any big money. Everyone pretty much broke even, uh, everyone except Wayne that is. Wayne gambled away his whole check. He didn't win a cotton picking thing. Not even a nickel.

It was a long ride home, y'all. That boy moaned and groaned all the way back to Los Angeles. And I'm talking literally. The closer we got to home, those moans turned into prayers. He must have been trying to figure out what he was going to tell his wife when he walked through that door with empty pockets. And he wasn't shamed to let us hear him either.

He was saying, "Lord, I know you heard me praying.

You know you could'a let me win somethin'. All I wanted was my share."

Guess he didn't feel his help come, so he kept praying, "Lord, you know I don't hurt nobody. I go to church when I can. I don't kill people. I follow most of the Ten Commandments. Why Lord, why?"

What got me was when he said, "Lord, why don't you like black people?"

Then his prayers started getting a bit more militant. "I mean, it's not like I ask you for much, you know. You the one with the cattle on a thousand hills. It wouldn't have been nothing for you to let me win a million dollars on that machine if you wanted to."

Finally Earl had enough and yelled, "Boy, you were playin' the nickel slots! How the Sam Hill you expect to win playin' the nickel slots? Who spends their whole check on the nickel slots! Don't make no kinda sense."

Well, everyone had been trying to hold it together until then. You know, laughing under your breath. But I'm telling you the truth, after Earl's irritated outburst, Mark almost ran that van off the road he was laughing so hard. We all busted up laughing at my hard luck brother.

And when I looked at Wayne out of the corner of my eyes, he was laughing too. That boy knows he a mess! Lord knows I'm gonna miss him. Thank goodness I have recollections like these to keep me company till I see him again on the other side.

* * * * *

A couple of days after the funeral, after Momma, Daddy, and Tina had returned to Memphis and we were trying to settle into our new life, Mae, Denise, and I were out for a drive. For days I had been thinking about deep stuff like life, death and why was I born in the first place. Why did God put us together as a family? Had Wayne fulfilled his destiny? Had Jean? I had all sorts of thoughts floating through my head, but the one that haunted me the most, was the one I found most unpleasant.

You see, in the beginning, there were ten of us, including Momma and Daddy. Then Jean left and there were nine. Now Wayne is gone and there are eight. I was thinking that as the years come and go, this number will dwindle down until there will be only one of us left.

Who will it be?

After having parents, brothers, and sisters around for our whole lives one day one of us will be all alone; the last surviving sibling. After years of sharing a common bond and developing a close relationship, each passing year brings us closer to the time that one by one, that bond will be severed. One of us would have to go through the ordeal of death seven more times. One of us will be the last one to die. And since I'm the youngest by many, many years, it could very well be me.

I marinated on this sobering thought for quite some time before I decided to share it with my sisters.

When I finished sharing my morbid declaration I said, "I don't think I want to be the last one. I think it would be awful to be here alone without any family."

Denise was thinking about the magnitude of what I said, and I could tell she was about to get emotional. That's how she is. She finally said, "I know what you mean. I can't image life without you guys. The thought is unbearable."

We both turned to Mae and waited for her words of inspiration and comfort. I mean, that's what you would expect with her being the oldest, right?

Mae looked me dead in the eyes and said, "I'll take it."

Now, that's just triflin'.

Read the Whole Story!

Meet the DeVaults, a strong close-knit family of ten that go together "Like Catfish and a Big Red Drink."

Order online at www.donnaderden.com